CURSED SWORD
CHOSEN LEGACY

CURSED SWORD
CHOSEN LEGACY

JAMES SELVY

Published by Wolfpac Books, LLC

Tucson, Arizona, 2026

Published by Wolfpac Books

Wolfpac-books.com

The Cursed Sword: Chosen Legacy / James Selvy.
Description: First Edition. | Arizona: Wolfpac Books, 2026

ISBN 978-1-968443-00-9 (ebook) | ISBN 978-1-968443-01-6 (Paperback)
| ISBN 978-1-968443-02-3 (Hardback)

Cover design: Bob Paltrow Design, bobpaltrow.com

For the woman who has seen me at my worst and still thinks I'm great.

Thanks for being in my corner, Mom.

CHAPTER ONE

Chisel and Hope — Ethrael

Come, gather close, and let me weave you a tale. I'm Yarnell, a human bard whose heart sings with stories, spun into rhyme and melody. I roam, collecting the world's whispers, but this tale found me in Keenroot's verdant embrace, where ancient trees cradle elven homes, their boughs aglow with twilight's grace. Hush now, our verse begins, where Ethrael, a slave of steadfast will, treads a shadowed path through boughs to tend a stranger's chiseled hope.

Ethrael arrived at the healing center as she did every day. Although most of her work involved menial tasks, changing beds, cleaning up messes, and scrubbing the floors, she kept her eyes and ears open and learned by watching.

On this particular morning, a guard brought in a young man—Human by the looks of it—severely wounded, bloodied, and unconscious. Her first task was to clean the body so the healers could begin their work. She cut away his tattered clothes, careful not to reopen the wounds.

With the clothes cut off, she rubbed her fingers across the gashes on the man's midsection, noticing the primary cause of the blood-soaked garments and extensive bruising.

She leaned close only then, voice soft as breath. "How long were you out there? Don't worry, you're not alone now."

Her master, Lord Thalen, mocked, "What takes you so long? He'll be long dead before you finish cleaning him up." His cruel speech, always unkind, stung her despite its familiarity.

"Get out of the way. Let the healers work," Lord Thalen snarled, shoving her aside.

Ethrael pulled back into the shadows.

Thalen's hands wove radiant sigils, conjuring a shimmering veil over the man. The light flared, then dissolved like mist under dawn's heat, leaving the raw wounds untouched. With his brow creased, jaw tight, mind racing, he thought curse or hidden ward?

"Stubborn as stone!" he snapped. "Ethrael, now!"

"Yes, sir," she said, shuffling toward the table, eyes downcast.

"We must return to our healing roots. Simple enough that even you can handle it. Start wrapping his wounds. Place one druidic water patch and one food patch on him to prevent death from thirst or starvation. We don't know how long he was out there."

Thalen clicked his tongue, loud enough for the assistants to hear. "Her family forgot themselves, too," he mocked, cold and casual. "Best she remember her place before she repeats their failure."

Ethrael's breath hitched. She smoothed her expression, steadying her hands with practiced will. She had learned long ago that showing hurt only sharpened his cruelty.

Her head dipped in a quick nod, trembling fingers pressing a damp bandage to the jagged gashes. She placed the druidic patches on unscarred skin on his back, their soft glow, faint hum steady where Thalen's magic faltered. Her breath caught as the man's ashen skin warmed to a healthy flush, the patches' power clear.

He turned to his assistants. "The head wound keeps him trapped in sleep. We could lose him. The king won't be pleased."

"We could watch him, pray the wounds knit themselves," an assistant ventured, wringing his hands.

"Wishing mends no wounds."

Thalen stalked off, shoulders tense, muttering to himself. "Why did the king drop him in my lap?"

As the days passed, the areas around his eyes grew blacker and blacker. Blood leaked from his ears, and his head looked larger than when he first arrived. When Ethrael pried open his eyelids, she saw no white or color in the eyes, only red. His pulse raced, and his breathing grew shallow and irregular. His condition worsened steadily.

Thalen summoned his assistants, face etched with resolve, "The pressure in his skull will claim him unless we act. Magic has failed us."

He paused, voice steady. "I'll bore a hole to ease it."

Ethrael's mind flickered to Thalen's lessons on ancient, rare tomes, their faded scripts of forgotten arts. Had they inspired this grim choice?

An assistant, eyes wide, stammered, "M-master, such a procedure, wise?"

"It risks his life," Thalen said, "Yet no other path remains."

Thalen pointed to a young nurse. "You shave his head." Pointing to a more senior nurse. "You collect the old hammer and chisel from the shelf in my office. Scrub them clean."

Gripping the instruments, Thalen drew a steadying breath, his stern gaze fixed on the unconscious human. Ethrael, standing rigid near the table's edge, watched him trace a small circle behind the man's left ear, his hands turning the instrument nervously with slow, deliberate twists. Her chest tightened, breath held, as if the room itself paused.

"Steady," he told himself, barely audible. Muttering to his assistants but still in a quiet tone. "I do not want to do this... but there is no choice! I am taking this slow."

Sweat began to bead on his brow. Each *tap-tap-tap* of metal on bone echoed in Ethrael's ears, a relentless drumbeat. A bone disc, no wider than a coin, broke free with a sickening crack. Blood and fluid surged forth, streaming over the table and pooling on the floor. The air grew heavy with a damp, musky stench that stung Ethrael's nostrils, her stomach churning.

Thalen stepped back, wiping sweat from his brow, his face betraying a flicker of unease. As the flow ebbed, an assistant swiftly pressed an herb-soaked cloth to the wound, binding it tightly, as the room held its collective breath.

• • •

They moved the man to Ethrael's hut and commanded her to care for him. For the first few days, her master visited at day's end. Stepping away, she watched as he checked the quality of her bandages. She thought it strange he never examined the wounds.

"You have done an adequate job. Remember, if he dies, it's on your head. I'll not protect you from the King's wrath. You aren't worth it."

"Thank you, sir," she said, hoping to appease him.

Thalen pulled an old rusty sword from his belongings and tossed it into the corner. "This sword was found with him. It is worthless. I don't want it cluttering up my center."

She didn't understand what made this man so special. Why did the king care about this man? Surely there were more deserving elves. But her place was not to question. If she were to risk saying such things out loud, she would be back to scrubbing floors or worse. Looking at the sword, she noticed it bore runes. Could it have some magic? She moved the sword so carelessly discarded, wrapped it in a blanket, and placed it under the stranger's bed.

Days blurred together, sunrise fading into sunset. She refused to sit there staring at him. Her master had dumped the man in her care, and if he died, she knew the blame would fall on her.

She resolved to do her best to care for the man. In her quest to heal him, she read books and scrolls on the healing arts. Some she snuck out from the healing center, others she retrieved from the library. In them, she found various ways to treat wounds and diseases. Each race or tribe had its bent.

Ethrael decided to experiment with her growing medical knowledge. She didn't limit herself to only techniques from elven lore. She created salves for his wounds and bruises. Thalen commanded her to replace the druidic water and food patches daily. Reflecting on how often a woke person ate and drank, she replaced them more often.

Some of the texts she read discussed exercising the body and the mind. So she did what she could. She would move part of his body to exercise it slowly at first, then more rigorously over time. But how to exercise the mind? The only thing she could think about was talking to him. But being human, would he even understand? What language would he even know? Would his injuries even allow him to understand?

"You're not getting better yet, but you're holding on. You're a fighter, fight your way back." Ethrael whispered as she stroked his head.

Thalen ordered an assessment of the patient and a report to be issued after a month. Having seen few humans, she noted the man's muscles had withered since he first arrived. Yet his hair began to grow back, and his head appeared normal for a human. His bruising had turned yellow, a sign of improvement. The bone disc began knitting to the skull, and the skin started to close.

When Ethrael collected supplies, the healers would taunt her, "He will die in your care, and I can't wait," or "He'll never wake up, and you'll spend your youth caring for that human."

CHAPTER TWO

Goblin-Killer Returns — Skarn

Gather 'round, ye folk, and hear Yarnell's tale of blood, dread. This verse unfolds in the goblin-haunted woods, where three battered goblins, fresh from a slaughter, cower by a bloodied river. A human wielding a rune-etched blade, whispered as Goblin-Killer, carved through their band, leaving heads rolling. Their eyes darting at shadows in fear, as they limped home to their crude stronghold. There, the squad leader faced King Gorath's wrath, his throne of bones shaking with rage. The court buzzed, tales of the magic sword spreading like wildfire. Gorath's command was clear: capture the human, seize the blade. A warband marched, hearts torn twixt vengeance, terror, into the Elven forest's silver gloom. Mark my words, that blade's glow promises doom, and the goblins' fate hangs by a thread.

*T*hree goblins huddled downstream from the battle, bandaging their wounds. The river gurgled with blood-tinged water, red with the blood of goblins, marking a brutal war. Twisted elven branches loomed like claws overhead. Skarn, the new leader, clutched a gash across his ribs and limped from a slashed leg.

"I didn't want to get promoted this way. Can't believe one stinkin' human offed three of our squad. The boss lost his head! We barely escaped," Skarn growled, wrapping a strip of cloth around his wounded leg. The two junior goblins discussed the brawl.

"Looked like a green fighter, but his swings were deadly."

"That sword—blue tint, fancy runes. Reckon it's the Goblin-Killer, maybe?" his eyes widened.

"Bet so. Better be just one! Don't wanna see a whole army armed with those swords."

"Human's gotta be dead." he paused, listening. "No movement now, but I ain't goin' back to check. Like my head right where it is." Unbeknownst to them, the man lay mortally wounded but alive, his blade at his side.

One goblin, shaking, muttered, "That blade's gonna haunt us all."

Skarn snorted. "Magic blade, no question. No human chops the boss's head and kills two mates, otherwise. Tellin' King Gorath's gonna suck, bed down here, keep watch. Head home at dawn." The leader's gut twisted, dreadin' Gorath's axe.

"Don't forget our boss's dad, the king's brother, mean arena champ. He'll lose it."

"Seein' boss's head hittin' dirt. Burned in my skull till I die."

"Figger Gorath'll send us back?"

The leader sighed. "Elven forest? Damn sure. That human's gotta be sidin' with the elves. King'll send more next time. Won't let this bloodbath slide. Elves gotta pay."

Weary from battle, their eyes darted to every shadow, spooked by the rune-etched blade. They settled for the night, avoiding a campfire to stay hidden. Each gust through the trees startled them, every noise sparking fear of the deadly sword.

At dawn's light, their boots pounded the path, glad to be moving from the sword but fearful of the wrath of the king when they arrived.

• • •

As they approached the Goblin Stronghold, their home, they finally relaxed. They had nothing to fear from humans or elves here. This was their land. The Goblin Stronghold stands deep in the goblin forest, a crude fortress of rough-hewn logs from twisted trees. Its walls, lashed with vine and caked with mud, were adorned with sharpened stakes.

A heavy wooden gate, reinforced with rusted metal bands, creaks at the entrance. Inattentive guards slump on the walls, half-asleep or bickering, barely scanning the forest. Crooked towers with rickety archer platforms teeter above at the corners.

Skarn stomped to the gate. "Oi, open up! Got news for the king!"

The guards looked down, rolling their eyes. "Oi, quit yer yellin'!"

It took a few minutes, but the gate opened just enough to let the small squad inside. Once inside, they shut the gate. Inside, smoky hearths light a maze of low tunnels and cluttered hovels, littered with scavenged weapons and bones, and thick with the stench of damp wood and goblin musk. Shouts and clanging forges echoed. Goblins scuffled over scraps in the shadows like cockroaches. A large log was placed across the gate to reinforce it.

"Hope that Goblin-Killer don't follow us," the third goblin muttered, eyeing the gate.

The squad leader looked to his companions. "Gonna dump my gear at home, then face Gorath's wrath. Scram and sleep." His gut churned, knowing Gorath's rage awaited.

The other two junior goblins, relieved to avoid the king's fury, hastened home. Whispering of the Goblin-Killer, they vanished into the tunnels. Skarn steeled himself, heading for Gorath's throne room, dreading the king's fury.

• • •

Skarn trudged through the Goblin Stronghold's tunnels, his battered armor clanking with each step. Torches sputtered on damp log walls, casting jagged shadows over piles of trash and gnawed bones. The air reeked of sour ale and goblin sweat, thick enough to choke.

Goblins scurried past, some hauling sacks, others brawling over a chipped axe, their guttural shouts bouncing off the low ceiling.

He passed a forge where a burly, soot-stained smith hammered a blade. Sparks leapt like angry insects. A scrawny goblin hissed to another sharpening a spear: "Heard 'bout that human? Swings a blade named Goblin-Killer. Butchered half a crew!"

Skarn's jaw tightened. Exaggerated, aye... but not by much. Word traveled too fast.

"Pfft, lies!" the other spat, but his eyes flicked nervously. "Ain't no human that fierce."

His chest tightened, and the memory of that rune-etched sword flashed in his mind. He quickened his pace, boots crunching on gravel-strewn earth. The tunnels twisted deeper, sloping toward King Gorath's throne room. Two goblins lounged against a wall, one picking his teeth with a splintered bone. "Oi, you from the raid?" one jeered, spotting the leader's bloodied face. "Heard Goblin-Killer got yer boss's head!"

"Shut yer trap!" Skarn snarled, shoving him aside. His heart thudded. Taunts were nothing. Gorath's wrath... that was death.

Every muttered rumor gnawed at him—and the king would have heard them all.

Ahead, the tunnel widened, the rumble of the throne room echoing like distant thunder. Skarn paused, wiping sweat from his brow, the weight of his report pressing heavy.

Goblin-Killer. Curse the name. It would be Gorath's first question. Steeling himself, he pressed on, torchlight flickering like a predator's gaze.

The stronghold buzzed with unease, whispers weaving through the crowd. Skarn squared his shoulders. The king waited. And so did judgment.

• • •

Skarn stepped into King Gorath's throne room, a cavernous hall of scorched logs and jagged bones, its air thick with the stench of burnt meat and goblin sweat. The throne loomed at the far end, a monstrous construct of massive beast bones, lashed with sinew and studded with iron spikes. Skulls grinned from the armrests and crowned the high back, their empty sockets glaring under flickering torchlight.

Tattered pelts draped the seat, stained with old blood. Piles of scavenged loot—rusted swords, cracked helms, and gnawed ribs—cluttered the floor, while gnarled banners hung torn and limp on damp walls. Goblins jammed the space, snarling warriors and skulking dogs, their growls a low rumble.

King Gorath, a hulking figure with scars crisscrossing his green hide, slouched on the throne, his scowl deepening, eyes burning with barely restrained fury. Beside him stood Krogar, his brother, a towering arena champion clad in spiked armor, knuckles scarred from countless brawls.

Skarn inched forward, boots scuffing the bone-strewn floor, his throat dry as ash, eager not to speak. The court's eyes bored into him, their chatter fading to a tense hush. He dropped to one knee, head bowed, heart pounding. "King Gorath, I... I got news from the raid on the elves." He paused, looking for the strength to go on.

"Spit it out!" Gorath roared, voice shaking the hall. "Where's my nephew? Why isn't he giving the report?"

Sweat beading, he said, "We was huntin' elves in their forest, like ya ordered. But one stinkin' human jumped us! Carried a bleedin' blue blade, runes burnin' cold-like. It... it... it hacked through us like straw! My team thinks it is the Goblin-Killer."

The court erupted, goblins hissing and cursing. A scrawny advisor near the throne snarled, "Goblin-Killer? That's just an old tale! It has been lost for years."

"Ain't no tale! Musta been found," Skarn barked, voice cracking. "It took our boss's head, yer nephew, sire! Cut down two more 'fore we ran. Them runes... saw 'em flare like the blade had hunger."

Gorath's eyes narrowed, his massive hand gripping a cleaver propped by the throne. "You ran?" he growled, rising, his shadow swallowing Skarn. The court shrank back, some clutching weapons, others trembling. "My kin's dead, and ya scurried off like rats?"

Krogar stomped forward, spiked gauntlet slamming into his palm. "I'll tear that human apart! Where's this Goblin-Killer now?"

"Dunno, sire," Skarn stammered, quailing. "Human was bloodied somethin' fierce when we bolted. Likely dead. But that blade's cursed, I swear it! I'd not touch it. You've heard the stories."

Gorath bellowed, hurling the cleaver. It thudded into a log pillar, quivering. "Cursed or not, no human spills my blood and breathes!" He jabbed a claw at Krogar. "You, brother, send two squads. Have them find this human, bring me that blade, and his skull! But I want you here in case they come for me."

Krogar's lip curled into a savage grin. "I'll take his head clean with that blade. Elves too, if they're hidin' 'im. My men'll bring 'im back here alive with the sword so I can defeat 'im in the arena before you and your subjects."

Skarn cowered, expecting a strike, but Krogar's glare swept the court.

Krogar barked to the assembled warriors. "All o' ya, ready the warbands! Grab steel, grab fire! We stomp the Elven woods till they crack!"

The goblins roared, a deafening wave of war cries, though some muttered nervously, the name Goblin-Killer slithering through their ranks.

Skarn's gut twisted, not knowing whether he'd be dragged into the hunt or face Gorath's wrath. Had his words doomed them to face it again?

Gorath's gaze pinned him. "You will join Krogar's warband. Fail again, and you'll face Krogar in the arena." Skarn nodded, backing away, visions of that glowing sword haunting him. Facing the sword or Krogar, he was not sure which was worse.

The court surged, goblins scrambling to sharpen blades and haul armor, their shouts echoing off the bone-laden walls. Krogar barked orders, his gauntlets gleaming, while Gorath sank back onto his throne, muttering of blood and vengeance.

Skarn slipped from the hall, Gorath's command to hunt the human echoing. His steps were heavy with dread.

. . .

Just inside the Goblin Stronghold's groaning gates, about thirty goblins gathered, their war cries tangling with the scrape of rusted blades. The fortress's jagged log walls towered, and the foul stench of sweat mixed with the torch smoke. Warriors swung crude axes, archers clutched warped bows, both eager to spill elven blood. War drums pounded, rattling the muddy earth.

Skarn, scars fresh from the human's attack, stood among them, conscripted into Krogar's warband by Gorath's decree. His ribs burned, his slashed leg faltered, and that blue-tinted, rune-carved blade, Goblin-Killer, haunted his every thought. Its presence clung to him like cold iron.

Krogar's lieutenant, a grizzled leader named Dravok, leaped onto a broken barrel, spiked mace aloft. "Oi, ya filthy lot!" he roared, silencing the clamor. "Krogar wants that human! Wields a blade called Goblin-Killer, sliced royalty! We'll capture 'im and that sword, and feed them elf trees elven blood!"

The troops brandished their weapons, but fear flickered in their eyes. "That blade hates us," a scrawny goblin muttered, fingering a dagger. "Runes glow like death." Skarn's hands shook on his weapon, that same glow crawling up his spine.

The lieutenant's glare swept over them. "Scared? Thinkin' of running? I'll gut ya first! March, or you'll die here!"

The contingent spilled from the stronghold, churning through the goblin forest's twisted trees. Torches cast writhing shadows, like beasts ready to pounce. Skarn staggered, jostled by snarling goblins, his pulse racing. Whispers of Goblin-Killer snaked through the ranks, their bravado a thin mask. Scouts slunk ahead, cloaks fading into twilight.

The goblin woods thinned, giving way to the road to the Elven forest. A sharp chill bit the air, colder than any blade.

At the forest's edge, silvery trunks rose tall, their leaves shimmering under the pale moon. The warband lifted weapons with a growl. A scout stumbled back, waving a snapped elven arrow, its tip stained red. "Tracks, human or elf, near!" he panted. Torches hissed, goblins snarling.

"We'll roast 'em!" Dravok growled. "No one escapes us!" Skarn said nothing, his stomach knotted, the cursed sword haunting his thoughts like a nightmare he could never wake from. Was it out there, waiting? Did elves wield it now?

Rage burned hot, fueled by Gorath's will, but fear of Goblin-Killer gnawed at their hearts. The Elven forest stood silent, its shadows hiding threats, maybe the human, perhaps that blade, its runes poised for slaughter. A twig snapped, and the leader froze, others clutching weapons.

The lieutenant charged forward, shouting, "Into the woods! Kill anything that breathes!"

They ran forward, their cries splitting the night, but Skarn trailed, scanning the darkness, certain the blade's curse lurked ahead.

The forest closed around them, a tangle of silver and gloom, primed for a battle to break the goblin host. Goblin-Killer hung over them all, a name heavy as doom.

CHAPTER THREE

Dwarven Chord — Ethrael

Gather 'round, ye weary travelers, and let Yarnell spin a tale of heart and hope! In this verse of our saga, I met Ethrael, a lass with fire in her soul, nursing a wounded man back from death's door. Her coin pouch light, her spirit heavy, she roamed the market, where my lute's tune caught her ear. Though she brushed me off, her sharp mind recalled music's power to stir a dormant soul. A bargain struck: I'd play for her silent ward while she toiled, and in return, a cot by her hearth. Weeks passed, and lo! His foot twitched to a dwarven ballad, sparking Ethrael's hope. She dove into dwarven lore, and soon, his hum joined my song. By tale's end, a royal summons stirred our humble trio—what fate awaits us at the king's court?

*E*thrael whispered sweetly to her ward, "You're still in there. I am going to the market now, but will return soon."

The coin pouch in her hand felt light, a familiar ache. No stipend, no help, once he wakes, how am I to feed him? Unable to offer more than broth, she purchased vegetables and herbs at the market.

A bard wandered the market playing his lute. He headed towards her, the music disrupting her focus. Can't he see I'm busy? She tried to be polite, but his persistence wore on her.

"May I walk you home? My name is Yarnell. Would you like to hear a tune?" he said, hoping to win her over with his charm.

"I don't have time for such nonsense. I am nursing a wounded man back to health."

Yarnell recoiled at the rebuff. His smile and charm usually wooed the ladies.

Ethrael stopped to think. Her mind recalled something from her studies. Music reaching a mind when nothing else could... wasn't there something about it in one of the scrolls?

A bard is a man of music. Could his songs reach him where my words fail? She decided to explore this avenue.

She restarted her walk towards home. "So what kind of songs do you know? Are your songs all vulgar tavern songs, or does your repertoire include heroic stories?"

"Uhm, uh," Yarnell stumbled for words.

"I have learned that stimulating the mind could speed recovery."

"I don't know what you are asking. I know nothing of the healing arts."

"Music is common across all cultures. My patient sleeps. Maybe music and song could stimulate his mind." As she was speaking, she was formulating a plan.

"You could play music for him when I go to the market. In exchange, you may have a cot in the corner to sleep. Think of it as a challenge to be more than a performer, perhaps a healer."

"So what kind of things would I play?"

"It probably doesn't make any difference. Maybe use it as time to rehearse or compose a new song."

Yarnell stroked his chin. "An interesting proposition," he said.

"What's the range of your material? What tribes and races are you familiar with? Do you know any songs in different languages?"

"I have travelled quite widely from small villages to large cities. I have played for humans and elves alike."

They arrived at her door. "Come in and have a seat."

Yarnell entered the home, placed his lute on the table, and sat. They struck a deal. Yarnell would play for the man in the morning, while Ethrael performed duties in the market and the healing center. While Yarnell played the taverns at night, Ethrael would watch over her ward.

At least two months later, when Ethrael returned from the healing center, Yarnell looked excited. "You have to see this. Watch his foot." Yarnell started playing a song. The man's left foot moved ever so slightly.

"He moved! He responded to the music." Her heart leapt; he's still in there, fighting. "Is it just that song, or is it any song?"

"It's a dwarven tune that stirs him!"

"So you visited the dwarven homelands?"

"No, I've longed to roam the dwarven hills. I was practicing a dwarven ballad, and his foot twitched."

"Luck smiles on us. Have you tried anything else?"

"I switched to a human ditty, nothing. Back to the dwarven chant, and his foot stirred again."

"Dwarves, huh. I wonder what that means? He is obviously human," Yarnell said.

"I don't know his roots, but he's heard the dwarves' songs, maybe grew up with their hammer-beat refrains. If dwarven melodies rouse him, I'll hunt down every dwarven verse. It'll tune my strings for the road ahead."

The pitch in Ethrael's voice rose with excitement. "If he heard dwarven music, then he likely ate their food. I need to research everything: their food, language, culture, and medicine. Thank you, Yarnell, you have energized my hope."

"Crafting dwarven dishes? A costly refrain! Their ingredients scarce grace Keenroot's markets, and when found, they'd demand a hefty purse." Yarnell pressed a few coins into her palm. "Take these for our sleepy guest. You've played the gracious host; let my voice join your chorus to lift him."

She threw her arms around the bard. "Thank you so much. With this additional coin, I can provide for his needs."

• • •

Ethrael threw herself into her studies. She often brought home stacks of books and scrolls with various dwarven topics.

Ethrael noticed that things were progressing much quicker now that she and Yarnell were focused on Dwarven culture. A scant two weeks later, while waiting for dinner to be served, Yarnell was singing a new dwarven ballad. Ethrael heard a quiet hum. Ethrael stopped stirring the soup, and Yarnell stopped playing his lute.

The humming stopped. Yarnell started playing again, and it restarted. Ethrael wandered the room and found it was coming from the man. She lightly touched his throat and could feel the vibration. Yarnell and Ethrael hugged in celebration.

From that day on, the humming became stronger, but only in response to the one song in dwarvish. No other human, elven, or dwarven song stirred the man's voice. A week later, he also started humming the same song, but when Yarnell sang it in Elvish.

Ethrael exclaimed with tears rolling down her face, "He understands the words, not just the music. He knows both the elf and the dwarf languages." She pondered, he's no ordinary man, her heart swelling. "We're going to bring him back."

Ethrael and Yarnell grabbed each other and danced around the room like schoolkids.

• • •

Things started improving quickly. There seemed to be something new and different almost every day. Next, he opened his eyes for brief moments. The blood was gone, and replaced by the bluest eyes Ethrael had ever seen. Those blue eyes would focus and track her movement. She took it as a good sign.

When he was awake, she would sit him up in the bed, leaning his back against the wall and feeding him bits of broth and water. She continued using the druidic water and food patches to ensure he was getting all his body needed.

She talked to him, but there wasn't any recognition that he understood. The following week, he began moving his feet and hands, followed by his arms and legs a few days later. But still, there was no direct interaction.

Ethrael was undeterred. She read and talked to him. Recalling the importance of physical exercise in the literature, she moved his limb to work his muscles.

Yarnell cautioned, "Ethrael, you are wearing yourself out."

But she felt renewed by each small victory, undeterred by the bard's warning. She knew it was only a matter of time before this human fully recovered.

Finally, it happened. Ethrael recited a story about elves and dwarves fighting together to press back a cave elf attack. The man opened his eyes and smiled. He seemed to be enjoying the story. As the story unfolded and the terrible price both elves and dwarves paid in lost lives, a tear leaked from his eyes. "Would you like me to stop?"

The man gently shook his head. No? He understands me! Tears spilled down her cheeks. Now, it was Ethrael crying. She reflexively reached over and hugged him. She composed herself, withdrew from the hug, and continued the story. He had understood her and responded.

He grew stronger each day, her hope flickering brighter. Though he couldn't speak, she carefully lifted him to a sitting position in bed, her heart sinking as he slumped, unable to hold himself up. He slept often, but she noticed his eyes growing more alert with every passing day, a quiet victory.

Determined, she moved him to sit on the bed's edge, her hands steady as she bathed, dressed, and fed him, grateful for the control this gave her. His physical weakness lingered, yet she saw his healed wounds as a triumph. As he struggled to balance, working new muscles, he flinched, but her resolve deepened. He was getting stronger.

Now that he was awake and could sit for a short period, Ethrael decided he was ready to graduate to solid foods. She introduced them to him slowly because he hadn't had solid food for months. But the extra nourishment of solid foods helped him gain strength. Soon, he was eating and drinking by himself and taking short walks around the room. Throughout all of this, he continued to respond to dwarven music. Other than humming, he had yet to talk.

She didn't know anything else to stimulate the mind, so she continued reading to him. She read mostly stories about the elves because that was generally available, but she also read as many stories as possible about humans and dwarves.

The man was getting stronger. Ethrael would take him for walks, which were short at first but a bit longer every day. It would exhaust the man. People in the village watched daily as Ethrael and the man walked.

One day, after a morning walk, Ethrael noticed a palace page standing outside her hut. As she approached, the page handed her a note stating she, Yarnell, and the patient had an audience with the king in the late afternoon. At the bottom gleamed the royal seal. Ethrael read through the summons, her mind swirling with questions. Why us? What does the king want with a slave, a bard, and a broken man? Ethrael leaned her head to the side so Yarnell could read the note over her shoulder.

When she looked up, signaling she had read it, the page said, "I'll be back to usher you to the palace."

While Ethrael was puzzling over the note's meaning, her mind swirling with questions, Yarnell turned to the page, his voice sharp and quick with questions. "What tune summons us to this royal stage? Why does the king call for such humble players as we? No grand deeds have we sung, nor shadows cast to rouse his wrath. Have we stumbled into some hidden verse of state, a crime unsung? And our garb, what chords of cloth could suit his majesty's court? Our threads are but simple refrains!"

The page answered, her voice steady: "I cannot answer any of your questions. I was told to deliver these items and return later to escort you to the palace." The page handed a package to Yarnell, and Ethrael watched as he opened it. She saw three sets of clothes, one for each of them, finer than any she had ever seen.

She reasoned they wouldn't be given these fine clothes if guilty of some crime. Who could be so set on us meeting the king, leaving no room for excuses?

That afternoon, Ethrael felt time slip away as she prepared. She bathed and dabbed on a flower fragrance, hoping it would keep her from offending the king. She noted that Yarnell and the man did the same.

The page returned as promised, joined by two armed guards, their swords glinting.

CHAPTER FOUR

Truth Unveiled — Ethrael

Come close, travelers, and hear Yarnell recount a tale whose ripples would reach farther than Keenroot's forest walls. A king called us forth—one slave, one wounded soul, and myself, a bard whose courage proved as scant as his coin. Beneath the palace's gleaming splendor, old grudges stirred, and truths lay buried deep—yet Ethrael's voice, trembling but unbroken, unmasked deceit before the High King's throne. Chains fell, names were given, and a silent stranger claimed a seat none could have foreseen. Little did we know then that this single day would tilt the balance of realms.

*E*thrael, as a slave, was accustomed to the palace's grandeur but never part of its activities. Passing through the banquet hall with their escorts, the trio moved in a quiet procession, their steps echoing in the vast hall. Yarnell, the bard, admired the opulence, his fingers itching to strum a tune inspired by the grandeur. The human paused to admire the tapestries on the wall, their intricate details and vivid stories captivating. Their escort motioned them forward, impatient with lingering.

A slave in the king's hall? I don't belong here, Ethrael thought, her heart heavy with doubt. Five elves in robes stood by the wall to the king's right, if the king had been sitting on the throne. A dozen guards were stationed around the room. Ethrael and her friends were directed to stand opposite the elves, to the throne's left. The elves whispered, their murmurs laced with disdain for the trio.

Ethrael whispered, "The robed elves are the healers." Her voice constricted as her eyes dipped. "The one in opulent robes... that is my owner, Lord Thalen." Yarnell, sensing her unease, longed to lighten her burden with a jest.

She continued, "This is the throne room of King Arkiel, High King of the Elves. Remain silent and respectful. He wields great power."

Their escort approached one of the guards and whispered something. He immediately left, and she returned to stand between Ethrael's group and the throne. The healers, confident in their status, had no such escort.

· · ·

In short order, the guard who left returned. Not long after, two guards, followed by the king, and followed by two more guards, entered the throne room. The king stood before his throne, and his guards took their place beside the throne.

The king's robes were regal and beautiful. Deep green like twilight's forest, they were woven with threads glinting like dew on moss, and the hem resembled roots. His long silver hair framed his eyes like curtains opened to reveal the fire in his soul.

The guards escorting the king were dressed in ornate attire. The king surveyed the room, pausing to look at each individual. His gaze lingered on Ethrael before moving on to the rest of the attendees. He sat.

When he spoke, the chamber itself seemed to still. His voice was a quiet tide—soft, measured, yet carrying a weight that bowed the air around him.

Ethrael looked at her ward and noticed he was holding his breath. She whispered, "I know this is a lot to take in, but remember to breathe. You have not taken a breath since the king entered the room."

Arkiel's gaze swept across the hall, and with quiet authority, he said, "Lift your heads. The matter before us is grave, and each of you is summoned with purpose. Let there be no fear—only truth."

No one answered, but everyone bowed their heads.

The king turned to the escort and said, "Bring the stranger to my side. Let me behold him with my own eyes." The human was taken and positioned as requested; his frail form was a puzzle that Arkiel studied with keen interest.

"Ethrael, I am told this man cannot speak. Does he understand what is said to him?"

"He cannot form words, your Majesty… yet he understands. He answers yes or no when I ask, with nods or a shake of his head." Her voice remained steady despite Thalen's piercing stare.

Yarnell added quickly, "Hail, mighty Arkiel. I'm Yarnell, a humble strummer o' tales. We're but minor notes in your grand refrain, me with my lute, Ethrael with her healer's touch, this lad a mystery wrapped in scars. Why summon such lowly notes to your throne's high melody?"

Arkiel's eyes flicked toward him—not harsh, but cool as moonlit water. "Peace, bard. Your tongue leaps ahead of wisdom. Speak when I bid it."

Yarnell shrank back, his face reddening with embarrassment.

The king turned his attention to the other side of the room. "The scouts told me how he was found. Now tell me how he fared once placed in your care."

Thalen fidgeted. The healers traded glances until Lord Thalen stepped forth, voice shaky. "Your Majesty. This human stood on death's brink when he reached us. His wounds were dire, as your scouts no doubt told you, lacerations, contusions. We wove our usual enchantments, but the magic failed. We turned to potions, herbs, yet his state worsened, blood issuing from his ears, his skull darkening with ruin, his eyes blood-filled."

He hesitated and drew a slow, deep breath.

"We knew of your interest, yet our efforts faltered. In desperation, we," he paused, swallowing hard, "we removed a piece of his skull. A barbarous act, untried among us. Slowly, the pressure eased, and we restored the bone."

Arkiel pressed, his voice still calm, but edged now with iron. "He improved afterward? Then speak plainly… what followed?"

"Well, yes, he did get better. His wounds were healing. The swelling in his head subsided. But he never woke up."

Arkiel stood with hands on his hips, the gentleness gone from his expression. "Must I drag each truth from you myself? Say what happened."

"Your Majesty, you have to understand, we figured he was going to die. We needed the bed space. We transferred him to the care of my servant girl. We instructed her on how to care for him. We regularly visited to check on his health and make changes as required. It is a miracle that he stands by you today. I am confident he will never be able to talk or perform more than the most menial tasks." The healer bowed his head, saying nothing more.

Arkiel relaxed and sat. "Very well. A few final questions, and then judgment. Did this man have any possessions?"

"No, sire. Only tattered rags, blood-soaked and ruined. We discarded them." The healer looked uncomfortable, though Ethrael couldn't discern if it was due to the king's questions or another cause.

Arkiel nodded that he understood. "And the rest of you— is any truth yet hidden from me?" They all shook their heads quickly without saying a word.

Ethrael fidgeted, uncomfortable with Lord Thalen's version of events.

Arkiel's gaze, softened yet firm, met hers. "Child, I sense unrest in you. Do your thoughts differ from Lord Thalen's tale?"

Thalen's glare pierced her, twisting her stomach into a knot. He'll punish me if I speak, she thought.

"Sire, I am but a slave. It is not my place to comment on my master's testimony," her eyes focused on the floor.

Arkiel leaned forward, compassion and command woven seamlessly in his tone. "You stand before your king. Your honesty honors this court more than misplaced obedience. Speak without fear—none here shall harm you."

Thalen began fidgeting, his unease evident to Ethrael.

She thought she must speak for the man, no matter the cost.

Raising her eyes, steady and firm, she replied, "Yes, sire. I'll share what I know, and you may distill the truth. Much was true, but he polished it. They scorned him for being human and checked him scarcely twice. Their visits gave no guidance beyond dressing changes."

Arkiel's scrutiny sharpened, like a blade honed. "So beyond those paltry efforts, you alone tended him?"

"Sire, not so. I took it on myself to study scrolls and lore of many folk. Unsupervised, I crafted remedies my master would've scorned. I called on this bard, Yarnell, to stir his soul with song and story. Those tunes and tales, I swear, woke him to life and response. I see his full healing ahead. His past may remain hidden, his memories lost, but his strength will return."

Ethrael sensed a storm brewing as Arkiel tilted his head in silence. "Without a healer's rank... you restored him?"

Thalen smiled, anticipating Ethrael's punishment for defying his instructions.

"Yes, sire," she said, firm as oak. "All others forsook him. I had to try."

He paused as if weighing her words. "...Then you have my respect. Courage is seldom found where chains are worn."

"And his effects, what of them?"

Ethrael shifted, unease flickering, yet remaining focused on the king. Focusing solely on the king steadied her will.

"Beyond the rags my master named, I recall three things. A coin purse, though I know not its contents, a ring, but I do not know its importance, and an old sword, rusted and dull, currently wrapped in cloth under my bed."

Arkiel leaned to one of his guards, whispering a command, and he hastened off.

"I have heard sufficient truth for now. I shall withdraw to weigh what has been spoken. No one leaves this hall until my return."

He rose and left the throne room with his guards trailing.

Thalen stared at Ethrael. He meant for his silence to loom over her, a threat without words. *He is trying to intimidate me,* Ethrael reckoned. Ethrael looked away, avoiding eye contact, hands still. The patient shuffled to her side, his frail form seeking her strength.

Time crawled. The stranger clung to Ethrael for support as his strength was fading. Whispering to no one, she said, "Not now, please, you've come so far."

Propriety tossed aside, she eased him to the floor, where he slumped against the wall, eyes fluttering, breath shallow. She knelt, tucking her shawl under his head, wiping sweat with her sleeve, as tenderly as possible under the circumstances.

A guard, seeing the stranger collapse to the floor, slipped out of the throne room. His expression was unreadable, but his urgency was not. Soon, he returned with one of Arkiel's retinue, clad in regal armor, formidable as a storm.

Thalen leaned close, smirking, and whispering loud enough for Ethrael to hear, "Now she will feel the king's wrath."

The king's personal guard strode forward and gently lifted the stranger, setting him on the throne. The gesture drew a hush. No one expected such honor for a human. He spoke softly to Ethrael and motioned for her to stand beside her charge. Ethrael arranged the throne's cushions to cradle her patient.

The healers murmured, their shock in their hushed tones. None dared voice it openly, but every face revealed the same disbelief: a slave's patient placed upon the High King's throne.

· · ·

A long while later, as Ethrael's back and legs were cramping, the door opened, and two of the personal guards entered with their king. He approached the throne, his poise steady and deliberate, smiled, and motioned for Ethrael to stay there. He stood beside his throne while a human was sitting in his position of honor, a rare, approving smile spread across his face.

His gaze traversed the hall, resting at last upon Ethrael. "Be at ease, child. Permit him to relax there. Minister to him as you see fit. My guard has retrieved the sword you spoke of from your dwelling."

He pivoted to the healers, his scrutiny fixing upon their leader, his tone edged with controlled anger. "Thalen, your quarters have been searched. The coin pouch and ring Ethrael spoke of? Discovered. You will answer for this. Explain yourself."

Lord Thalen faltered. Ethrael could see he was searching for an acceptable answer, scrambling for a defense. "Your Majesty... we kept them only for safekeeping. When... when he recovered, we... we meant to return them. Assuredly, sire... assuredly." Perspiration began beading upon his brow; his companions' eyes remained glued to the floor.

"Convenient words, offered only once you were caught," Arkiel scoffed, his tone cold as tempered steel. "Yet why were these articles in your private quarters rather than the center's repository? Is it customary among your profession to convey patients' effects to your home for 'safeguarding'? Do not insult this court further." His exasperation was barely contained beneath a mantle of regal composure.

He leaned toward a guard, issuing a muted command. Then, with heightened timbre: "Guards, remove these blights on the honorable healing profession! Their sentencing shall be addressed tomorrow."

The healers were escorted from the throne room under firm guard, their pride shattered. Ethrael watched as the healers filed out, her heart pounding, the enormity of the moment settling over her like a weight.

• • •

His visage softened, gentleness breaking through the anger. "My honored guests." His voice, imbued with benevolence, carried through the hall. "You have my profound gratitude. I take pride in reigning over those like you. Unknowingly, you have rendered a service of great magnitude to me, this realm, and realms beyond. For this, I offer rewards."

Arkiel gestured toward the man, reposing upon the throne. "His identity and history remain veiled. In the absence of his own voice, I would name him *Lorin*, after a cherished comrade of my youth. Should his speech return, he may choose his name."

He turned to Ethrael, his countenance gracious. "Ethrael, for your valor amidst perilous odds, I decree thy emancipation."

Free? After all these years? Ethrael's heart soared.
"As of this moment, you are free.
No chain binds you.
No oath claims you.
No elf holds dominion over your life."

Arkiel paused, letting the words settle. "You shall enter the ranks of my royal healers. They shall instruct you in their disciplines: pursue the unorthodox, arcane magics, divine magics, remedies beyond elven tradition, or other studies as your inclination directs. You shall receive a stipend commensurate with my healers. Lorin's recovery is your charge; you answer only to me."

Leaning close, he whispered, "I have known who you were from the day you entered my kingdom. Your family's calling was once a light to every elven hall. I believe it shall be so again. Your lineage is yours to reveal when your heart allows, but know this... it eased my spirit to find Lorin in your care." Confusion washed through her, her heart hammering harder with each breath.

He knew her heritage... he believed in it... the truth felt both distant and unreal.

His attention shifted to Yarnell. "Bard, thy desires elude me, yet you are welcome within these halls. My aegis extends over you, wherever your melodies may lead, bear this ring as its testament."

He withdrew a band from his finger. "I request you remain, though. My servants say you are quite the artist. Your talent deserves a performance before me. Seek the artisans of my court. They shall guide you where an instrument befitting your talent may be fashioned, at my expense."

Arkiel paused, his tone resolute. "One final matter, Lorin's possessions: coin, ring, and sword. I shall retain them presently and restore them at the appropriate hour. I eagerly await our next reunion, when our silent guest might grace us with his voice."

A faint smile graced his lips as he turned to depart, then pivoted once more to address the trio. "Ah, I nearly forgot, as a more immediate token of my gratitude, accept this."

He bestowed upon each a pouch, the clink of coins resounding within. "Night descends, but tomorrow, embrace the dawn of your new paths."

With that, he exited the throne room with a stately stride, his guards trailing behind.

Yarnell and Ethrael had to help Lorin home. By the time he was eased into bed, exhaustion had overtaken Ethrael, too, her mind swirling with freedom and the weight of her new responsibilities.

CHAPTER FIVE

Scourge and Mercy — Lorin

Gather 'round the fire, friends, let Yarnell's lute hum a tale both grim and tender. In Keenroot's heart, where justice's whip met mercy's touch, our trio—freed healer, the silent stranger, and a bard whose jests failed him—witnessed a courtyard's cruel dance. Lashes tore flesh, tar sealed wounds, and King Arkiel's voice carved truth deep into our bones.

Lorin's eyes, haunted by pain's old echo, watched Thalen's pride break. Yet Ethrael's heart, ever steady, ever kind, stirred us toward the infirmary's shadows. There, amid cries, we bound what was torn, choosing healing over hate.

Hush now, for this is a story of scars shared, of a silent man's ember stirring to life, and a vow to rise nobler, forged in a realm's stern crucible of scourge and song.

Lorin sat at breakfast, the weight of yesterday's throne room lingering. His new name, a king's gift, anchored him, but it felt foreign, its connection to his past elusive. The king's interest marked him as more than a broken stranger, stirring a sense of self yet to be grasped. Across the table, Ethrael sat with a steady gaze, Yarnell fidgeting restlessly, their presence echoing his tentative hope. Her freedom and his new seal brightened the world, sharpening its edges.

Their morning walk carried them through Keenroot's vibrant market, the air crisp with birdsong. But the usual hum was pierced by urgent chatter. Ethrael paused at a fruit vendor's stall. "What's happening?"

"Punishment in the courtyard at noon," the vendor replied, eyes darting.

Lorin's gut tightened. The healers' fearful glances from the throne room flashed in his mind, Thalen's cold stare, the others' averted gazes. They were the condemned, their sentencing imminent. The trio joined the swelling crowd at the palace courtyard.

The courtyard thrummed with an unseen pulse, as if the ancient oaks channeled Keenroot's magic into their knotted roots. Lorin's skin prickled, the air heavy with a faint hum, elven chants woven into the canopy, blessing or cursing this judgment, he couldn't tell. The crowd pressed close, highborn elves in silks standing aloof from merchants and servants, their eyes cold on the human in their midst. A stark wooden frame stood at the center, flanked by barrels of black ooze. Guards held the crowd back, their armor glinting coldly.

Lorin leaned toward Ethrael, gesturing faintly toward the black ooze.

"Nightroot resin," she murmured back, eyes darkening. "It seals wounds, prevents fever... and makes sure the scars never fade. We use it in old justice rites."

Lorin stiffened. The purpose was suddenly, brutally clear.

A trumpet's blare cut the air. King Arkiel stepped onto the balcony, his green robes shimmering like dew, flanked by guards. His voice rang out, stern yet steady. "Bring out the accused."

Lorin's eyes followed the healers, now chained, their faces pale, stripped of robes. Their hunched shoulders bore the crowd's stare, pride replaced by fear.

Arkiel's words crashed like a tide. "I charged you to care for this man," he said, voice a honed blade. "You neglected him, lied to me, scorned his human blood. Thieves, betrayers, you've shamed your craft."

A faint tightness crossed Arkiel's eyes—fleeting, but Lorin saw it. The king did not relish this.

"Ten lashes for all," Arkiel continued. A faint tremor touched his hand before he steadied it against the railing. "But

Thalen—your crimes cut deeper. Your title is stripped. Then the dungeon."

Lorin's breath was unsteady, the accusations stirring a nameless ache. The crowd murmured as guards bound the healers to the frame, their backs exposed, whips poised.

"We are compassionate," Arkiel said, voice heavy. The edge of formality cracked slightly—a human note beneath the king. "Yet justice must resound. Ten lashes. Count with me."

As Arkiel raised his hand to signal the start, Lorin saw a tiny pause—a heartbeat of sorrow the crowd might miss, but unmistakable to him.

Lorin's chest tightened, the air bracing for a storm.

"One."

The whips cracked, a thunderclap. Metal tips tore flesh, blood bubbling on their backs. The healers' jaws clenched, eyes wide with silent torment. Lorin flinched, the whip's crack stirring memories of familiar pain. His hands trembled, Thalen's contorted face searing into him, a mirror to his remembered pain.

"Two—three."

Wounds widened, blood surging, staining their backs crimson. The crowd's low whispers faltered, women's sobs soft against the leather's snap. Lorin's hands trembled, Thalen's contorted face searing into him, a mirror to his recent pain. Lorin glanced at Ethrael, her jaw tight, eyes locked on Thalen's bleeding back. Her hands, usually steady with bandages, trembled, as if torn between healing and the justice she'd demanded. Yarnell lingered behind them, fingers twitching in small, nervous bursts. His face had gone pale, mouth drawn tight, the usual mischief drained from him. Lorin felt their weight beside him, their shared scars binding them tighter than any oath.

"Four—five—six."

Cries shattered the stillness, raw and piercing. Blood streamed, the ground darkening. Lorin's stomach churned, the violence a blur, his eyes locked on the healers' anguish.

"Seven—eight."

Screams tore free, backs a sheen of red.

Arkiel's count was steady, but Lorin heard strain beneath it—as if each number etched pain onto the king as surely as the lashes tore the healers.

"Nine—ten."

The whips fell silent. Healers slumped, broken. The coppery scent stung Lorin's nose, a tremor running through him as the courtyard held its breath.

Silence deepened, the forest's boughs whispering grief.

Arkiel's voice rose, laced with pain. "These men wronged you all. Witness their judgment, share their sentencing. Punishment carves; mercy heals. All must partake."

When Arkiel said mercy, his voice thinned—Lorin sensed the weight in it, as if the word itself carried years of hard choices.

The crowd hesitated, guards, men, women, and children following, all hands stained black. Lorin hesitated, a flicker of Ethrael's mercy urging him to aid the healers. Lorin's breath caught as resin was smeared across the healers' torn backs, the acrid scent sharp in his nose. He felt drawn to Thalen. His feet moved, fingers shaking as he dipped them in barrels of blackness, its bitter warmth coating his hands. Rubbing it across the healer's ravaged back, he recalled Thalen's throne-room glare. His gaze lingered on Thalen, torn between justice's clarity and a leader's burden to command such punishment.

The crowd ebbed, every palm darkened. Arkiel descended, casting off his robes, silks pooling like wine. Plunging his hands into a barrel, blackness mixed with blood fell to the ground as he anointed each healer. Lorin's heart pulsed, awe and ache mingling, watching tears carving through Arkiel's tear-streaked face. He watched Arkiel, awe mingling with doubt over balancing strength with mercy.

"It grieves to scourge our own," his voice was heavy with pain. "Let this burn in your memory, an indelible mark to spare its return. Teach the young. These healers bear scars of their sentence; I bear commanding this judgment; you bear its witness. Vow to rise nobler, depart, and comfort one another."

He turned to the guards. "Bear them to the infirmary. They remain our brothers." Head bowed, stained hands limp at his side, he retreated to the palace, shoulders sagging under an unseen weight.

• • •

At the hut, silence cloaked Lorin, Ethrael, and Yarnell, heavy as the courtyard's echoes. The dim glow of a single lantern flickered across the wooden walls, casting shadows that danced like the ghosts of the day's violence. Lorin sat at the table, his hands still sticky despite scrubbing, the acrid scent clinging stubbornly to his skin. His chest ached, not from his old wounds, but from the weight of Thalen's screams. Arkiel's heavy words weighed on his mind, drawing tight around him, stirring a gnawing uncertainty over whether this was justice or something crueler.

Ethrael sat across from him, her hands clenched around a clay mug, steam rising untouched. Her eyes, usually bright with purpose, were shadowed, fixed on stained fingers. Her jaw tightened, a flicker of resolve breaking through her exhaustion, as if she were fighting a silent battle inside. She glanced toward the window, where the infirmary's path lay beyond, hidden in the twilight.

Yarnell slumped in a chair, his lute untouched in the corner, its strings silent for the first time Lorin could recall. The bard's fingers twitched, as if itching to pluck a tune to banish the day's scars, but his face was pale, lips pressed thin. "No celebrating tonight," he mumbled, voice barely breaking the hush. His eyes darted to Lorin, then Ethrael, seeking something, comfort—or even absolution. Lorin met his gaze, nodding, his jaw tight, feeling their shared silence weave a bond stronger than words.

The fire in the hearth crackled, spitting embers that mirrored the unease in Lorin's chest. He tried to eat, the broth Ethrael had warmed bitter on his tongue, each swallow heavy with the coppery tang of memory, blood on the courtyard stones, stains on his hands. A shadow flickered through his thoughts: a forge's glow, the clash of steel, a voice cursing his name. Was it his past, or the courtyard's cruelty seeping into his broken thoughts? He pushed the bowl away, the clink of clay loud in the stillness.

Ethrael's voice, soft but firm, cut through the quiet. "Their pain doesn't end with the whips." She looked at Lorin, her eyes searching his, as if testing his heart. Her words resonated deeply, her gaze kindling his resolve that hate could not heal.

She added, "They're in the infirmary now, suffering. I keep seeing Thalen's face, not the sneer, but the fear. I hated him, but..." She trailed off, her fingers tracing the mug's rim, tar smudging the clay. Lorin's breath caught, her words echoing his own turmoil, and he sensed her urge, a quiet pull to mend what was torn.

Yarnell shifted, boots scuffing the floor. "You're not thinking of helping them, are you?" His voice carried a tremor, half disbelief, half awe. "After what they did to both of you?" Lorin's chest tightened, Thalen's cold dismissal flashing in his mind, yet Ethrael's glance held no vengeance, a tired, quiet reflection.

"I don't know," Ethrael said, her voice steadying. "But I know what it's like to be forsaken. So do you, Lorin." Her eyes locked on his, and he felt exposed, as if she saw the scars beneath his skin, the ones no healer could touch. He nodded slowly, deliberately, her words settling like a vow. The infirmary's path called to him too, a faint tug, like the sword's hum in the courtyard, urging him toward something he didn't yet understand.

The silence returned, but it was different now, less a shield and more a shared resolve. Lorin's memory drifted to the old sword wrapped in cloth, its presence a mystery stirring questions that weighed on him.

Ethrael rose, setting her mug down, her movements deliberate. "We should rest," she said, but her eyes lingered on the door, on the path beyond. "I'll see how I can assist in the infirmary tomorrow."

The lessons of mercy settled like a vow in Lorin's chest. He felt a resolve to join Ethrael at the infirmary come dawn, drawn not by duty but by mercy's answer to the courtyard's scars.

· · ·

Dawn rose, dimmed by the courtyard's ache in Lorin's bones. He and Ethrael left early for the healing center.

Lorin's legs were unsteady from the start, a deep trembling threaded through his calves. Each step reminded him he was still recovering, not yet built for a day of tending others. But Ethrael moved with quiet purpose, and he followed, leaning on that resolve when his own faltered.

The families of the condemned were struggling to care for their loved ones. Their heartache and lack of healing skills frustrated them.

The families of the healers were crying, struggling to grasp the brutality inflicted on those they cherished. Lorin overheard comments from the families:

"He was merely human—why would the king shield him so fiercely?"

"What lie could justify such a severe penalty?"

"It's so brutal... will he ever recover?"

The patients were all lying on their stomachs to avoid pressure on their whip-torn backs.

The sharp scents of resin, blood, and sweat hung in the air, turning Lorin's stomach and making the lingering dizziness from his injury pulse at his temples.

Ethrael, unfazed, moved with quiet purpose. She took a wet lavender-scented towel and placed it over their eyes and nose. It had a calming effect; some even fell asleep.

She examined their wounds and was surprised to see that no blood oozed and that they were starting to mend.

Lorin did as much as he could to help her.

More than once, his hands trembled, forcing him to pause and steady himself on a bedframe or wall. The room swayed when he bent too long over a patient, his breath coming faster than it should. Ethrael noticed once, opening her mouth to intervene, but he shook his head—gently, stubbornly—and kept going.

He wasn't strong enough for this work—not yet—but leaving her alone with so much hurt felt worse than the ache in his limbs.

By dusk, Lorin and Ethrael returned to the hut, her face weary but fierce, his exhaustion mirrored in the shadows beneath his eyes.

Every muscle in his body throbbed, a deep, lingering tremor running through his legs. He could barely lift his arms by the time they stepped through the door, every movement a dull burn.

Yarnell opened his mouth, but Ethrael's raised hand stilled him.

"The punishment struck us deeply," she said, voice firm yet pained. "We chose to heal, not hate, spending this day in the infirmary, tending their wounds. The resin staunched their bleeding, but their scars teach us integrity. A lesson to carry forward."

Lorin clung to her strength, a warmth blooming in his chest. He nodded, her words settling like a vow in his clouded thoughts, binding them to a path of mercy.

CHAPTER SIX

The Forge's Rekindled Voice — Lorin

Gather, friends, and hear a forge's song, where Keenroot's embers spark a stranger's tale. In the village's smoky heart, our silent Lorin, tethered by a king's name, feels a hammer's call. Will fire and steel rekindle his voice, or leave his past a locked door? Hush now, for his steps tread the anvil's edge, forging purpose from a clouded soul.

*L*orin walked through the village at dawn, boots brushing dew-soaked earth. The air stung his lungs, sharp with grass and smoke. Ethrael's voice broke the stillness, soft but clear, tinged with a familiar elven cadence. "I believe the gods placed us here to help and care for one another," she said, her eyes fixed on the path ahead. "Work is one way we do that. Mine is healing, tending to others. Yarnell's is lifting hearts with song, teaching through tales. But Lorin...has no work." She glanced at him, her gaze steady. "He needs to find what the gods mean for him."

His chest tightened, not from the chill, but from the weight of Ethrael's words echoing in his mind: Lorin has no work. The name still felt foreign, a gift from a king, not his own. He glanced at Ethrael beside him, her silver hair catching the first light like a river under moonlight, and Yarnell, trailing with a restless stride, his lute silent. The village hummed with life, but Lorin felt like a shadow, adrift, his past a locked door.

Lorin's throat tightened, words he couldn't form trapped inside. Who was I before? What was my profession? The questions gnawed at him, as they had since the courtyard's punishment. They wandered the village, passing market stalls where merchants hawked fruits and cloth, and artisans offered mended boots or sharpened blades. Lorin's eyes skimmed the bustle, searching for something to spark recognition, but nothing stirred. *Without Ethrael, would I even be here, grasping at shadows?* The faces blurred, their voices a distant hum, like memories he couldn't hold.

Yarnell nudged him, pointing to a new path, one they'd never taken. It led away from the village, where the air grew thick with smoke and a metallic tang. Lorin's pulse quickened, his steps heavier, drawn by a heat he felt before he saw it. The forge loomed ahead, its coals glowing red, spitting sparks that danced like stars in his clouded mind. He moved closer, the warmth washing over him, pulling him like a tide. A shadow flickered in his thoughts, hammers ringing, steel glowing, a voice calling a name not his.

Lorin stood frozen, inches from the forge's glowing coals, their heat searing his face. The world faded, the village's hum drowned by the fire's pulse, a rhythm echoing deep within, like a forgotten song. Sparks danced, fleeting stars in his clouded mind, whispering of hammers and steel he couldn't name.

"Lorin!" Ethrael's voice cut through, loud and sharp. Blinking, he saw the Forge Master's soot-streaked arm barring his path. Ethrael stepped closer, silver hair catching the firelight, her eyes flicking between him and the blacksmith.

"Please stand back, this is a dangerous area," the Forge Master said, his voice sharp. Lorin barely heard, eyes locked on the junior blacksmiths. Some thrust irons into the coals, flames licking the metal red, then plunged them into water barrels, steam hissing like a sigh. Others pounded rough shapes, the hammers' cadence stirring his chest. His arms burned, a pull to grip a hammer surging within, muscles trembling. The forge's heat enveloped him, familiar, a home he couldn't recall.

"Sir," she said, her voice steady but soft, "this man was gravely injured, his memories gone, even his name. King Arkiel tasked me with his recovery. Watching him now, I think… something in his past pulls him to your forge. Could you show him around, perhaps let him help with small tasks? Work might aid his healing. I don't know what you'd need, but we'd find a way to repay you."

Lorin's pulse quickened, Ethrael's words stirring a spark in his chest. The forge feels right; its heat was a memory his body knew, even if his mind didn't. He met her gaze, nodding, a silent plea to stay.

The Forge Master, a burly elf with eyes like flint, glanced between them. "Here's my offer," he said, voice gruff. "He can help with basic tasks, nothing risky or too heavy. I need grunt work done, and he looks frail, but it'll put muscle on his frame. He starts tomorrow at sunrise. Agreed? Name's Falere, Master Falere."

Lorin's chest surged, a warmth spreading through him, like the forge's glow. Ethrael looked at him, and he nodded, eager, his hands trembling with something like hope. "He'll be here," she said. "One request, sir. The king himself charged me with his care. Please tell me if the work's too much or he risks harm."

"Young lady," Falere replied, a faint smile breaking his stern face, "I run this forge, craft weapons, and keep my people safe. If His Majesty values him, I'll treat him like my own. No offense, but I'll check your story with the palace before dawn. If it holds, you have my word."

• • •

The next morning, Lorin woke before dawn, his body tense with purpose. He dressed quickly, boots scuffing the hut's floor, and stepped into the chill, the forge's distant smoke calling him. Falere waited, silhouetted against the coals. "You'll stoke the forge," he said, pointing to a coal pile. "Hard work, but you'll manage. This is Brynvar, my laborer. He'll show you."

Brynvar, a towering elf with broad shoulders and an easy grin, nodded at Lorin. His strength dwarfed most elves, but his eyes were kind. Following Brynvar, mimicking his movements, he shoved coal into the fire. His arms burned, each motion a strain, but the forge's heat steadied him. He thought he couldn't fail here, not when this felt like home.

At noon, Brynvar guided him back to the hut, his voice gentle, "Falere says you're done for today. You're not strong enough for a full shift."

Lorin slumped onto the bed, his arms limp, exhaustion sinking into his bones. Ethrael's eyes widened as she looked at him. "Does Falere think he shouldn't return?" she asked, her voice sharp. Lorin's breath caught; the thought of losing the forge was like a blade in his chest. Brynvar shook his head.

"No, ma'am. Falere says Lorin's got grit. He worked to exhaustion but wouldn't stop until we made him. Falere's worried he'll push too hard, hurt himself, or others. He says mornings only, till Lorin's stronger."

Ethrael's shoulders lowered, and she nodded, pouring water infused with her herbs. Lorin drank, the liquid cool against his parched throat, and sank into sleep. For weeks, this became his rhythm: mornings at the forge, stoking coals, sweeping ash, his muscles aching but growing. By month's end, he worked full days, hauling supplies and cleaning tools, his body tougher, and the forge's pulse his anchor.

One day, Ethrael visited, and her arrival brought a quiet warmth to Lorin's heart. Falere approached, his face stern but his eyes less sharp. "The palace oversight is new to me," he said, glancing at Lorin. "But your man's doing well. He thinks I give him grunt work, but small tasks test character. Excel at them, and greatness follows. Lorin's the best I've seen. Our forges run smoother because of him."

He turned to Lorin, a rare grin breaking through. "You've even taught Brynvar a thing or two. That oaf's been here for years, always sloppy. You've made him useful, saved his job."

Falere began teaching Lorin forge techniques, his voice sharp with instruction. Lorin understood the ideas, shaping metal and tempering blades, but his hands fumbled, the hammer was awkward, and his strikes were weak. Weeks passed, each failure a weight on his chest. In frustration, Falere changed tactics. "Do it your way," he said, stepping back. "Show me what you know."

Lorin hesitated, the hammer heavy in his grip. He closed his eyes, the forge's heat washing over him, a memory flickering, dwarven chants, a blade glowing red. How do I know this? His hands moved, guided by instinct, striking the metal with a rhythm he didn't understand. When he finished, the tool, a simple knife, was flawless; its edge was sharp, its curve was elegant, and it was fit for a lord, not a commoner. Falere's eyes widened, Lorin's chest tightened, the forge's heat pulsing like a memory in his blood. Was this who I was?

Falere faced Ethrael and Lorin, "He knows the forge, his ways unique but effective. I'll keep challenging him. I will give him more complex tasks, but he will have to figure out how to accomplish them. I will guide as needed, but to date, it has become increasingly unnecessary. The simple objects he has created are beyond most of my other students. I can imagine the day when he will surpass me. I welcome that day and the challenge it will present me."

A smile cracked Lorin's face, warmth surging in his chest.

"Thank you, master. You have been very kind." Ethrael replied, "His body has responded beyond my greatest hopes. Were I as successful with his mind as you are with his body, he would be fully restored."

Falere put his hand on Ethrael's shoulder. "Lass, the body is much easier to rebuild than a mind. All it took was hard work on his part. I don't know about such things, but a mind is a much more complex thing. All of my students can make the simple things, like a sword for hacking through bushes. It takes a great bit of skill, experience, and sometimes luck to make something fit for a royal guard. His mind is just such a thing. You have brought him a long way, and it will be you who brings him back to full health, full mental health. Remember how far you have brought him. The king is wise and would not have left him in your care if he did not believe in you."

Lorin's throat tightened, Falere's words of confidence a light in his fogged thoughts. True to his word, he gave Lorin greater tasks. Before long, he stood out as the forge's finest apprentice, his work exact while others' wavered. He caught the other apprentices' glances as their hammers rang and blades took form. Yet his own strikes seemed steered, as if a hand from his past guided each blow.

One day, Falere brought all the apprentices together to show them what he had been working on, a shaft for a hammer. It was still glowing red because it had just been pulled from the flame. "Lorin, what do you think of my workmanship?" Master Falere asked, his voice loud and confident.

Lorin studied the shaft, its craftsmanship gleaming. Then his gaze caught a flaw, a hairline crack. Words rose unbidden, his voice rough from disuse. "Sir, no disrespect, but here's an imperfection. In battle... it could break. It's fine for decoration, though not a weapon. Am I wrong?" He froze, the sound of his own voice a shock, like a dam bursting.

Falere's jaw dropped, then he laughed, checking the shaft. "You're right, Lorin. None caught it, though we worked on this for a week."

The forge master faced the apprentices, voice booming. "You saw it and stayed silent. Our craft can kill if we fail. I'd rather be embarrassed here than before the king for a guard's death. Clear?"

He grinned at Lorin. "You'll be a master craftsman. Time to head home."

• • •

When Lorin entered the hut, Ethrael's eyes widened, startling him. "Word already reached us that you spoke," she said.

Yarnell spoke, questions tumbling out. "How long have you been able to speak? Why not talk to us? Have your memories returned?"

Lorin's voice, still strange to him, answered. "I don't know. Falere asked, and I spoke. I didn't think about speaking. It just happened. I was completely focused on the hammer. My speech is back, but my past... still gone. I pray that changes, but now I can be part of this community, thanks to you both. I couldn't say it before, but thank you. I wouldn't have survived without you. I can never repay you."

Ethrael's gaze lingered, and Yarnell's lips curved into a grin. They headed to the tavern to celebrate.

Lorin leaned forward, the tavern's din fading as he watched Ethrael stare into her mug, the ale's amber glow reflecting in her eyes. Her fingers traced the mug's rim, hesitant, as if weighing words too heavy to speak.

"You don't have to say it," he offered softly, sensing a storm behind her silence.

She shook her head, her voice barely above a whisper. "I want to. It's just... hard." Her gaze remained fixed on the liquid, as if it held the shape of her past. "I come from Aelthar, a small elven hold in the northern glades. My family tended the Starbloom Grove, sacred, glowing like embers under starlight."

Lorin's chest tightened. Her words sparked images: moonlit glades, flowers pulsing like the forge's heart he knew so well. Her pain mirrored his own, a locked vault of memories he couldn't face. "What happened there?" he asked, voice low, bracing for her answer.

Her fingers stilled, her voice faltering. "I was five when the cave elves and goblins came. They... burned everything. My parents, siblings, and the guards who sang to me, slaughtered. The meadow, the starblooms... just ash." A tear slipped down her cheek, and in Lorin's mind, flames roared, screams clanging like hammer strikes.

Her despair settled over him, heavy as an anvil, yet he glimpsed something beneath it, roots enduring, like steel forged in fire, waiting to bloom again. His own buried past stirred, a faint hope he clung to. Her sorrow cut sharper than his, but it kindled a resolve. If she could face her pain, so could he.

CHAPTER SEVEN

The Grove's Fading Whisper — Lorin

Gather, friends, and heed a tale of ash and ember, where Keenroot's hearth cradles a healer's heart. Ethrael, born of Aelthar's starlit grove, bears a shadow's weight, her roots enduring beneath ruin. Lorin, our smith, hammers steel and dreams, a spark to lead where shadows falter. Will her whispered past kindle his flame, forging a path to guide them both? Hush now, for their bond weaves a song of hope amid the fading whispers of a lost glade.

Now that Lorin was physically strong, employed, and able to communicate, he decided it was time to branch out. He would find a new place to live with Yarnell and give Ethrael back her space; her hut was far too small for three adults.

Days passed in his new home, warmed by Ethrael's visits. Watching her arrive, her healer's bag slung over her shoulder, Lorin noted her steps were slower than before. Sensing a weight in her silence, a shift from her usual warmth, he wondered if his independence dimmed her purpose, as the forge had kindled his own.

Tracing the hut's beams, their grain worn smooth by time, he caught the scent of pine mingling with earth. Yarnell's lute rested in a corner, reflecting the hearth's glow, a reminder of their shared journey. The space felt open, too vast after Ethrael's cramped hut, his fingers twitching, longing for the forge's hammer to ground him. He wondered if this move had changed their bond, the hearth's warmth a faint comfort against the chill of his still-locked past.

Lorin deemed his personal life to be going well. Though not his full-time caregiver, Ethrael regularly stopped in to chat about his health and studies. His favorite times were when she visited for talks or walks through the village. He couldn't share much beyond his forge training, but loved hearing about her experiences and past. At times, her voice softened, eyes distant, but often her words came faster as they talked and walked together. Those visits filled his evenings, her healer's bag clinking with vials as she settled by the hearth.

He described his forge work, like shaping a new blade with Brynvar, hoping her eyes would brighten as they once did. But her responses grew short over the days, her gaze fixed on her hands, fingers tracing her cloak's hem. Lorin's chest tightened, a familiar ache from his early recovery days, unsure if his growing strength pushed her away. He thought, was he forging his future at the cost of her light? Did she think he had abandoned her? He remembered her standing firm in the throne room, defying Thalen's scorn, and worried he had done something to weigh her down.

One day, she was even more withdrawn. Her gaze softened toward Lorin, but she hardly spoke as they returned to the hut. Trying to engage her on different topics, he found nothing worked. When they made it back, she quietly excused herself and walked out. Very confused, he thought, why did she pull away, as if he had hammered a wedge between them?

• • •

Lorin paced the hut, the hearth's glow fading as dusk crept in— the hurried exit replayed in his mind, her silence a mystery he couldn't unravel. Has my forge talk and pride in a new blade pushed her away? His boots scuffed the floor, the quiet pressing like the forge's heat. It wasn't until the evening meal that he saw her. The door creaked, and Ethrael returned, her face shadowed with a basket of bread and stew. Lorin's resolve hardened, a need to shape his future like steel.

She brought him food, but was still very quiet. Her hands trembled slightly, setting down the basket, her eyes avoiding his. As they sat down to eat, she said, "I am sorry I have been so distracted lately, but things have progressed much quicker than I expected them to."

Still confused, Lorin thought, wasn't he becoming self-sufficient, allowing her to resume her normal life? What was the problem? Wasn't this what they both had been working towards? Brow furrowing, he noted her words clashing with the distance in her eyes.

She continued, "Your wounds are fully mended, your strength increases daily, and you excel at the forge. I am proud of you." But her eyes, when they met his, shimmered with unshed tears, and her hands twisted the edge of her cloak, the green fabric fraying under her fingers.

"I owe it all to you," he said, voice earnest, a warmth in it that hadn't been there months ago. "Without your care, I'd have perished. Yet something still troubles you. What is it?"

She paused, then drew a shuddering breath, her gaze dropping to the table, where Lorin noticed a sprig of dried sage, left from her last visit, a faint reminder of her presence. "It's not simple," she began, her voice soft as a whisper in the wind. "Tending, you taught me much in my work and beyond. I've learned new ways to mend body and mind and served the king himself in your care. I have seen a whole new world. How can I return to the limited world of my old path, just another healer at the hospital, stitching wounds and brewing tonics? It feels small now, a shadow of what I've known." She halted, her breath catching.

His pulse quickened, and he felt her words stir a mix of gratitude and unease; he hadn't realized how his recovery had reshaped her life.

"And in truth, I've come to care for you. I know it's not proper. I'm but a healer in the king's shadow. I fear being sent away, cast off now that my use wanes."

He thought, did she care for him? Had her heart forged a bond he never dared hope for?

Lorin's gaze followed Ethrael's hands, twisting her cloak until threads frayed, her voice faint over the hearth's crackle. Noticing her tremble, he envisioned a shadow of Thalen's scorn in her faltering gaze, as if she dreaded being cast off. His chest tightened. Her strength, once his anchor, faltered, like a blade under strain. Wanting to promise her a place as a friend, he found his past, heavy as iron, holding his words.

Her clenched hands, a sign of resolve, stirred him to keep her near. Looking to his heart, Lorin ached for her. Thoughts flickering to the forge, its steady rhythm mirrored the resilience he saw in her trembling form, now seemingly shaken by fear. Realizing he felt the same way about her, stunned she might feel similarly, he thought, did her care mirror his, a spark in the dark he couldn't name? Her words stirred a vision of leading, not just surviving, a path where he could guide others as she had guided him. He figured it was natural to be drawn to someone so instrumental in his long recovery.

"Ethrael, I don't know what the future holds, but I hope we can still be friends even though I am not your patient anymore. I don't have many friends and don't want to lose you. Please say that we will still be close even if you aren't burdened with my recovery anymore." His words seemed to ease her burden a bit.

Her eyes darted as she searched for words. Taking a deep breath, she spoke. "Lord Thalen found me amidst the Aelthar ruins on his return from a pilgrimage. He took me in, not as an act of kindness, but as a slave, claiming my survival was his mercy."

Lorin's fists clenched under the table, the image of her bound by Thalen's cruelty burning in his mind.

He heard her voice tighten, a bitter edge that sent a chill through him. "I've served under his lash ever since, learning the healer's craft to earn my keep, but always at the edge of being cast off if my use faltered."

Lorin heard a bitter edge in her voice, her words sharp as a blade's edge. They struck him like a hammer's blow, their weight settling in his chest. Yet, as difficult as her servitude was, her face revealed more to share, more to her story.

"I can't imagine the pain of your slavery."

"He looks down on me, always has, he sees my blood's a threat. My family line, though broken, stands above him in the old ways, and he'd sooner see me broken, too, than rise beyond his shadow."

She looked into Lorin's eyes, "Tending you gave me purpose and a kind of independence, more than I've known since Aelthar fell. I'm afraid of losing that, losing you, and being nothing but a shadow again. Though the king has freed me, I can't shake Thalen's influence."

Lorin heard her voice break, a sob escaping as she clutched her cloak tighter, and his throat tightened, her pain echoing the weight of his own shadowed past. How could Thalen chain her spirit so? Her strength hums like tempered steel.

Leaning back, Lorin felt his shoulders tense as if struck by a forge's blow. Seeing her anew, he saw her tale of royal blood and bondage shift his view through her trembling words and haunted eyes. Perceiving her not just as a healer but a survivor, her strength forged in fire like his own, unbowed despite Thalen's cruelty, he felt a fire kindle within. The defiance in her tear-streaked face spurred a call to rise beyond the forge, to lead others as she had led him through darkness. The sword, a relic of his shadowed past, whispered of a purpose yet to unfold, perhaps tied to the king's knowing gaze.

He felt her survival, forged in loss, echo his own, though his past stayed dark, like unlit coals. Her royal blood and defiance, evident in her resolute words to Lorin, made her more than a healer, a kindred spirit. His throat tightened, wanting to share his hopes, to speak of the forge's rhythm that anchored him, the sword's mystery that tugged at his mind. The rusty sword's origins were as lost as Aelthar's blooms but seemed to hum in his mind, urging him to uncover the past that weighed on him like the forge's anvil. What secrets does this blade hold? Could it forge my path as she has? Like a blade forged in fire, her struggle, evident in her words to Lorin, kindled his resolve to anchor her as she had him. Heavy as the forge's heat, her tale lingered, stirring a deeper call within him. He yearned to rise beyond the anvil, lead others as she had led him through darkness, and forge a destiny greater than his shadowed past.

"Besides," he added, seeking to lighten her spirit, his voice brightening as he stood, "I need someone to share my thoughts, one to aid me in pondering what comes next. Your counsel would be cherished, you whose strength I've seen endure so much yet stand so firm." He smiled, the expression softening the hard lines of his face, a warmth that echoed the fire's glow. "And I suspect the king has not revealed all. I believe he knows my past, perhaps even my true name."

Lorin saw Ethrael's eyes meet his, a spark of curiosity glinting through her tears. A faint hope kindled in his chest, warming the hut's shadows, as her gaze lingered on him. Feeling the air lighten between them for the first time that evening, like embers flaring in the forge, he thought, did her care mirror his?

CHAPTER EIGHT

The Sword's Enchanted Call - Lorin

Gather, friends, and heed a feast of kings, where Keenroot's halls gleam with torch and tale. Lorin, our smith, bears a sword of shadowed lore, its past a whisper to stir royal hearts. Dwarven crown meets elven grace, their eyes on a smith's rising valor. What secrets will the blade unveil, what bonds forge in the king's hidden chamber? Hush now, for destiny's song weaves through the clink of goblets and the weight of crowns.

Opening the door, Lorin found the king's page, the same one he'd met previously, bearing a parchment stamped with the royal seal. The page broke the wax and read aloud: "You are summoned to a feast at the palace in seven days."

As before, the king would provide raiment, yet he and his companions were to visit the tailor for the attire. The missive offered no hint of the feast's intent. He thought, who could decline a royal summons? Why would they be asked to a feast at the palace?

To prepare, they visited the tailor, who knew his craft well. Watching the tailor measure Yarnell, Lorin noted the bard's choice of bright, flamboyant fabrics suiting his flair. Ethrael chose a gown, fair yet modest. Holding out for simplicity, he faced the tailor's push for vestments grander than a blacksmith's lot. Yet after much debate, he settled on modest regality.

· · ·

The week passed swifter than expected. The page led the trio to the palace, flanked by two royal guards. Entering the banquet hall, Lorin noted its familiar tapestries overshadowed by folk clad in dazzling attire. Their ease sharpened his unease, a knot tightening in his chest. Seated at the immediate right of the king's chair, a place of honor, his eyes widened. As a commoner, Ethrael could not sit, while Yarnell, being a bard, was directed to the musicians' nook and handed a lute.

Looking at the weapons on the walls, Lorin whispered to Ethrael, "These are more than decorations. They are real weapons of war." The wooden walls and tables, their polished grain caught the torchlight. Lorin gazed at the banquet table, its polished wood gleaming under torchlight, festive yet daunting in its grandeur. It seemed to grow out of the floor, with a tabletop that could easily seat fifty.

Most guests were seated, but the king had not arrived. Lorin didn't know the protocol, so he just nodded and smiled at those who looked at him. They all seemed to know something he didn't. Why am I seated in such a privileged position?

"I'll be right here if you need me," Ethrael said as she stepped back a few paces behind him. What was unusual was that she was the only one positioned so close to the table, neither seated nor actively serving. As a server approached Lorin, Ethrael stepped forward, took the water from the server, and personally poured it into Lorin's cup. The servant was taken aback, but after a few whispers, it seemed all was settled. The rest of the court noted the exchange, but said nothing. Her care anchors me, even here.

Moments later, music filled the air. The seated rose, servants straightened, and Lorin glanced about, expecting the king. Yet, following the guests' gazes, he spied a man enter, not Arkiel. Ornately clad, with a full beard, he was shorter than Lorin yet bore a presence that commanded the hall. Broad and muscled, devoid of excess, he moved as one who could wrestle a bear unscathed. His aura demanded reverence, a man of stature, and not of this realm. Lorin recognized him immediately as a dwarf.

Lorin watched as he was guided to the seat across from him, to the king's immediate left.

Ethrael leaned close and whispered, "That is Tarul, King of the Yankul dwarf clan."

Before Lorin sat, he squared his shoulders and said, "King Tarul, I am honored to meet you. King Arkiel hath shown great grace, overseeing my restoration. I'd surely have perished without his aid. I am called Lorin." He took his seat. He was reasonably sure he was understood.

Tarul paused, his eyes narrowing briefly, then replied, "The honor is mine, Lorin. I am privileged to join in the celebration of your recovery."

Lorin's gaze flickered. What did this king know that he did not?

Tarul lifted his goblet to the side, and a servant filled it with wine. He downed it in one gulp and motioned for it to be filled again.

Lorin said, "If I overstep, I beg pardon, yet why don't I see an entourage? You're a mighty king; such solitude would seem uncommon."

Tarul let go of a deep, hearty laugh. "True, matters of state often demand a host of assistants. Yet this is a rare occasion, more personal rather than political. I wish to keep them separate, a luxury seldom afforded me. I'd hear of you, though. How do you fare? What do you recall of thy past? What are your plans?"

"Sire," Lorin said, "I know not why a lord such as you would care, yet I cannot deny you. I recall nothing before a few months ago. My first memory is waking in a small hut, my head grievously wounded. They pierced my skull to mend it." He recounted his recovery within the elven halls.

"A dwarf's name carries weight. Mine, Tarul, means 'Tested Iron,' earned through battles as Captain of the Guard. So, where did 'Lorin' come from? What does it signify?"

"Well," Lorin replied, "having no name of mine own, King Arkiel proposed Lorin, after a friend from his youth. I had no better notion, so I accepted it. As for meaning, it is but a label to me. I don't know if it bears any meaning. But your name fits you well. I marvel even that I speak your tongue."

Tarul's face tightened momentarily, as if stung, then smoothed swiftly. "So it serves as a mark until you remember your true self? Is that so?"

"I guess that sums it up." Lorin took a long drink of his water.

Most of the others at the table were sipping their wine, but no one offered him any. He assumed that his ever-watchful caretaker thought better of it. He surmised the wine could affect the healing process.

The music swelled anew, this time much more regal. All stood, yet Tarul knelt, head bowed. Lorin, catching the dwarf's lead, knelt as well. Like Tarul, Lorin deemed the act more fitting than standing. As Arkiel took his place at the table's head, Tarul and Lorin rose and sat. Lorin's gaze dropped, recalling past meetings with Arkiel. He felt regret.

Arkiel chuckled knowingly, his gaze shifting between Tarul and Lorin. "Too long has passed since we last welcomed the Dwarf King among us. This day is a singular cause for elves and dwarves to rejoice. We shall feast before the celebration in honor of our dwarven brother."

As the fare arrived, Lorin leaned forward, his brow furrowed as if wrestling some past misstep with the elven king. "Sire, I apologize for failing to show you the reverence you merit when first we met. I wish I had borne myself with greater respect. You've been nothing but gracious. I am sorry."

King Arkiel smiled gently. "My young friend, I recall it so differently. I saw no discourtesy, merely one lost and suffering. Given your plight, I expected nothing else. Don't give it another thought."

Ethrael refilled Lorin's water and served his meal.

"One matter more, sire," Lorin added. "I know it is uncommon, yet I'd thank you for permitting Ethrael to aid me this night. I lean upon her utterly. She is a great comfort. Judging by the others' stares, I see it must be highly unusual. I hope it stirs no discord among your people."

"Lorin, you're remarkable," Arkiel said. "Scarce a few months alive in memory, yet show me greater reverence than my entire court combined. I am proud to name you a friend and honored to aid your restoration. My only trepidation is that your regard might lessen once your memories return."

"Sire, you've got me at a loss," Lorin replied, "yet I cannot fathom holding you in lesser esteem."

King Tarul interjected swiftly. "I stand with Lorin, Arkiel. You're the paragon of a leader, an emissary to the world. As king of my folk, I thank you for including me in this festivity."

"Tarul," Arkiel said, "our peoples have known discord, matters we shall not unearth in this time of joy. This celebration would be incomplete without you. This moment unites our people, though few may perceive it."

Lorin noticed that he was being served less than those around him. He knew that his caretaker was monitoring his intake. The food was excellent, but he decided he had better not overdo it. The dwarf, on the other hand, was eating and drinking more than the next five people at the table combined. Finally, the food was taken away, and the next phase of the celebration began.

King Arkiel rose and addressed the hall. "To my court, I present King Tarul of the Yankul dwarf clan. Tarul and his kin have been allied with the elves for generations. We've faced trials, as allies do, yet they remain steadfast. We are privileged to host him. Yet this night is for Lorin. He came unto us nearly dead, struck by a goblin blade's venom in the forest. Wounded, he felled three goblins alone, one, the mightiest, beheaded. It's a feat indeed. What you and he don't know is that this beast was the Goblin King's nephew, a scourge to our scouts and neighboring human farmers. We owe him much."

Shocked, Lorin's jaw dropped. He thought, how could he, a man with no past, have done such a thing?

Tarul looked back between him and the elven king, smiling but confused.

"I mean not to overshadow our guest," Arkiel continued, passing a sword to Lorin. "Raise it aloft for all to behold."

Lorin drew the blade from its scabbard and lifted it overhead. A blue tint shimmered along the edge, unveiling magical runes.

King Arkiel continued, "This is no common weapon. Some here may have already surmised that it is the lost 'cursed sword'. Named by master swordsmen who could not wield it. It imperiled them more than their foes. Yet, this magnificent weapon was not cursed in the hands of our guest. That is all I am at liberty to say right now: save this, it must be returned to its maker. In time, Lorin, with our support, will make that journey and return it to its rightful resting place."

CHAPTER NINE

Truths too Heavy, Mind Unquiet - Lorin

Listen, friends, to a song of secrets stirred in a chamber's flickering heart, where torchlight weaves truths too vast for one soul to bear. I lingered, my lute a silent witness, as kings bared a smith's hidden name, a blade's cursed weight, and kin long lost to shadow. Goblins' wrath hums beyond the walls, a storm to test the ties of blood and heart. Hush, for a weary mind quakes beneath a destiny it cannot yet grasp.

Murmurs rippled through the court, but Tarul finally spoke, breaking the whispers, "A stirring tale, Arkiel, yet are you certain Lorin should embark upon so perilous a quest? He prevailed once by luck. He may not fare so well next time."

Arkiel smiled, "I understand your concern, Tarul. I didn't say he'd depart soon, only in time. He has much to learn, and I promise he will be prepared when the hour comes. We have private matters to discuss. Follow me to my chambers."

He nodded to Ethrael. "You need not ask. I've placed Lorin in your care."

Looking to the bard, "Yarnell, join us. I expect both you and Ethrael not to watch over him until I release you."

Arkiel rose and strode from the hall, trailed by King Tarul, Lorin, Ethrael, and Yarnell.

. . .

As they sat down, the king dismissed his normal servants. Ethrael took over, serving the kings wine, while Lorin received only water.

His head swimming with new thoughts, he wondered what the sword was, why it glowed, what its runes meant, why it must be returned, and how he could wield it so well when great masters could not.

Arkiel's voice cut through the stillness, steady as a drumbeat rolling across a battlefield. "Gentlemen, we've business too sensitive for my court's eager ears, secrets that demand this shadowed nook. First, the sword. Lorin, place it here."

Lorin hesitated, then placed the blade on the table, its scarred steel dull and unassuming. As his hand lifted, the faint glow snuffed out, like a candle pinched dark. Arkiel flicked a finger, elven finesse in a single gesture, and the light surged back, bathing the runes in pale fire rippling like moonlight on a restless sea. The air hummed, a whisper of power stirring the stillness.

"You've felt it," Arkiel said, his tone low and certain. "This isn't some simple sword hammered out for coin. It's a wizard's blade, forged for one with the spark, a rarity even among relics."

Breaking in, voice sharp and baffled, he said, "But I'm no wizard!"

Arkiel's smile curved like a crescent moon, wise and faintly sly. "The world's a maze, lad. A swordsman's worth, learned or born? Both are true. The truest masters, though, are kissed by the gods, born with a gift that yearns to be shaped. You're one, magic humming in your bones, unseen until now. The sword knew you before you did. I'll teach you more when your strength returns. Then it must be returned to its wielder's family, its maker. Her blood still stains it, and honor calls it home." Lorin's mind reeled, the idea of wizardry as foreign as the heritage he couldn't feel.

King Tarul's face twisted, a knot of doubt and shock unraveling. "How's that possible? A dwarf can't be a wizard!" The words burst out, raw and unguarded, and his meaty hand clamped over his mouth, eyes widening like polished coins. A secret had slipped, but Lorin, still reeling, was too stunned to seize it.

Arkiel's laughter rustled like leaves in a gentle wind. "My blunt friend, I was coming to that. You dwarves wear your hearts plain, no guile to muddy the truth. Let me unveil this for our guest.

Remember, I just gave you the name Lorin; it's a mask. You're Barzul, the sole son of King Qartul and Queen Luzula, dwarves of ancient blood. Your mother poured her last breath into your birth, poisoned by foes, cut free by elven hands that couldn't save her. Tarul, born of Qartul and Queen Kiran, is your half-brother, younger by years."

Lorin stood completely dumbstruck. He thought, How could this be? Lacking the great dwarf's bearded bulk across the table, the dwarf king's sturdy build, he believed there had to be some mistake. Chest seizing, the name Barzul, a king's son, struck like a hammer's blow, jarring and unfamiliar. Staring at Tarul, his brother's dwarven strength stood stark against his own. Brother? Fists clenching, nails biting palms, the chamber's torchlight blurred into molten sparks. A prince? Absurd. Yet Tarul's steady gaze tethered him, a bond beyond grasp, Ethrael's quiet presence anchoring him, a lifeline in the fog.

. . .

Arkiel pressed on, voice firm yet kind. "There's more to unearth, but this is certain: he's your blood. We've waited until the body mended before stirring the mind. Memory's a fiercer beast than flesh. Strength will be needed for it. Tarul and I will peel back the past, but it must be guarded closely. Enemies circle, ravenous for ruin, and anyone bound to you. Can we be trusted, just for now?"

Lorin's voice was unsteady but resolute, a thread holding against the strain. "I'm lost here, and you've all been kind. Yes, I'll trust you. I ache to know who I am, but I'll keep silent. If I'm to stay, I won't be a burden. What can I offer in return?"

Yarnell grinned, leaning close, his whisper sharp in Lorin's ear. "A dwarf prince with no beard? Tarul's got enough for the whole lot of us!" His fingers twitched on his lute, poised to strum a tale of a smith's royal blood. Lorin caught the glint in Yarnell's eye and the smile spreading on his face, a bard's jest lifting the chamber's weight.

Tarul leaned forward, his gruff warmth cutting through the haze. "This wizard nonsense, I don't swallow it, not yet. But back home, Barzul, you were a blacksmith. Not the burliest, not the loudest, but your hands wove wonders. 'Barzul' means 'Golden Maker' in our tongue. Father named you that, frail as you looked, fresh from Luzula's death, his 'Precious Jewel' gone, and you touched by elven magic. Proved it true, though, with that hammer you forged for him, solid as a mountain's root, a masterpiece I carry still. Next time, I'll bring it for you to hold."

Lorin's chest tightened; the idea of crafting a king's hammer was both thrilling and unreachable, locked behind his lost memories.

Arkiel nodded, eyes glinting like struck flint. "Elves smith well enough, but dwarven forges birth marvels. We'd be richer with you at our hearths. Master Falere says you've taken to the anvil like it's family. Your hands recall what your mind has lost. Work heals the soul."

"I do enjoy the forge," Lorin's shoulders sagged slightly, the weight of Tarul's words pressing against his fading strength. "It feels right, even if I don't remember dwarven fires. Master Falere's been a steady guide. I could be content there, past or no past. But you spoke of returning the sword. Why me?"

Tarul grunted, nodding as if in agreement. "It's been lost for years. Why not bury it with your other treasures in some vault?"

Anger flashed across Arkiel's face, but quickly disappeared. His gaze darkened, his voice forceful and direct. "Bury it? No, Tarul, that would only stoke the fire. This sword chose Barzul, binding itself to him as surely as a root grips stone. Beyond its first master, a figure lost to time, only he can wield it without its power turning inward, a blade sparing its bearer while cleaving foes. Its tale has twisted. The goblins know it struck down their king's nephew, his blood-kin, in a skirmish that stained my forest, turning our streams red. They've named it 'Goblin-Killer', a title it was never forged to claim, a curse born of fear and fury. To them, it's no mere weapon but a taunt, a splinter in their pride. Even now, they scour my forest searching for it and its master."

Lorin's mind raced. Were goblins hunting him for this blade? Why had it chosen him?

Arkiel leaned forward, the torchlight carving shadows across his angular face. "They won't rest, Tarul. Their scouts skulk closer, and their war drums echo louder in the deep woods. Each raid swells, ten goblins become fifty, and fifty become hordes. They seek the sword not just to destroy it but to reclaim hope among their people. To the goblins, it's a beacon of defiance, a threat that must be snuffed out. If it stays here, my realm bleeds."

Lorin's hands clenched, the chamber's torchlight flickering as if echoing Arkiel's warning.

The elf king continued, "Every village razed, every elf felled, would be a wound this blade could have prevented, yet its presence invites and fuels the storm."

Lorin's breath caught, the air growing heavier as Arkiel's gaze turned to him, softening yet piercing, as if peering through the man to the soul beneath.

"This sword isn't a trinket to be locked away; it's a key to your past, purpose, and a legacy older than these walls. Its wielder's family, a lineage of wizards, dwindled to a single heir and dwelt far beyond our forest. Her blood anoints this steel; her spirit lingers in its hum, a woman whose name echoes in tales around the hearths. The sword yearns for her line as if it knows its unfinished story. Honor demands its return, yes, but more: it's a summons. The goblins' wrath is but one ripple; greater tides stir. Ancient foes waking in the dark, forces that crave this blade's power for their ends. Only returned can it be safeguarded, its purpose fulfilled."

Arkiel's voice dipped, heavy with prophecy. "But there's a deeper thread, Barzul, woven into your very being. You are its bearer, not by chance. You're no blacksmith to toil in quiet nor a prince to sit on a throne. You're a royal of a rarer sort, marked by the gods, your spark a flame the sword recognized before you did. Returning it isn't just a task; it's your destiny. The road will temper you, through peril, through discovery, into the man who'll bless nations, not merely mend their tools. Hide it here, and you doom my people to endless war. Return it, and you step into the world you were born to shape."

Arkiel made it sound as though Lorin were some great leader, part of some grand prophecy, and the notion left him deeply uncomfortable.

• • •

Ethrael's eyes locked on Lorin, catching his slumping shoulders, trembling hands, and exhaustion from Arkiel's truths. Her grip tightened on the wine pitcher, torn between royal deference and duty. Tarul's gruff voice and Arkiel's heavy words were breaking him. She met Yarnell's nod, her resolve steeling. She'd defied Thalen for Lorin; kings wouldn't stop her now. Ethrael stepped forward, her voice slicing clean through the thickening air. "Sirs, pardon me, but my charge is fading. He's nearly spent. I'd take him to rest." Looking to Yarnell, she continued, "I told Yarnell how I fought for him when he came to Keenroot, bloodied and broken. The healers scorned him, but I talked to him, defied their sneers, for I saw his spark. That duty binds me still, and I'll not let him falter now."

Ethrael's voice shielded Lorin, guarding the frail prince who bore a world's fate. She's still fighting for me, even before kings. I owe her more than I can repay—and my heart aches to try.

The kings laughed, a rare duet, Tarul's rumble blending with Arkiel's lighter timbre. "Kings we may be," Tarul said, "but not fool enough to cross you, lass. You guard him as a mama bear watches over her cub, fierce to the last. Thank you for nursing my brother. You've got a friend in my halls forever. Ask, and it's yours."

Tarul rose, bowing deeply, and pressed two rings into her palm. He whispered something in her ear.

Arkiel's voice flowed in, calm as a mountain lake. "Leave the sword with me for now. I'll guard it until the hour comes."

Ethrael bowed gracefully and escorted her charge out, his body sagging under a weight he couldn't name. He thought, was she still fighting for him, even before kings? Did he owe her more than he could repay? His heart ached to try. Was he a prince, a wizard, with destinies too heavy to bear, his mind unquiet?

CHAPTER TEN

Forged in Friendship — Lorin

Let us continue our journey, ye hearers of tales, and let my lute sing a soft refrain, for this verse burns like embers in Keenroot's twilight heart. I strum for Lorin, a smith whose soul wrestles shadows, his hammer striking not just steel but sparks of hope. He seeks a place among elves who crown him prince yet call him stranger, tethered by Ethrael's healer's heart, a melody woven through their shared scars. Can a name be forged from lost flames, or a home kindled from ruin's dust? Hush now, as dawn's first light spills soft, and Lorin stirs from dreams, his heart a song yet to find its tune. Walk with me, where friendship's glow lights the winding path.

After a night of restless dreams, Lorin awoke to find Ethrael seated across the room. She rose as he stirred, crossing to him with a cool, damp cloth to wipe his brow. "You had a hard night," she said softly. "Tossing and turning, murmuring in your sleep, so I watched over you. I've never tended royalty before, and do not know what's fitting. I mean no offense."

"Ethrael, until yesternight, I didn't know I was royalty," he said, his eyes softening, voice gentle. "Yet even had I known, you've been a blessing. You tended me without complaint when I was but a peasant. I could never be angry with you. I count you a trusted friend and hope you'll see me the same. I face a long path of healing and learning. I'd trust none more. Will you be my friend, not merely my caretaker?"

Excusing herself, Ethrael nodded and returned with a breakfast fit for a dwarf. "I thought we agreed to be friends," Lorin said, looking at the vast amount of food and back at her, a hint of warmth in his tone. "You're as hungry as I, likely more, having watched me all night. I won't eat while my friend goes hungry. Please sit and share this with me. I'd love to speak of what comes next." Hesitant, she joined him, taking a piece of fruit.

Breaking a piece of bread, Lorin continued, hands steady but eyes distant. "Much has changed for us. You've been freed, and I've been named prince to a people I don't know. This truth sits heavy on me. I feel the weight of a past I cannot recall, a duty I'm not sure I can bear. I dreamed of a sword last night, a black sword. It called to me, Ethrael, in a voice I cannot unhear. It holds answers, but I fear what they might be."

At the mention of royalty, her body tensed, fingers tightening about the fruit. "I am sorry, I'll excuse myself, sire," she said, rising to leave.

"STOP! I understand you just learned I am royalty, but it changes nothing. I'll not ask you to serve me as a subject," he said, sensing her discomfort. "I need a friend, Ethrael, not a servant. I'm as lost as when you first saw me, voiceless and broken. This title changes nothing about who I am to you." He offered a small smile, one that carried more weight than words. "Please, eat. Let us speak as equals, friends."

She sat and nodded slowly, finally taking a bite of the fruit, its juice staining her fingers. "I'll try, Lorin," she said at last, her voice soft. "It is difficult for me. I have been raised in the king's halls and taught to act this way. I will endeavor to try. I thank you, though. Friendship is a new path for me. I've seen your heart. You don't lord over me or command me. You're Lorin, the man I've tended and who's fought to live. I'll stand by you as a friend."

• • •

The room warmed with their shared promise, dawn's light casting long shadows across the floor. Lorin felt something inside him loosen, a quiet relief rising like a neglected forge catching flame. For the first time since waking in this strange world, he felt anchored not by duty or destiny but by connection.

"Thank you," he said softly, his voice easing the tension in the air.

Yarnell stepped into the doorway, hair tousled and lute in hand. He paused, looking between them with a half-smile. "Breakfast still peaceful, or do I need armor?"

Ethrael managed a faint smile, although Lorin saw how quickly it flickered away.

He took a slow bite of bread, choosing his words carefully. "There is something I have been thinking about, something that might help us all." He watched Ethrael, noting the subtle shift in her posture. "You told us of Aelthar, of the Starbloom Grove your family tended before its fall."

Ethrael stilled, the fruit hovering at her lips.

"What if it is not gone forever?" Lorin continued, leaning forward slightly. "What if it can be restored?"

Her eyes widened, and the reaction struck him with unexpected force. No spark of hope surfaced. Instead, he saw fear tighten her features, sorrow deepening the shadows beneath her eyes.

"The grove?" she whispered. Her voice trembled. "Lorin, I saw it burn. Nothing survived."

Yarnell stepped fully into the room, his brows drawing together, and sat near Ethrael, gently taking her hands. His voice softened. "The starblooms were born of the sky. Magic like that does not vanish quickly. You have been gone for years, and there may still be something beneath the ruin, something waiting."

Ethrael shook her head, the motion small and quick, as though fending off a memory. "You do not understand," she murmured. "To return and see it destroyed... it would break me."

Lorin watched the exchange, trying to understand the depth of her reluctance.

"Ethrael," Yarnell said, still gentle, "when you spoke of it before, you made it sound alive even in memory. Places shaped by old magic have a way of lingering."

She did not look up. Lorin saw her grip tighten on the fruit, her shoulders drawing inward as if bracing against a blow.

"That was a long time ago, and a lifetime long gone," she said quietly. "A faint memory, nothing more."

Lorin leaned in a little, careful not to close the distance too much. "Dream of what can be. Dreams can carry truth," he said. "And you are a healer, the last steward of that grove. If anyone could bring it back, it would be you."

Ethrael's gaze dropped, her expression guarded.

Lorin could not read everything behind it, but he felt the weight of her resistance, solid as stone.

"I cannot," she whispered. "Not now."

He nodded, accepting the truth even as a small ache stirred in his chest. He had hoped this idea might give her direction, and perhaps himself as well. But he would not push her into pain she was not ready to face. "All right," he said gently. "Think about it. There is no need to decide today."

Yarnell added in a low, steady tone, "When you are ready, if you ever are, we will stand with you."

Ethrael did not answer. She kept her gaze lowered, her shoulders tense, her silence saying more than words could. Morning light continued to brighten the room, but Lorin felt the lingering shadow around her, the old wounds she still carried.

He wished he knew how to guide her toward healing, or toward whatever future waited for her. And he hoped, quietly and without certainty, that the vision she once held of the grove was more than memory, and that somewhere beneath the ash, something still breathed.

●　●　●

Heart shining like tempered steel, Lorin steadied his hands as he dressed. By the time he had washed and clad himself, Ethrael returned, now in simple garb, with an elf in tow.

"Lorin," she said, "I asked around and found a teacher. This is Hirel, a scholar from the royal court. The king has sent him. You must have already known our language, but he'll teach you the foundations of elven customs and history. As you grow, we can decide together what's next. He'll seek one who can aid if it's beyond his knowledge."

A cool breeze drifted through the room, carrying a faint sweetness Lorin couldn't name. Ethrael's shoulders tightened for the briefest moment before she composed herself again.

Hirel spoke. "I hear you toil at the forge. I'd prefer you full-time, yet we'll begin with a few hours each evening after your labor. We'll weigh progress in a few weeks and adjust as needed. Acceptable?"

Lorin nodded and offered his hand, which Hirel clasped. "Sir," Lorin said, "I don't know what you've been told, but I was grievously wounded; I recall nothing of my past, not even my name. The king has granted me a great favor, welcoming me into your community. I wish to honor it by contributing. Your aid will let me repay his generosity. I am grateful for your time and hope to respect your labor as I mend. The king told you to help me, but treat me like any pupil. I'll diligently strive as my frame permits. Ethrael tends my health, though; I yield to her. In all else, I am yours to guide."

Hirel blinked, struck by Lorin's earnest reverence, rare in a learner. Ethrael added, "It's set, then. Starting tomorrow, evenings belong to Master Hirel at the library."

By day, Lorin's hammer sang at the forge, its rhythm steadying his hands; by night, elven words flowed like molten steel under Hirel's guidance, rekindling embers of a buried past. Within months, Hirel conceded he had nothing left to impart. Hirel called a gathering at the library.

"I've taught him all I can," Hirel began. "He knows enough to function in the elven community, even at the palace. He might learn more, but he does not need me for it. He's adapted enough to study alone now. If he seeks counsel, I'll gladly aid, yet presently, I hinder him."

Lorin's chest swelled with a mix of pride and uncertainty, like steel tempered yet untested, Hirel's words a milestone, leaving him both freed and adrift.

Lorin smiled. "Sir, thanks for all you've done. I cannot fathom you slowing me down, yet I cherish your praise. I've pondered what comes next and hoped you could steer me. I am drawn to dwarf history and ways. Are there writings for that?"

"We hold some texts, primarily where our people work together. I'll seek them from the archives. Ask for them when you visit the library, grant me until week's end, for it may take time to unearth. If there's nothing else, I'll take my leave."

The library's hush enveloped Lorin, Hirel's parting words a spark against the shadowed void of his past. Tears welled as he turned to Ethrael, his voice breaking. "I know not who I am. A dwarf? A prince? It troubled me little when my past was a void, yet now it haunts me. Where do I belong?"

Ethrael took his hand, meeting his gaze. "Lorin, I cannot untangle those riddles for you. You are on a strange road. But I know you: strong, steadfast, unflinching before hardship. You have come far. The gods must have a purpose for you. You'll always have a home here."

Her words eased his burden a bit, like a hammer's steady strike smoothing rough steel. The future remained a mystery to him.

CHAPTER ELEVEN

Starbloom Grove Calls — Ethrael

Come close, travelers, and listen well, for not all battles are waged with steel. Some are fought in the quiet chambers of the heart, where memory and fear weave snares sharper than any blade. A healer once told me that wounds of the soul bleed slowest, yet it is those wounds that bind our steps most tightly to fate.

So hear now of Ethrael, last steward of a dying grove, who tried to turn from her past, though the past would not release her. While Lorin sought his name and I my next verse, a different summons stirred beneath the roots of the world, whispering through her dreams. The land remembers its keepers, and when its light falters, it calls to those who once tended it with love and sorrow both.

What she saw in sleep was not mere fancy, nor the wandering of a weary mind. Shattered lands sometimes speak in visions, and their truth can strike harder than prophecy. When she woke, trembling with the weight of what she had witnessed, the choice before her was no longer one of courage but of duty, carved into her very blood.

And so our tale turns toward the Starbloom Grove, forgotten by many, mourned by one, and waiting still for the day it might breathe again.

The scent reached her first. Cool, sweet, and faint as morning dew, it drifted through her sleep and beckoned her forward. Ethrael followed it into a world she knew and did not know, her breath catching as the shadows parted.

She stood in Aelthar. Not the Aelthar of memory, charred and broken, but a grove reborn—lush, glowing, impossibly whole.

This had to be a dream—but it felt real, more real than waking moments ever did.

Starblooms blanketed the glade in shimmering clusters, petals glowing with soft sky-born radiance. Their light washed over the trees in hues of silver and pale blue, settling into her skin like a familiar embrace. The air hummed with quiet magic, the kind her mother once said was older than the kingdom itself.

A path opened beneath her bare feet, warm and living. Moss sparkled underfoot, releasing tiny motes of light that drifted upward like fallen stars returning home.

Her breath trembled. She had dreamed of this place as a child, imagined its heartbeat as she slept against her father's chest. But this—this was more vivid than memory.

Movement stirred at the grove's edge. Druids stepped forward, cloaked in woven leaves and starlit threads. Their faces were peaceful, their eyes gentle in recognition. The eldest bowed to her.

"Ethrael," he said, voice deep as rooted earth. "You have returned to tend the grove."

Emotion tightened her throat. She dropped to her knees beside a young sapling, its bark soft as velvet beneath her fingers. When she brushed a stray leaf, a pulse of warmth answered her touch— alive, trusting.

She felt whole, seen, purposeful. Together with the druids, she shaped the light, coaxing new growth from old roots. Blossoms opened wherever her hands passed, singing faint harmonies that curled through her bones. The grove breathed with her, rose with her, welcomed her home.

A soft wind whispered through the branches.
Stay.
Grow.
Become.

She closed her eyes, letting the warmth settle through her like healing.

But when she opened them—

The petals were black.

They shriveled inward, crisping like burnt paper. The nearest blossom collapsed into ash. A chill swept across the grove, stealing the breath from her chest.

"No," she whispered. "Not again."

The druids were gone.

In their place stood twisted silhouettes—rootlike limbs, hollow eyes, shapes warped by fire and shadow. They watched her without moving.

The ground trembled. Cracks tore through the glowing moss, splitting the earth to reveal charred roots writhing beneath. A deep groan rose from the soil, a sound of pain she remembered all too well.

Flames erupted along the far treeline, devouring leaves in a rush of heat. Smoke rolled toward her, thick and choking. The sky reddened, drenched in firelight.

A voice whispered from the shadows, soft as breath against her ear.

You left us.

Ethrael stumbled back. "I didn't—I couldn't—"

Another voice joined it.

Then another.

A chorus of accusations carried on the wind.

You turned away.

You let us die.

You abandoned the grove.

The heart-tree in the center pulsed weakly, its light flickering like a star on the verge of collapse. Ethrael lunged toward it, reaching out—but the branch crumbled before her touch, turning to black dust that clung to her fingers.

"Please," she begged. "I'm here now. I'm here."

The grove shuddered. Roots twisted violently, pulling back from her. Fire raced toward her feet. The sky cracked with a sound like splitting stone, spilling darkness into the glade.

The last surviving starbloom melted into ash.

The grove's final whisper carried its verdict:
Too late, Ethrael.

A scream tore from her as the flames closed in—and she woke, gasping, drenched in cold sweat.

Her hands still trembled. She stared at her palms, half expecting to see soot.

The scent of the grove—sweet, faint, impossible—lingered in her lungs.

· · ·

Ethrael woke with her pulse racing, the dream still clawing at her ribs. The grove's cries echoed in her ears, the scent of burnt starblooms lingering like smoke in her lungs. She pressed trembling hands to her eyes, but the darkness behind them only sharpened the memory.

It wasn't just fear.
It was warning.
It was calling her back.

As she walked into Lorin's hut, she noticed the morning light crept in, soft and indifferent. Lorin and Yarnell murmured nearby, unaware of the storm rising inside her. They had not felt the ground split beneath her feet. They had not heard the grove accuse her. A weight gathered in her chest until she could no longer bear its silence.

"We need to speak of the grove," she said abruptly.

The quiet shattered. Lorin turned toward her at once, concern tightening his features. Yarnell's hand stilled over his lute, brows lifting as he studied her trembling posture.

Ethrael swallowed hard. "I've been dreaming... no, *seeing*. The Starbloom Grove. What it was. What it has become." She met their eyes, her own raw with fear and determination. "I thought I could turn from the past. But the grove won't let me."

Lorin stepped closer, voice gentle. "Ethrael, what did you see?"

"A vision of the grove reborn," she whispered, "and then destroyed." She drew a shaky breath. "It felt real—too real. I believe it was a warning. Or a call. If I turn away again, I will lose it forever. I feel that truth in my bones."

Yarnell's voice softened, threaded with instinctive understanding. "Dreams like that often come from deeper places than sleep."

"Yes," Ethrael breathed. "And I cannot ignore it anymore."

She steadied herself, lifting her chin despite the fear coiled beneath her ribs. "Lorin... you once asked if the grove could be restored. I told you I could not face it." Her hands curled into fists. "But I must. I cannot turn away again."

Lorin nodded slowly, something fierce and steady entering his gaze. "Then tell us what you need."

Ethrael's voice strengthened. "We go to Aelthar. To the grove. If there is even a flicker of life left, I must answer it."

Lorin held her gaze, the vow forming before he spoke it. "You're a healer, Ethrael, and the last steward of that place. If anyone can bring it back, it's you. Is the grove far?"

She paused, gathering the last of her breath. "No... it's not far."

"Then let's go to Aelthar," he said softly. "Let's see if the Starbloom Grove can be reborn after all these years."

Ethrael straightened, determination spreading through her like fire taking hold. "If there's a chance—even a flicker of hope— that the grove could live again... I can't turn from that. It's my duty. My blood."

Her pain washed through Lorin; she could see the way it struck him, sharp and familiar, echoing his own lost past. Yet her resolve ignited something within him too. Leaning closer, he steadied his gaze with an unspoken promise.

"We'll face it together," he said. "A shared duty."

Yarnell brushed his fingers across the lute's strings, coaxing a soft note into the air. "A noble quest, though the road be tangled and shadowed. The Starbloom Grove, or what's left of it, lies within Keenroot's borders—a sacred place once, now a wound in the elven lands. Cave elves and goblins may still haunt those woods, their greed unslaked. A journey there might unearth more than starblooms."

"It's settled," Lorin said. "You, me, and Yarnell. We're a trio now, bound by more than chance. I'll not let you bear this alone. And perhaps, in healing the grove, we'll find healing for ourselves."

Ethrael drew a steadying breath, then nodded. A spark of resolve lit her eyes. "Very well. To Aelthar, then—to the Starbloom Grove. It's a dangerous road. We must prepare. There's peril in those woods, and I'll not lose another home to it."

Yarnell plucked a low, resonant chord, the note humming with promise. "A song in the making. To Aelthar we go, chasing a lost light in the forest's embrace. May the stars guide us, and the grove welcome us home."

Lorin's gaze softened as he outlined a plan. "Then we start by laying the groundwork. We can't begin the restoration now, but we can prepare. Druids will be the first we seek when the time is right—those who can tend the land and guide the starblooms' growth over the years. After that, we'll need more hands for labor, tools to build, perhaps even Arkiel's support."

"I think that is wise," Ethrael said, voice steady with purpose. "There's much I can do beforehand. Our library was lost in the fire, but perhaps Arkiel's resources can help. I must research the starblooms—their care, their history. Anything that might aid us. I don't know how to find druids yet, but that can wait."

Her expression tightened, vulnerable but resolute. "This is all so sudden. I need time to come to grips with seeing my homeland again. I'm afraid of what we'll find."

"A journey for another day," Yarnell murmured.

"That is our future," Lorin agreed, "but there is something more immediate I wish to begin. Beyond the care you've set for my body, I desire to hear your thoughts. If I am to dwell among the elves, I need to learn their tongue and ways."

"A good thought," Ethrael said. "Your body is stronger now, and working the mind will help the healing too. Learning will serve you well." She rose, gathering herself. "I will clean up, and you wash and dress. I have a few ideas we can discuss when I return."

CHAPTER TWELVE

Strings of the Heart — Yarnell

Harken, ye dreamers, and let my lute hum a wistful strain, for this tale sings of ancient tomes and starlit lore. I, Yarnell, weave new ballads from dwarven refrains, while Lorin seeks his shadowed kin and Ethrael chases a grove's lost light. In the library's hush, our hearts align, threading melodies through truths half-buried. Can songs rekindle a fractured past? Listen close, as dawn's breath stirs, and our quest begins anew.

The morning after Lorin's resolve, Yarnell sought the craftsman who'd forged the remarkable lute he played at the king's celebration, guided by whispers from the royal band. His fingers twitched, yearning for his lute's familiar strings, but a restless hope stirred in his chest, perhaps a new instrument to weave the tales he carried.

The shop's humble facade, tucked in Keenroot's shadow, belied its master's renown. Within, an aged man sat in the corner, frail as weathered wood, his eyes sharp with unspoken craft. Yarnell's heart thrummed with eagerness and doubt.

"Sir," Yarnell said, his voice tentative yet earnest, "they say you can craft an instrument to surpass my beloved lute. I'm unsure what I seek, but I hope you can guide me."

The craftsman regarded him for a long moment, his gaze piercing. "Play for me."

"What would you hear?" Yarnell asked, a flicker of unease in his chest.

"You are a bard: you know what to play. Play for me."

Yarnell's fingers tightened on his lute, the weight grounding him. Taverns and halls were his stage, not this hovel, yet an audience was an audience. He began a tavern mainstay, strumming a few bars before the craftsman's sharp cry halted him.

"Cease! Spare my ears such common rubbish. Play one of your own, something you love, from the heart."

Yarnell hesitated, his mind on a piece he'd never shared, a tale so personal it threatened to consume him. Yet a quiet certainty stirred, as if this moment called for it. He commenced strumming, his voice weaving the song's raw truth.

The shop faded, leaving only the lute's hum and his soaring melody. The music took life, carrying him on its waves, adrift from the world. When the final note faded, Yarnell felt both at peace and utterly spent, the song having claimed all he had. He opened his eyes slowly, finding the craftsman smiling, a young woman beside him, her face streaked with tears yet alight with joy.

They had journeyed with him through the song, their eyes reflecting his own stirred heart.

"Young man, we can aid you," the craftsman said, his voice warm with conviction. "I craft common instruments for those without passion, but word in the village and palace spoke of greater talent. Your song proves it. You love your lute, as you should, a comrade through years of journeys. Yet the next path calls for a new companion.

"When you play," he continued, "it is not just strumming but melding with your instrument. Every great minstrel wields their craft uniquely. I see your way now. I can fashion a lute as natural as the fingers on your hand, merging with your artistry. You're destined to be a master bard, playing palaces for royalty, turning away more requests than you can accept."

Yarnell loved praise, but he was unsure what to make of his interpretation of his performance.

The craftman paused, his tone softening. "Two matters, though. You must leave your lute here for us to study as we shape the new. Crafting this is no small feat. It will take time."

Yarnell's grip tightened, his chest aching as he handed over his lute. It felt like severing a limb, this weathered friend that had sung with him since his youth. A fear gripped him. Could he still be a bard without his oldest friend? He'd never entrusted it to another, and the loss cut deep.

The young woman spoke, her voice gentle. "This is hard, we know, but we vow you'll be overjoyed. Take this lute we've just finished. It is not as loved as yours, but it will serve until your new one is ready."

Yarnell took the offered instrument, its unfamiliar heft heavy in his hands. Words failed him, so he nodded and left, his eagerness replaced by a hollow ache, as if he'd abandoned a treasured friend.

• • •

Yarnell's fingers lingered on the borrowed lute, its strings silent as Keenroot's dawn, his heart adrift in the echo of a lost chord. He drifted into mourning for a week, his songs silent as the borrowed lute lay untouched. When he finally tried his songs, the notes felt foreign, lacking the warmth of his old companion. The sound was fair, yet he hadn't realized how much he relied on his weathered friend. Playing the usual rounds felt like a betrayal, and his heart remained adrift. Yet in that drift, Yarnell wondered if new songs could fill the void his lute had left.

One night, as Yarnell watched Lorin poring over parchments, books, and scrolls of dwarf lore, his eyes alight with a hunger for knowledge, a spark of inspiration struck him. Lorin's furrowed brow betrayed a struggle to grasp his heritage, and Yarnell realized he could pursue music from other realms, broadening his craft beyond the worn rut of familiar tunes. He plunged into the library's quiet embrace, joining Lorin in a shared pursuit that formed a silent bond. Friends likely thought them mad, two recluses lost in lore.

Yarnell wove new songs from dwarven tomes, their ballads brimming with truth. A tale of Lorin's clan, born in strife when cave elves poisoned the dwarf queen, stirred a chord in his mind. Being part of the story pulled at his soul. Would he even be able to perform it?

Yarnell wrestled with whether to share this discovery, but Lorin deserved to know his past. One night, over supper, he spoke. "Lorin, I found the story of your birth, a horrifying, sad tale."

"Yes," Lorin replied, his voice heavy, "I found a similar account, written from the elves' perspective." As they compared findings, Yarnell learned the elven tale matched in significant details but bore the healers' anguish at failing to save the queen, a sorrow Lorin described with a weight that resonated in Yarnell's bardic heart. The surgery to save Barzul was a desperate act, doomed to spark the rift between kingdoms.

• • •

The library's amber glow faded with the supper's end, Ethrael's quest for starlit lore stirring in Yarnell's mind like a ballad yet to be sung. That morning, Yarnell had seen Ethrael head to the library alone, her steps purposeful, a shadow in her eyes hinting at a burden. He'd offered to join her, lute ready to lighten her load, but she'd shaken her head, a faint smile touching her lips.

"I need to do this myself, Yarnell," she said, her voice soft but firm. "The grove... It's my blood, my duty. I need to know what it was and could be again."

Yarnell watched her go, her healer's satchel slung over her shoulder, silver hair catching the dawn's light as she vanished into the city.

Yarnell did not see her the next day. He started to worry, so, come evening, he sought her out. He found her seated in a secluded alcove, surrounded by open books and unrolled scrolls. Stained glass cast jade and amber across her face, her brow furrowed in deep focus. A quill scratched across parchment, her fingers ink-stained, a lock of hair falling across her cheek. She didn't notice his approach until he set his lute against the table, the soft thud breaking her concentration. She looked up, her eyes bright with wonder and resolve.

Yarnell smiled, seeing this spark in her eyes. "What have you learned?" Yarnell asked, pulling a chair beside her. On the table was a map, scrolls with faded elven script, a tome with a starbloom embossed, and a sketch of the glowing grove. Cold tea sat untouched, hinting at hours lost in study.

Ethrael set down her quill, her hands steady despite a faint tremble of fervor. "The Starbloom Grove," she said, her voice a reverent whisper, "is more than I knew. I knew my family were stewards, but the grove was a place of magic and healing, woven into the heavens and earth."

She pointed to a passage, its script flowing like starlight. "This tells of the grove's origins," she said, tracing the lines. "It was born when the sky wept celestial fragments that fell to the earth before Keenroot's halls were built. The starbloom trees grew where they landed, their roots drinking the heavens' magic. The blossoms held power and magic to heal wounds; no mortal remedy could touch them. It could soothe broken minds, or mend the spirit."

Listening to Ethrael's vision, Yarnell felt his ballads yearn to echo her healing vision. Yarnell leaned closer, scanning the unreadable script. "Healing," he murmured, a note in the quiet air. "Your family used healing magic, didn't they?"

Ethrael nodded, her gaze distant, as if seeing the grove at its prime. "Another tome spoke of the stewards, my ancestors, chosen by the grove's light to tend its magic. They harvested blossoms with care, crafting remedies to knit flesh, calm fevers, ease dying souls. The dust, the harmful byproduct, was too potent, buried deep with warded chants. The grove was a sanctuary, where the wounded found wholeness, the lost peace."

Her voice faltered as she turned to a brittle book, its ink smudged by time. "But this tells of its fall," she said, her tone darkening. "The cave elves and goblins came to quell its light. Dwarves and elves fought them, an alliance of stone and star, and won, but the cave elves burned the grove with dark fire. Aelthar withered, the magic lost, or so the records say."

Yarnell reached for the sketch, imagining the magical forest. "A place of magic and healing," he said softly. "If it was so powerful, could some magic remain?"

"I hope so," Ethrael said, her eyes meeting his, determination blazing within her. "The grove's magic was rooted deep in the sky's fragments. If any survived, it's wild now, untended. The starblooms could heal again and be a sanctuary, but they need time, knowledge, and skilled hands. Druids, perhaps, to guide their harmony. Tools, wards, a community to tend it over the years."

She gathered her notes, her purpose a flame burning brighter, the grove's legacy reigniting her spirit. "I'll learn more," she said. "The library holds fragments, but the rituals and wards were consumed in the fire, awaiting discovery in other archives or from druids. We haven't seen the grove yet, Yarnell. We need to go to Aelthar to know what remains. But this is a labor for the future, a legacy to rebuild when we're ready."

Yarnell plucked a soft chord, the sound a promise in the alcove. "A song for another day," he said, his voice warm with admiration. "You've found the grove's heart, Ethrael, its magic, its healing. We'll carry that knowledge until the time comes to see if it can bloom again. For now, let's share this with Lorin. We've much to plan."

Ethrael smiled, a rare light in her eyes, as if the starblooms glowed within her. "Yes," she said, gathering scrolls and tomes into her satchel. "Let's go back and share with Lorin. The Starbloom Grove waits. I can foresee that, one day, we'll make it a place of magic and healing once more."

CHAPTER THIRTEEN

The Road's Kindled Spark — Lorin

Gather, friends, by the fire's glow, and hear a tale of hearts forged and paths yet to roam. In a city of stone and song, a smith with a shadowed past grips a hammer, its weight a whisper of dwarven blood lost to time. Across the cobbled streets, a bard cradles a lute born of sacrifice, its strings humming with dreams of distant lands. Together with a healer, whose hands seek new wisdom, they sit at a table, their fates entwining like threads in a tapestry. A journey beckons—to a homeland of deep halls and guarded thrones—where memory, music, and mending may find their truth. Listen closely to their first steps, where craft and courage meet, and let the winds of fate guide their tale. Now, listen, as the forge's embers spark the story's heart...

Lorin felt the forge's embers when Master Falere summoned him. "I am very impressed with you. You are probably my best student, and I didn't even teach you that much. Your work is remarkable."

Lorin's chest swelled with pride, yet a shadow lingered. How could he excel with a past still locked away?

Falere continued, "One last task to finish your training: make something that's art but functional. I won't say what, but I'll check every inch. If it ain't as good as my own, you start over. Got any ideas what you'll craft?"

Lorin recalled Tarul's tale—a hammer for his father. Could he wield such a tool as a warrior? Lorin gripped a hammer from the forge's rack, its weight a nod to his dwarven roots, though he could not recall them. For a throwback to his heritage, a hammer seemed the perfect project.

"Sir, I remember that hammer you made during my apprenticeship. I want to make a hammer that is magnificent in beauty but also worthy of the palace guards in battle." Yet a flicker of doubt stirred. Could a hammer reclaim the dwarf he was, or was a sword his true path?

"Good choice! I look forward to it. You may use any materials at the forge. If you need any others, you must acquire them on your own. I suggest you take some time off and work out the design of your masterpiece. Perfect execution requires perfect planning. Good luck."

A hammer felt like a key to his lost past, its weight in his mind both an anchor and mystery. Could its creation unlock the dwarf he'd been, or would it only forge new questions? As Lorin's thoughts turned to his hammer, Yarnell sought his own craft's renewal.

• • • (Yarnell)

Yarnell's heart thrummed with excitement and trepidation when the craftsman's shop summoned him, the new lute complete. He knocked, and the young woman ushered him inside, her eyes soft with unspoken sorrow. The absence of the old craftsman struck a discordant note in his chest. "Where is the master I spoke with last time?" Yarnell asked, disappointment shadowing his voice. "I thought he would present it to me."

She sighed, her voice gentle. "He passed away. He labored day and night on your lute, obsessed with its perfection. His health faltered, and his body could no longer match his heart's fire. We often spoke of his vision. I finished it for him. He called it his finest work."

Yarnell's chest tightened, grief muting his excitement. "If I had known he would push himself so..." His words faltered, heavy with guilt and regret.

"Do not let your heart be troubled," she said. "He died crafting what he loved. Few are so fortunate."

Yarnell nodded, still adrift in sorrow. "My old lute, where is it?"

She smiled faintly as she handed the new instrument to him. "Father saw your soul entwined with it when you played. He said it should not sing for another. So he wove its essence into the new lute. It may look different, but its heart is yours."

Yarnell turned it over in his hands. He tried to grasp its beauty. He thought, this instrument is no mere tool but a vision of art's breath, its very form a melody unspoken. It might hum without my hand to stir its strings.

Looking closer at its body, hewn of rosewood and glowing with the deep, ruddy warmth of twilight's embers, while its spruce neck, pale as dawn's first light, stood in tender contrast, the pairing sang of nature's own accord. Rubies, set like drops of captured flame, adorned the frets and bridge, their elegance a silent proclamation of grace. The neck, smooth as a river's caress, nestled into palms like a companion long-known. Its contours are a welcome homecoming.

With care, he tuned its voice, fingers brushed the strings in gentle reverence, and lo, a test-strum bloomed forth, clear and bracing as a breeze born of mountain heights. He plucked a cascade of chords, each note ringing true, its timbre as pure and unbidden as the morning songbird's anthem. To cradle this masterpiece felt as innate as the beat of his own heart, an extension of his flesh and soul.

He imagined its chords lifting their spirits on the road ahead, a companion for the trials he'd face with Lorin and Ethrael. Each chord felt like an extension of his fingers, as natural as his old lute yet richer, its polished curves gleaming with the promise of countless songs.

"If I may ask," the young woman said, "would you play the song you shared with my father? It would honor him and reveal your new partner's range."

"Of course," Yarnell replied, his voice thick with reverence. "He deserves to be remembered through this song."

The notes flowed effortlessly, each sound more vivid than any he had known, a magical duet between bard and lute. The world faded, his heart riding the melody, the instrument no longer separate but part of him. When the final chord lingered, Yarnell stood, exhausted yet alive, the music a testament to the craftsman's legacy.

The young woman's eyes glistened, her smile radiant through tears. "Thank you. I see him smiling. He will live on in your music."

As Yarnell left the shop, lute cradled in his arms, he felt a pull to share its song with Lorin and Ethrael, their journey together waiting just beyond the horizon.

• • • *(Lorin)*

Lorin sat at the dinner table with Yarnell and Ethrael, the forge's heat still lingering in his mind as they shared their triumphs. Yarnell's tales of his new lute and Ethrael's quiet pride in her healing sparked hope in Lorin for the next chapter of their lives, yet her sudden silence caught his attention as they spoke of the future. A pang of concern tightened his chest, mirrored in Yarnell's glance.

Lorin's gaze lingered on Ethrael, her fingers twisting a sprig of dried herb, a relic of the dwarven salves that had steadied his pulse. Her usually bright eyes dimmed with a quiet weight, her silence thick with unspoken resolve, as if bearing an unseen burden.

"Sorry to overshadow your thoughts, Ethrael," Lorin said, his voice softening, "but your silence worries me. What's happening with you? How are your healing studies progressing?"

Ethrael hesitated, her voice soft, eyes tracing the table's grain. "Keenroot's herbs saved many, but they're spent for me. When I tended you, Lorin, dwarven songs and stone-mixed salves brought you back, where elven magic failed. That lore opened a door I can't close, yet I fear losing the natural healing that's my root. Dwarven healers weave natural healing deeper than elves."

Yarnell leaned forward, his voice animated. "Well, for me, I need to experience different cultures, music, and literature. I suspect I'll have to start traveling again. I have spent too long here and must share my new instrument with the world. I don't know where I'll go, but you can come along."

Lorin saw Ethrael's face light up, her voice eager. "That would be great. I'm sure new cultures and flora would reveal new healing techniques." She paused and looked at Lorin, "I would love to join you, but don't want to leave Lorin behind. I am not ready to say goodbye."

"Well, let's bring him along. He can always find a job as a blacksmith wherever we go."

Lorin's eyes brightened as a thought crossed his mind. A journey home might unlock my past, but what if my brother sees me as a threat?

"I've been thinking of a journey too, to my dwarven homeland. It might spark my memories and help finish my project for Master Falere. I'll travel as Lorin, not Barzul, to avoid troubling my brother's throne, but I'm unsure how to handle him."

Ethrael stood with excitement in her eyes, "That would be great! The dwarves have very different healing techniques, and I would love to learn them. Yarnell has learned a few dwarf songs, but he could expand his repertoire by being there. As far as the dwarf king issue, I have an idea there, too. Perhaps we could obtain a letter from King Arkiel introducing us and expressing our interest in examining and learning from their culture as a bridge-building exercise between the two realms. It would benefit him, so I think he would be willing to pen an introduction for us. What do you both think?"

Lorin nodded enthusiastically, his heart lifting at the thought of their shared adventure, though a flicker of unease lingered about facing his brother. "I agree," he said, his gaze meeting

Yarnell's nod of assent. "Tomorrow, we begin preparing for our adventure. Yarnell can pen a note to the king requesting his aid."

Lorin lay awake that night, excitement warring with the weight of his unknown past, the hammer's design still vivid in his mind.

Since Yarnell had traveled before, they relied on his guidance for what they would need, his memories of dwarven roads lost to the void. None of them was rich, so it would be a walking journey. They would need a map to the dwarf king's homeland, as Lorin's mind held no trace of its location. A letter from the king would likely ease encounters, though Lorin's thoughts drifted to the dangers, brigands, and goblins, like those that had once left him broken. Without a warrior, their journey would test them all.

Lorin watched as Ethrael sent the message Yarnell penned to the king, informing him of their plans and requesting the royal announcement.

As Lorin readied his belongings, he watched Ethrael pack a vial of stone-ground salve, her hands steady with purpose. "This helped you heal," she said, eyes bright with hope for dwarven lore. Lorin saw her strength, binding them for the road ahead.

• • •

It was only three days later when Yarnell declared, "Ok, I think we're ready. We have the basics. Really, all we are missing is a map and a letter of introduction. I have a vague idea of where the dwarf kingdom lies, but we can ask other travelers along the way. We will have to find our way to the dwarf kingdom somehow."

Lorin adjusted the heavy pack on his shoulders, wondering if they'd carried too much for the journey. Yarnell's response to his concern was to sell excess items later. A sharp knock at the door jolted Lorin. Opening it, he found a young servant, her satchel slung over her shoulder, her arrival stirring a mix of hope and unease.

Lorin's gaze followed the servant as she spoke, her voice steady with royal authority. "This note will ease your journey," she said, handing it to Ethrael. Lorin's heart quickened with hope. "It describes how you are under King Arkiel's direction, and any impediment will be considered an insult to the throne." She placed it back in the satchel and pulled out another note.

This had the royal seal, but it was sealed shut. "This is your introduction to King Tarul by our king," she continued, and Lorin's thoughts raced to his brother's throne. "The exact contents are only to be known by both sets of royalty." She placed it back in the satchel and pulled out the final item.

This one had no royal seal. "I suspect this one will be of the most important use. It's a map showing a path between the two kingdoms. It is suggested that you stay on the main roads and travel by day to avoid brigands."

Lorin's grip tightened on the table's edge as she handed the map to Yarnell, the weight of their journey pressing heavier on his shoulders. Could these gifts truly pave the way to my past, or deepen its shadows?

Behind her was a horse pulling a wagon, and Lorin's eyes widened at the sight. "There are two barrels of wine as a gift to the dwarf king," pausing for a moment, she continued. "The forge master has added a barrel with scrap metal to support your final project since you won't be here. The satchel has a few coins to help you on your way." Lorin's heart swelled with gratitude as she handed the satchel to Ethrael.

Lorin listened intently as the servant continued, her words sparking a fragile hope.

"The king would wish you well on your journey. He wished to meet with you himself, but he is dealing with goblins in his forest. But, he expects you to return this way. There is still the matter of returning the sword he would ask of you in the future. He believes this is the best course of action for the three of you and the two kingdoms. If you find others like yourselves in the dwarf clan who would like to engage in a cultural exchange, he would be delighted to host them. In his message to King Tarul, he said as much."

Bowing slightly, Lorin felt her words bolster their mission, though the shadow of his brother's throne loomed, a lingering doubt.

CHAPTER FOURTEEN

Stones from Heaven — Lorin

Gather, friends, for a tale of shadowed roads, where Gooseberry's humble heart hides a heavenly curse. Lorin treads to dwarven lands, a hammer's call in his blood. Will Ethrael's healing fire mend the sky's strange blight, or deepen our smith's quest? Hush, the path unfolds.

A quick glance at the map revealed a path through the forest, leading to a human hamlet named Gooseberry, where an inn, or at least a farmer's barn, might await. Lorin's heart surged with purpose and excitement for the journey. Ethrael's tight grip on her satchel and the steady pluck of Yarnell's lute caught his eye and lifted his spirit. Lorin guided the wagon, its creak mirroring his unsteady hopes.

The road, path really, was easy to follow, though uncomfortably narrow with a wagon. Lorin decided it must have been well-traveled because it was not overgrown, and no trees had fallen across the trail. Yarnell's lute complemented the birds' song, easing the knot in Lorin's chest, though the forest's quiet made him scan for goblins—the memories of his near-death were never far from his thoughts.

He leaned back as dusk settled, the day's smooth travel lifting his spirits more than expected. Lorin signaled to stop as darkness crept over the forest, the path fading into shadow like his own uncertain past. A stream's soft gurgle caught his ear, steps away from the path, its ripple a faint comfort in the gathering dusk. He started a fire, and Yarnell headed to the stream to catch a few fish.

He watched while Ethrael carefully sorted her herbs. After emptying her backpack into the wagon and slinging it over her shoulder, she said, "I think we should save our supplies until we need them. The forest has quite a delicious bounty. I'll be back soon." Her words, 'I'll be back soon,' sent a flicker of unease through him, as if the forest might swallow her as it nearly had him.

Yarnell returned with three fresh trout and fresh water. Ethrael had come back with an herb-and-vegetable bounty. Lorin had a decent fire burning, its crackle a small comfort against the forest's deepening chill.

Ethrael's stew simmered, a hearty mixture of root, leaf, and fish, its savor enriched by the wild air. It felt like a feast to Lorin, the road's hardships seasoning the meal with a magic that stirred faint echoes of dwarven hearths, Ethrael's care warming him like the forge he left behind.

For a fortnight, Lorin settled into a rhythm, the road's gentle cadence guiding their steps. Each day, Lorin felt the road draw him closer to the dwarven lands. The forest's dense ranks began to thin.

•   •   •

On the final eve among the trees, he caught a faint curl of smoke in the air, a prickle of unease stirring his senses. Lorin shot a questioning glance toward Yarnell.

Yarnell said in a low voice, "I think we should camp within the trees tonight. Tomorrow, we can venture out of their protective embrace with the sun high in the sky. Not all hearts strum kindness."

Lorin nodded, his unease deepening at the thought of unseen threats, his hand reaching for a weapon he did not have. At dawn, golden light pierced the leafy lattice, rousing Lorin with a jolt of purpose. He guided the wagon forward. His eyes were sharp as they bid farewell to the woodland's shelter.

At the forest's edge, the earth bore scars of labor, stumps like silent tombstones where trees once stood. Lorin saw Gooseberry's dozen roofs clustered tightly, like sentinels around a hard-won camp. Beyond, fields stretched in neat patches, their order a stark contrast to the forest's wild tangle.

The wagon rattled into Gooseberry under midday's harsh light, its gnarled wooden walls sturdy as a weathered outpost. Fields of oats and rye rippled beyond, tended by hands he pictured as rough as his own from the forge. Gooseberry stood alone amid the farmland. The hamlet's humble roofs stirred a pang in Lorin, a reminder of how far he was from the dwarven lands he sought, yet Ethrael's steady presence at his side grounded him, her healer's skill a beacon of hope in his shadowed journey. Its geese strutted the lanes with proud steps, a hound bounding up with a stick in its maw, eager as a smith with a finished blade.

• • •

Lorin felt the folk's sidelong glances, their eyes sharp as honed flint, studying him, Yarnell's lute, and Ethrael's elven grace. When they returned to their tasks, he sensed a cautious acceptance, as if the village had sized them up and found no threat.

At the hamlet's heart stood two businesses: the Goosefeather Inn, a timbered roost of cheer, its faded sign creaking in the gusts. The scent of ale and stew, rich with goosefat and thyme, wafted from the inn, promising rest on straw beds in Lorin's mind.

A sign for Oren's Hollow, a healer's den thick with nettle and lavender, caught his nose. A passing villager mentioned Oren, a healer tending the ailing. The overheard whispers spoke of a farm beyond the walls, where a strange malady lingered, strangely limited to one family. Glancing at Ethrael, her healer's satchel at her side, he wondered if this mystery might draw her skill or if the dwarven halls alone held her desire.

Ethrael headed to speak with Oren, Lorin by her side. "I hear there is a farm outside town whose family is deathly ill. What is going on and what is being done to help them?"

Oren, at a loss for words for a moment, took a deep breath and said, "It is a most unusual malady. Their skin is turning black, and they can't keep food or water down. It has not spread outside the family."

Oren's words echoed the whispers Lorin had caught in the village, talk of a curse. He quickly added, with a resigned tone, "We're just waiting for nature to take its course."

Lorin was ill at ease with the healer's lack of compassion.

Ethrael's face turned red, and she started raising her voice, "So you don't know anything, for sure?" She paused as she searched for the right words. "You are just going to let them die?"

Lorin beamed with pride while watching Ethrael's passion for the sick. Her fierceness reminded him of Keenroot, when she'd defied all to save his life, a debt that anchored him now as he stood by her side.

Oren looked to the floor, "What can I do? I don't want to be cursed."

With her hands on her hips, she forcefully said, "At morning light, I am heading out there. Gossip is not a tool of the healer!"

Lorin followed Ethrael out, the healer's fire kindling his own resolve to uncover truth. What curse could strike only one family? Lorin wondered, his gaze sweeping the village for answers.

As he strolled through town, he observed everyone, but especially the children. He could not determine who their parents were. The villagers' care for every child stirred a longing in Lorin. The children's curious gazes made him feel, for a moment, part of their world. They started coming up to him. Like his speech at the forge, he could speak with them. It was not Elvish or Dwarven. Yarnell told him later they were speaking Common, the language of most humans. Lorin felt a flicker of recognition as the children's words took shape. The Common tongue stirred something familiar, as if his lost past had once known it. Could a prince's life, as Tarul claimed, have taught him this, or was it something else entirely?

• • •

The family was in dire straits; their breath was faint, stinking of rot. They'd been sick in their bellies for days, unable to hold food or water. Their skin was blotched, black patches spreading; their hair fell away. Too weak to tend their farm, Ethrael's grim expression told Lorin she feared they'd soon perish without aid. Speaking with the parents, she learned the children had fallen ill first, the girl and boy sickened, their parents following a week later.

Ethrael pressed them on the 'curse', but no cause surfaced. The father swore, "All is the same as ever, no new goods, visitors, or dead beasts."

Ethrael said, "If you have not interacted with anyone, I would think a curse unlikely. So what changed on the farm in the last month or so?"

The young girl spoke meekly, "Father, what of the fireballs from the sky some weeks back? They were like balls of flame falling, so bright I shielded my eyes. They struck the ground past our farm, near the stream by the groves where you hunt deer."

The rest of the family hadn't seen it, so they dismissed her tale as a child's fancy. Lorin saw Ethrael's eyes narrow at the dismissal, her focus sharpening as if she sensed truth in the girl's words. The story's clear and consistent details held her attention, a spark of hope that warmed Lorin's chest despite the tale's strangeness. It grew late, so Ethrael gave them herb-steeped water, a remedy for poisoning to calm their bellies. Lorin followed her back to the inn, the weight of the family's suffering heavy in his steps.

At supper, Lorin listened as Ethrael spoke only of the family, her eyes alight with the same healer's spark he'd seen when she fought for his life in Keenroot. Her renewed fire warmed his chest, a reminder of her relentless care, unbound by race, devoted only to easing pain. They filled their bellies with inn stew, and Lorin watched Yarnell strum a few tunes, the music a brief respite before they turned in.

Come morn, Ethrael dragged Lorin and Yarnell back to the farm, insisting on the wagon to haul her healing chattel. She could not be swayed. Yarnell sighed but followed, joining Lorin as they accompanied her.

On the road, Ethrael said to Lorin and Yarnell, "I think somehow the sky's fire poisoned their world. The children hold the key, though I don't understand how."

Her words sent a chill through Lorin, the talk of sky-fire stirring unease he couldn't name. Sky-fire and poison, could such a thing be real, or was it a child's tale grown large in fear?

Ethrael sent Lorin and Yarnell to search the fields for something unusual. Their protests were unheeded and in vain, so they wandered, dreading returning empty-handed. When Lorin and Yarnell finally gathered enough courage to return, Ethrael was with the children, her healer's bag open, likely tending their sores and questioning them about the illness.

Around midday, the boy cried, "What of the 'black rocks'?" He sprinted to his room, returning with one. "I found this by the river. It's small and fits in my pocket, yet there are greater ones. Some as big as a goat."

Ethrael's eyes gleamed with hope's first ray. The rock was black as night, dusted with ashy powder, solid yet oddly light. She tasted the powder, bitter.

"Lorin and Yarnell, come with us. The children will show the strange rocks that have fallen from the sky."

Lorin saw the boy's words proved true: beside the stream's rippling flow lay a dozen black stones, scattered like debris from an unknown source. Most were small, fist-sized, while some matched a goat's bulk; the largest stood as tall as a steed. Each matched the boy's dark, solid yet strangely light rock, dusted with powdery ash. The powder clung to Lorin's fingers like ash from a long-dead campfire.

"Draw them from the stream and load them into the wagon," Ethrael commanded. "Search the banks for others and gather those too!"

The largest stone was massive, unwieldy as an unworked anvil, yet strangely light. Lorin and Yarnell called the children to aid, their steps splashing through the stream as they gathered the lesser stones, dark pebbles piling in the wagon.

Ethrael's voice rang with certainty as she declared these rocks brought the 'curse': Ethrael's voice was firm, "The rocks in the drinking water sickened the family."

Lorin followed her gaze to the stream, realizing the town's upstream wells had spared them by sheer luck. The children, who played in the stream where the rocks landed and fetched water for tasks, fell ill first. The family used that water, too, which is how the sickness spread to the parents. Lorin felt the puzzle pieces falling into place. But the powder on his hands, what was it? Was it a danger to him?

Ethrael declared that with the rocks removed, the stream would cleanse itself in time. Ethrael had Lorin and Yarnell wash their hands with soap from upstream water, lye, and leaves. She bade the family do the same, commanding them to fetch water upstream only and cast out tainted vessels. She brewed a stew with herbs to guard against poisons, promising to check on them until they mended.

True to her word, Ethrael visited daily for a week. Each day, the family's nausea ebbed, their sores dried, and color returned, though full strength would take time. Lorin felt hope stir, like a new refrain in Yarnell's lute.

CHAPTER FIFTEEN

Shadows of the Road — Lorin

Gather, ye wanderers, and let my lute strum a tale of roads dust-worn and secrets borne on dawn's first breath. A smith named Lorin treads from Gooseberry's humble hearth, his hammer's pulse a dwarven echo, yet his past a shadow unclaimed. The wagon creaks, heavy with stones fallen from heaven's vault, their poison a riddle to stir a healer's fire. A stranger joins, his blade dull but his gaze sharp, kindling sparks of doubt in our smith's heart. And lo, a healer's whispered vow binds their fates, her strength a beacon to forge a new path. Hush now, for the road stretches wide, and destiny's chord trembles beneath the morning's rose-hued veil.

Lorin felt the dawn's rose-hued veil on his skin, the road's promise stirring both hope and shadow. The wagon groaned as it rolled from Gooseberry, dawn casting amber and rose across the fields. Yarnell plucked a wandering tune on his lute, notes mingling with hoof-clops and the goat's bleats, a gift from the family. Gripping the reins, jaw tight, he glanced at Ethrael in the rear, her eyes fixed on the sky-fallen stones amid turnips and greens. The air carried a fresh promise, but those stones weighed heavy, their riddle haunting his thoughts.

"Fare thee well, Gooseberry," Yarnell hummed a song, "Your curse is lifted, your tale unwritten."

Lorin flicked Yarnell a look, his brow creasing. "Keep it light, bard," he grumbled, "I've no stomach for odes to stones that rain sickness while driving this cart."

Yarnell's grin flashed, but Lorin saw his fingers pause briefly on the strings, as if his jest hid a flicker of unease, before continuing.

The elder's coins clinked, payment for Ethrael's healing, and the family's gifts, vegetables, and that ornery goat, crowded the wagon. Yet the sky-fallen stones gnawed at Lorin.

Ethrael's voice cut through the morning air, sharp with conviction, making Lorin tense. "They're no ordinary stones," she said. "They dropped from the sky, and that dust, it's no natural plague. I need to learn more before disposing of them." Her words stirred his unease, hinting at a purpose he couldn't grasp.

Yarnell leaned back, his voice light, "And until then? We cart them about like some grim treasure?"

"There's a way," she replied. "I'll wrap them tight with cloth and herbs to bind their malice. We can't allow it to be loosed on the wind."

Lorin glanced at the fading farmstead, catching the youngest child's faint wave by the gate, his face less hollow. Ethrael's care had set them on the mend, kindling a quiet pride in Lorin's chest, though the stones' mystery stirred unease.

Lorin felt the road widen beneath the wagon, the breeze sharp with earth and dew against his skin. Yarnell's lute softened, its notes steady, calming Lorin's racing thoughts like a heartbeat. Lorin kept his eyes ahead, while Ethrael murmured at the rear.

The goat bleated, drawing a chuckle from Yarnell. "The band's livelier now. What's her name?"

"Something mulish," Lorin grumbled.

"Like you." Ethrael's laugh rang clear, a rare sound that eased the weight in his chest.

Yarnell quipped, "Call her Mirth. It'll serve us where we're bound."

Lorin shook his head but drove on, sensing a bond with Ethrael and Yarnell he couldn't fully name, but was the road stretching toward answers or deeper shadows? The stones' faint rattle echoed his unease, but with Ethrael and Yarnell beside him, the road felt less daunting, for now.

Now, upon a well-trod road, and covering more ground each day, few travelers passed the other way, scarce bustling despite the road's worn ruts. Out in the open with a laden wagon and no true guard, Lorin feared they'd be an easy quarry for brigands. A dense forest trail was one matter; this broad road, with no stout arm to shield them, was another. Yet the gods seemed to favor them. The first day passed without peril.

As night fell, Lorin settled the wagon by a quiet campsite, his thoughts drifting to the dwarven lands, though an unease lingered he couldn't name.

. . .

Come daybreak, a young man with mud caked on his boots stood in their camp, his hand resting lightly on the hilt of a sheathed sword. His steady gaze fixed on Ethrael, stirring not, speaking not, just watching her. Lorin sat up quickly, noting the gleam in the stranger's eyes, a hunger of youths dreaming beyond their current circumstances. "Who are you?" Lorin called, his voice sharp in the morning chill.

"Jarek," the man replied, his tone steady but offering no more. Lorin studied him, the worn boots caked with mud and the dull sword at his hip suggesting a life of restless travel, perhaps seeking coin or glory beyond the fields.

Yarnell said, "Morning, join us, we're just getting ready to have some breakfast."

"Thank ya kindly. I'll take you up on that offer. Just left the farm and lookin' to do a bit of adventuring. Ya look like ya in need of a sword arm. Mind if I tag along?"

Yarnell answered, "Can't hurt. We're on our way to Parcelridge. You're welcome to join us that far."

Lorin shot Yarnell a look, mouthing, "We don't know anything about this man."

Yarnell waved his concerns off. "You got yourself a deal. Was heading that way anyway, maybe I can find work there."

That night, Lorin glimpsed Jarek under the stars, swinging a dull blade in clumsy arcs, its edge barely fit to cut twigs. Jarek's stubborn swings mirrored Lorin's own drive at the forge, yet the stranger knew his path. Lorin, dwarf prince or not, still groped in the dark for his true name.

Lorin watched Jarek over the days, his quiet demeanor suggesting more comfort with labor than banter. His sturdy frame hinted at fields left behind, and each night, Lorin saw him practice with that dull sword, its clumsy arcs belying a stubborn determination.

Jarek's gaze often lingered on Ethrael, fetching her water or piling leaves for her rest, his eyes bright with unspoken admiration. Ethrael appeared not to notice, her focus fixed on the stones. Jarek's eyes on Ethrael twisted a knot in Lorin's chest, wariness mingling with a sharper pang, jealousy, perhaps, though a man without a past felt unworthy of such claims on her.

Lorin and the others spoke of their path to the dwarven mountains by the fire one night, sharing little of their purpose. Jarek listened, his silence either courtesy or lack of curiosity, asking no questions of their past or aim.

Lorin unfolded the elves' map, his finger tracing the path to Parcelridge, two weeks away by his reckoning, with the dwarven mountains a similar span beyond.

Days blurred into weeks, the road's rhythm lulling Lorin, though Jarek's lingering glances at Ethrael still stirred a restless unease in his chest. Travel fell into a steady way. Yarnell drove the wagon, Jarek sitting beside him, calling it 'on watch' with a seriousness that grated on Lorin's nerves. Lorin's hammer sketches steadied his hands, but Jarek's self-proclaimed 'watch' felt like a challenge, a reminder of their vulnerability without a true warrior and his failure as a protector.

Ethrael fidgeted at the rear, and Lorin wondered if Jarek's constant attention wore on her, though her true thoughts remained a mystery. Sometimes, Lorin took the wagon's reins, and Yarnell lifted their spirits with song.

Nearing Parcelridge, Ethrael's fidgeting peaked, her glances darting toward Jarek, who lingered too close. She surprised Lorin with a kiss, her lips warm and sudden. Lorin's heart raced, guessing Jarek's constant attention had spurred her, though her whispered "I'll tell you later" left him uncertain.

• • •

Days later, the road widened, and Lorin's heart still thrummed with Ethrael's kiss as the city's clamor rose ahead. The wagon rattled into Parcelridge, its stone walls and bustling streets a stark contrast to Gooseberry's quiet fields. Lorin's eyes widened at the crowds, merchants hawking wares, animals bleating, and children darting through the chaos. The city wasn't vast like Keenroot, but its buildings huddled closer together, their cramped stone facades looming like stacked cages in Lorin's mind. Its clamor set his nerves on edge, a reminder of their vulnerability. As he guided the wagon through a narrow street, a figure lunged from the crowd, snatching the coin pouch from Lorin's belt and bolting. Lorin's heart lurched, his shout caught in his throat as the thief took off running.

Before he could react, Yarnell's hand flicked, a blur of motion sending bolas whistling through the air. The ropes snared the thief's legs, dropping him with a thud. Lorin stared, his pulse pounding, as Jarek leapt from the wagon, strolling to the fallen thief with a calm that grated on Lorin's nerves. Jarek retrieved the pouch, delivering a sharp kick to the thief's side for good measure. Lorin's jaw tightened, gratitude warring with irritation at Jarek's swagger.

The city guards glanced over, their faces impassive, before returning to their patrols, as if such thefts were routine. Lorin clutched the returned pouch, the weight of the coins a small comfort against the city's dangers.

They found refuge at The Wanderer's Rest, its sign creaking above a timbered facade. The scent of ale and stew wafted from within, promising rest, but the innkeeper's gruff voice dashed Lorin's hopes. "Only two rooms left," he said, eyeing their group. Lorin's stomach twisted as Ethrael suggested he share with her, her glance at Jarek sharp with something he couldn't read, discomfort, perhaps, or defiance. Yarnell shrugged, agreeing to room with Jarek, his easy grin doing little to ease Lorin's unease. The arrangement left Lorin both relieved and anxious, the memory of Ethrael's kiss burning in his mind as they climbed the creaking stairs.

• • •

Morning light spilled through the inn's narrow windows, stirring Lorin from a restless sleep. Ethrael's words echoed in his mind, her confession a warmth that battled the chill of his uncertain past. As he rose, the city's hum called him to action, his hammer's promise urging him forward.

As Yarnell slipped off to The Rusty Plow tavern below, the bard's voice carried through the floorboards, vibrant with a joy Lorin envied, each note a reminder of Yarnell's ease in any setting. Yarnell had urged them to explore Parcelridge, but Lorin's thoughts lingered on Ethrael, who sat across from him in their shared room, her satchel open, herbs and cloths spread out.

Ethrael's voice was soft, her breath warm against his ear. "Jarek's stares made me realize I don't want to lose you," she said, her eyes searching his. Lorin's heart surged, but doubt whispered he wasn't worthy. Her words kindled hope, yet the shadow of his lost past, prince or not, made him question if he could claim her heart.

In the morning, Lorin, Jarek, and Ethrael headed to the blacksmith's forge, its fiery maw glowing through a haze of smoke that stung Lorin's eyes. A thought struck Lorin as he watched Jarek's clumsy grip on his sword, his irritation flaring. "Why don't you seek out someone to help you with your sword work?" he said. "You could ask a guard, but they probably wouldn't be helpful. Maybe the blacksmith would know of someone who could teach you."

The forge reeked of sweat and molten iron, its heat wrapping Lorin like a familiar cloak. The blacksmith looked up from his work and said, "My name is Torric, Torric the Hammer. What do you need?"

Jarek stepped forward, his voice steady but eager. "I am looking for someone to help me with my swordwork. Would you know of anyone?"

Lorin's eyes roamed the forge, taking in the routine wares, horseshoes, and plow shares, sturdy but unremarkable.

Torric pointed down the street, "If you head down the street and take a right, there is an older gentleman who can help you."

Jarek walked off in the direction Torric pointed. Lorin watched Jarek walk off, his swagger grating, as if he already fancied himself a swordsman.

Torric's gaze shifted to Lorin, his eyes narrowing as if reading his thoughts. "By what your eyes are taking in, I suspect you know your way around a forge."

Lorin nodded, a spark of pride warming his chest. "Yes, I come from Keenroot and have been studying. I have completed my training, and now I only have the final project left. It is going to be a hammer. I am traveling to the dwarven kingdom of Cragmoore to learn their techniques."

"No call for such fancy work here. Even the weapons I repair are not much to look at."

Ethrael interjected, "I am looking for a healing facility. I want to talk with them. Where would I find them?"

"Ah, you would be wanting Mira's Haven. It is a wooden structure down there," Torric said, pointing down a different street.

Lorin's gaze followed the gesture, his mind drifting to Ethrael's relentless drive to heal, a drive that had saved him. Lorin and Ethrael walked off together.

Mira's Haven smelled of polished wood and sharp herbs, stirring memories of Ethrael's hut in Keenroot. Lorin stood by as Ethrael asked about their cases, her voice eager, learning they had a head-injury patient like him. He felt a flush of unease as she explained his surgery, pointing to him as proof of its success.

The healers' faces twisted in horror at first, their eyes darting to Lorin, but their nods suggested they saw its logic. Lorin shifted, feeling like a specimen under their scrutiny, yet a pang of pride stirred as Ethrael's words flowed confidently.

The healers wrote down her description of the entire care and treatment, their quills scratching as Lorin watched, their thanks polite but guarded. He wondered if they'd dare try her methods, their hesitation a faint echo of Keenroot's scorn. Ethrael's eyes shone with purpose, and Lorin's chest warmed, her strength anchoring him as they left the haven.

Evening settled over Parcelridge, and Lorin's thoughts turned toward Ethrael's strength as they returned to The Wanderer's Rest.

CHAPTER SIXTEEN

The Sword's Farewell Whisper — Lorin

By the fire's glow, I'll spin a tale of shadowed blades and shadowed fates. In The Wanderer's Rest, Lorin hears whispers of a cursed sword, its song entwined with his soul's quest. Yet farewells weigh heavy, as trusted companions turn from the path, and the road to Cragmoore beckons with secrets. Beneath the mountain's gaze, strangers clad in stone's resolve will test his heart. Will trust or treachery greet him in the dwarven halls? Listen, and let the tale unfold.

At The Wanderer's Rest, Lorin sat with Ethrael and Yarnell for dinner, Jarek's absence easing the tension in his shoulders. A local bard strummed in the corner, the monotonous tune and poorly tuned lute grating on his nerves. Barely listening, his mind drifted to the sky-fallen stones and Ethrael's whispered confession until a song about a 'cursed sword' pierced his thoughts. Meeting Ethrael and Yarnell's eyes, he saw recognition in their eyes too.

When the bard finished, Yarnell beckoned the man over, offering a tankard of ale with a grin. The young bard's eyes widened as Yarnell displayed his lute, its polished wood gleaming under the tavern's dim light, and Lorin noted the young man's awe, recognizing a master's instrument. As the ale flowed, the bard grew chatty, and Yarnell deftly steered the conversation to the cursed sword. Lorin leaned forward, his pulse quickening, as the bard shared a tale from a dozen years past.

The young bard drained his tankard of ale and started his tale. "When she reached the age of 15, she announced to her family that she would leave on her next birthday. She was tired of living under her parents' rule and wanted to see the world. But her father knew her naivety put her in danger. He had done the same at her age. Her parents promised to give her a magical sword on her next birthday."

The bard lifted his tankard to be refilled. "Her father and mother were great magicians. They spent the entire year working on enchanting a sword with magic. On her 16th birthday, they presented her with the sword. It was bright and shiny, and the girl was happy knowing her family supported her."

The server filled his tankard, and he took another gulp before continuing the tale. "She was no swordsman, but she didn't need to be. She didn't need to know how to fight, as the sword's magic fought for her. The magic sword spoke to her on their journey. Raised in a magical family, she was not scared of such artifacts. It was a trusted companion. When brigands saw a young, unprotected traveler and attacked, the sword would 'swing into action' and dispatch her foes. It sang in battle, thrilled to be alive, useful, and strong. But it was loyal only to her. If anyone else wielded it, the blade injured or killed them, earning its 'cursed sword' reputation."

Lorin's grip tightened on his mug, the story stirring a shadow in his mind. He glanced at Ethrael, her brow furrowed, and Yarnell, his easy smile not reaching his eyes.

"So what happened to the girl? If the sword was always protecting her, how did she come to lose it?" Yarnell asked, his tone light but probing.

"That's the saddest part," the bard replied. "A band of brigands, bitter over the defeat she dealt their comrades, snuck into her camp one night, slit her throat, and took the sword as a prize. Unaware of its power, the thief who wielded it slew his friends and then himself. Others found it, and the tale continued until it was lost forever. No one knows where it is now." The bard slumped over and fell asleep.

Lorin's chest tightened, the tale's grim end leaving a hollow ache. The sword's loyalty, singing, and curse felt too close to his path. Was he destined to wield such a blade, its power unclaimed?

How had it found him? The questions gnawed at him, each a riddle as heavy as the sky-fallen stones.

Yarnell pressed a few coins into the sleeping bard's hand.

Lorin stared into the tavern's flickering light. The story raised more questions than it answered, and Lorin wondered why he, of all people, might wield a blade that spared no other.

• • •

As the tavern's echoes faded, Lorin sat in the quiet of their room, the cursed sword's tale heavy in his mind. Morning ushered in the task of packing, facing the unenviable duty of speaking to Jarek.

"I'm sorry, Jarek, you cannot join us for the next leg of our journey. The dwarves are wary of strangers, and our letter of introduction from King Arkiel does not include you." His chest tightened, seeing heartbreak in Jarek's eyes, likely from parting with Ethrael as much as the journey itself.

Jarek's shoulders slumped, his gaze falling to the ground.

Lorin felt a pang of sympathy. "I suggest you hone your skills," he continued, "perhaps take on mercenary work. It'll make you a stronger asset to any party. Who knows, we may return and need your strength." Lorin wondered if their paths would cross again, the road's uncertainties as heavy as the sky-fallen stones.

Before Lorin could process Jarek's departure, Ethrael's voice cut through the morning air, firm and resolute. "I will not be traveling with you either," she declared. "I'm staying to help the head injury patient at Mira's Haven. I'll ensure all is well and join you in the dwarven kingdom later."

Lorin's heart nearly stopped, her words a sudden blow. Ethrael's strength and steady presence would be absent, and the thought of traveling without her stirred great dread. Could he face the dwarven halls, his shadowed past, without her steady presence?

He nodded, trying to harden his resolve despite the ache. He and Yarnell turned to the wagon, the road to Cragmoore looming ahead. With heavy hearts, Lorin and Yarnell set out for the dwarven kingdom. The absence of Ethrael and Jarek pressed heavily on Lorin, the first time their band had been parted in months. How would Ethrael find them in the vastness of the dwarven lands?

The road from the city was rougher and less trodden than the road to Parcelridge. It was wide enough for the wagon, yet with scant room aside. He guided the wagon cautiously, wincing as the wheels sank into deep ruts, the narrow bounds offering no escape.

He found the first day dragging, lonely, and still. His thoughts kept drifting to Ethrael, her absence a void beside him, and he wondered if the dwarven halls would hold any answers. Would the dwarves see him as an outsider, or could they unlock his past?

At the mountain's foot, Lorin and Yarnell camped at day's end, forced to leave the wagon on the road, with no other option.

• • •

The mountain loomed closer, its shadow cooling the air, and Lorin felt the weight of their solitude. Lorin surveyed a small clearing, noting an old fire pit, and began hewing wood for a blaze. They lit a fire and took turns keeping watch. The reduced band size stretched each watch stint longer than before.

On Lorin's watch, the second shift, a small band approached from the mountain road, their figures stark against the moonlit path. No concealment was possible for them or Lorin's camp.

His pulse quickened, and he roused Yarnell with a low whisper, eyes fixed on the newcomers. Were they foes, or just wary travelers like us? As they drew near, Lorin saw three dwarves, afoot, tough as stone, and plainly scrappers, one limping from a wound.

"Well met, gentlemen," Lorin said, his voice steady despite the fear of being unarmed gnawing at him. "What brings ye down the mountain?"

The largest dwarf bristled, hand on his hammer, his eyes narrowing. "Not all of us are fellows, sir! This one is my wife, and hurt."

His tone was sharp, and his companions gripped their weapons, too. Abruptly, he swung his hammer at Lorin, who dodged with startling swiftness. Twirling around, Lorin swept his walking staff over the dwarf's ankles, felling him.

"I meant no disrespect, sir," Lorin said. "I'm a simple man and have never met a female of your kind. While some human men have beards, females don't. I apologize to you and your wife. Please join us at the fire."

The dwarf got back on his feet and laughed. "You, sir, are delightful. Where my wife is concerned, I tend to let my emotions get the better of me."

The dwarf's wife laughed harder than her husband. When she caught her breath, she said, "Don't let him lie to you. He's always quick with his temper and weapon. Too often it gets him and me into trouble, my leg's the latest casualty of his shenanigans."

As they sat, keeping their weapons close, Lorin continued. "What brings you down the mountain? I don't see any goods to trade in the city."

The dwarf's wife replied, "We're not on a trading journey but a more mundane one. As you can see, I'm injured and need medical care."

"I assume you're from the dwarf kingdom, and there must be healers there. Why not get aid there instead of undertaking a difficult trek while injured?"

"You'd think so, wouldn't you? But you see, my husband decided his anger should be directed at the head healer's youngest son, putting him in the hospital. In the brawl, he threw the boy toward a table. My bad luck was that his aim was poor. The youngster missed the table and landed on me instead. My leg's broken in multiple places, and this journey hasn't helped it heal. We thought we might be able to indenture ourselves to a patron in the city for a season to pay for the care I need to become whole again. I'm a wonderful cook. My husband and his brother are strong and can do whatever needs doing."

Yarnell piped up, "Madam, I'm sorry to hear that. You met us a day too late. We left a companion in the city, a healer who saved my friend from a deadly head wound."

"Just more bad luck, I'm afraid," she replied. "Let us camp with you for the evening, and we'll be on our way. Where are you headed? There's nothing up this path but the dwarven mountain home."

Yarnell smiled, "Perfect! That's our destination."

"You might as well turn back. They're not kind to strangers," she warned.

The quiet dwarf spoke, "Please, sir. I hold you no ill will, especially after your kindness, but dwarves aren't keen on outsiders. I suggest you turn around. Even if we vouch for you, they're not as open-minded as my brother. They distrust strangers."

Yarnell replied, "Thank you for your candor. We know your king's reputation. We carry a diplomatic message from the elven King Arkiel to King Tarul, accompanied by a gift to secure an audience. Your kinsmen likely wouldn't risk the wrath of either king."

"I see," the quiet dwarf said. "Many charlatans have claimed such things to enter our homeland. Can you prove your intent is noble?"

"You're wise," Yarnell said. "We're no threat, barely provisioned for the journey. As proof, here's a royal dispatch with the royal seal. I'm not privy to its contents nor free to show them to anyone but King Tarul, but it proves our honorable intent." Lorin wondered if the seal would sway them, or if they'd face more distrust.

The quiet dwarf, examining the seal, said, "Of course, it would be an honor to escort you to our home. It's lucky for you that we met. Too many of our brethren fight first and never ask questions. I'm guessing such an important message should be delivered promptly. Shall we start now?"

Lorin was relieved by the shift in tone, "As much as I'd value your help, I can't in good conscience delay treatment for this fine woman. We'll be fine." Lorin exhaled, the tension easing as the dwarves seemed convinced.

Yarnell pulled out his lute. "It's time to lighten the mood. Enough of future trials, let's warm up by the fire." Lorin shared some medical water that Ethrael had insisted he carry with the dwarf's wife. Yarnell sang a few songs, and soon, all drifted off to sleep.

In the morning, Lorin noticed the swelling in the dwarf's wife's leg had lessened slightly, but it was discolored and still clearly broken in need of medical attention. The dwarves spoke in hushed tones, their gestures suggesting they'd reached a decision.

The husband strode to Lorin and Yarnell, saying, "I'll escort you to the kingdom. My younger brother will take my wife to the city for treatment."

Lorin answered, "Thank you, sir, but your wife needs you. We'll manage."

"You don't understand," the dwarf insisted. "I wasn't asking. I'd be remiss not to assist if you're on a diplomatic mission. As the elder of my family, it's my duty to serve my sovereign to the best of my ability."

"Thank you, then," Lorin replied. "We'd welcome your company and aid. I'll write a letter for our companion Ethrael at the healing center, Mira's Haven. She'll help your wife—she saved my life. Hopefully, they can travel back to Cragmoore together afterward. I've worried about her traveling to the dwarven kingdom alone."

CHAPTER SEVENTEEN

Forging Resolve Through Trials — Lorin

Friends, hear a verse of forge and fire, of a lad named Lorin, whose heart burned fierce to craft a hammer worthy of Cragmoore's fabled anvils. Traveling from Parcelridge's bustling city, we set forth, I with my songs, and Lorin with his dreams. Hikal, a dwarf of iron and grit, guides us through the mountain's maw. The road to Cragmoore promised trials, blades that gleamed in ambush, and dwarven eyes sharp with mistrust. Yet Lorin's resolve, like a spark in the dark, lit our path. Sing with me now, of ambition's weight and the forge's call, as we tread the rocky road to destiny's gate.

Resolving to master dwarven forging in Keenroot, Lorin set out for Cragmoore with Yarnell and a gruff dwarf. He felt the journey's weight, the rutted road jarring his bones as Cragmoore's peaks loomed closer. The mountain air chilled his skin, sharp with pine and dust, eased by their talk of many things. Yarnell's lute hummed softly beside him, a tune to pass the hours, while the dwarf trudged ahead, hammer swinging at his hip. A casual remark from the dwarf sparked Lorin's interest.

"We don't travel much. My wife always works long days in the kitchen, and I work at the forge. By the time I get home, I want to eat, drink, and sleep. I'm Hikal, by the way."

Lorin's head snapped up. The reins slipped from his calloused hands as the forge's heat flared in his memory.

"You are a blacksmith?" he asked, his pulse quickening. "I'm an apprentice, working on my final project. I have the plans mostly drawn up, but I'm hoping to gain inspiration from your people. I'd wager a cultural exchange could benefit both. Do you think the forge master would be open to such a request?"

Hikal scratched his beard, his gaze wary. The wagon creaked as he spoke, his gravelly voice cutting through the hum of Yarnell's lute.

"Ain't sure, lad. He's a sour anvil, cold to outsiders. My countrymen've had rough dealings, battles with goblins and dark elves, but even our allies have wrought us pain." He shrugged, eyes softening. "I wish ye luck, though. What's this project of yours?"

"I plan to make a hammer for myself. It seemed the best place to learn would be at a dwarven forge. I expect I could learn a lot. The elven forge master made a decent hammer, but I can only imagine it would not match the mastery of one of your dwarven masters."

Lorin noticed Hikal's scowl crack, a grin breaking through. "I forged my final piece only a couple of years ago." He leaned closer, boots scuffing the dirt. "I guarded my design like gold, but I'd love a peek at yours, lad."

Lorin's gut tightened, his mind weighing the risk. Could he share his work with Hikal, or would it reveal his novice flaws? Always guarding his work closely, he hesitated, unsure if he could trust the dwarf. Resolve steadied his hands.

"Where'd ye get these?" Hikal growled, his tone rumbling low. "You shouldn't have them, none should!"

"I swear," Lorin said, hands raised. "I drew them from my mind. Why such a reaction?"

"'Tis different," the dwarf said, "yet 'tis too similar to our king's royal hammer. Sized for a man, yet still cousin to King Tarul's weapon. You couldn't have mirrored it so closely without theft."

"I assure you, I've never seen your king's weapon," Lorin said, holding his ground. "Maybe King Arkiel mentioned it in council, or I glimpsed it in elven or dwarven sketches. I didn't mean to mimic his hammer. I can alter it to be different, but do you have any other counsel?"

• • •

With Hikal's suspicions eased, Lorin turned his thoughts to perfecting his hammer's design, unaware of the solution fate would soon offer.

Hikal eased, his breathing steadying as he removed his hand from his weapon. "I'll take you at your word. Know my kin won't yield so easily to royal echoes. One major flaw, though, it will be too heavy for you to wield. You are no giant, and that hammer's a beast."

"I've pondered that too," Lorin admitted. "I don't want to make it smaller, but I'm thinking of lighter material, mithril, maybe."

"Mithril's a beauty," the dwarf said, "like elven mail, light but softer than steel. It'd be riddled with dents before the first battle is complete. So adorn with mithril, but the core weight issue would persist."

As if by divine providence, one of the largest sky-fallen stones rolled toward the back. The rock hit the backboard and bounced out onto the road. Lorin halted the wagon while Yarnell and Hikal turned to inspect the commotion.

Lorin said, frustration flaring in his voice, "It is these damned rocks. We still haven't found a place to dump them. Let's dump them here."

Yarnell countered, "Ethrael would kill us both. For now, we have to carry them in the wagon until she finds a safe place to dispose of them."

Ethrael's warnings about the stones' danger weighed heavily on Lorin. They heaved the stone back into the wagon. He washed his hands as Ethrael instructed on the farm. He counseled Yarnell and Hikal to do the same. Urging the wagon onward, Lorin glanced at Hikal, who trudged in silence, brow furrowed.

Hikal pilfered a suggestion. "You know, if you could put that rock in a forge under the right conditions, it might melt and form. It would be light enough for your weapon. It seems durable, too. I don't know the material, but my brethren might have ideas."

Lorin's heart stirred with cautious hope. Was this stone the key to his hammer's success, or just another false hope?

"Fantastic, I'm sure you're right! The final piece of the puzzle is falling into place. I need to understand how to work with this new material. With my design and this new material, I'll create a weapon that not only passes my test but also one I'll want to use. Thank you for the inspiration."

For days, the smiths debated designs and smelting, their lively shop talk easing the journey's extended hours. Yarnell, eyes glazed, plucked at his lute, his focus elsewhere.

• • •

Lorin's hopes soared with the stone's potential, but the road to Cragmoore held perils that would test his mettle.

The sun rose one morning, and Lorin sat quiet, his mind wrestling with the sky-fallen stone's potential, doubts clouding his resolve. He engaged with no one all day. Yarnell and Hikal tried, but Lorin seemed deep in thought. As midday approached, a band of three goblins blocked the road. Lorin stopped the wagon. Lorin noted the sides were even, three against three.

Goblins jabbered, their hostile gestures revealing their desire for the wagon's cargo. Hikal drew his hammer, Lorin grabbed a hammer left in the wagon by Hikal's wife, and Yarnell pulled out his bolas. The goblins, wielding crude swords, faced Lorin and his companions.

The two sides stood still, awaiting someone to make the first move. The goblins continued jabbering, growing louder by the minute. They waved their weapons, though crude, to intimidate Lorin's group.

Finally, the goblin leader moved toward Hikal and swung, but missed. Lorin saw Hikal strike the attacker's head, drawing blood as the goblin staggered, still dazed but standing. The other goblins attacked. Yarnell's bolas wrapped around the legs of the second goblin. Lorin jumped from the wagon, swinging the hammer, and fell flat on his face.

Lorin's arm burned and bled as the goblin's blade struck, his heart pounding with fear of failure. How could he prove himself if he faltered now? His resolve sparked to prove his worth. Luckily, the injury was on his off arm.

Hikal took another swing at the goblin leader while he was dazed, dropping him dead to the ground.

Lorin swung the hammer at his goblin, his motions clumsy, like a child with his father's tool. As Yarnell defeated his foe, Lorin's goblin fled, ending the skirmish quickly.

Lorin sat quietly as they cleaned his wound, shame gnawing at his clumsy fight, yet he wondered how he would master the hammer, vowing to make Ethrael proud.

$$\bullet \quad \bullet \quad \bullet$$

The clash with goblins left Lorin shaken, his clumsy swings a harsh reminder of his untested skill. As Lorin restarted the journey, he was even more self-absorbed.

Finally, Hikal approached him. "I know you're thinking about the battle, but consider your performance. The hammer clearly wasn't your weapon of choice. Even the most spectacular weapon is only a useless decoration if you're not proficient with it. Find what suits you best. That should be your final project." He walked off, not waiting for a response.

Lorin's party traveled for the rest of the day and made camp. As they sat around the campfire, Lorin slowly admitted, "Maybe the hammer isn't the best weapon for me. Besides, it might stir trouble in the dwarf community, resembling the king's weapon too closely. I made a fool of myself today. The only thing worse than not using a weapon I made would be looking foolish using it. I'm back to the drawing board, with no design." His shoulders and head fell in defeat.

Hikal sat beside him and whispered, "I know you're embarrassed. But we're your friends, and it's better to learn now than after crafting it."

"I am glad Ethrael was not here to see my failure. She has done so much for me. Nursing me back from death after my last gobin encounter."

"I have a suggestion: until you develop a new design, why not make something for Ethrael? She has nursed you back to health over several months. You can present it as a 'thank you' gift."

Lorin felt life return to him, his eyes lighting up as ideas stirred in his mind. Hikal and Lorin wandered off out of earshot of Yarnell and devised a plan. They retrieved the hammer design and started sketching on the back side. Though secretive, Lorin's enthusiasm was sparked, thoroughly enjoying himself. For the rest of the way to the dwarf kingdom, they often slipped away to work on the new design.

Lorin and Hikal huddled together through the remainder of the trek to the dwarven realm, cloaked in murmurs, hands sketching in the air or scratching on scraps they scrounged, their craft a flame stoked in shadow. Meanwhile, Yarnell filled his days with quill and vellum, penning a strain of verse, of goblins felled in battle's clangor, their ruin a song to echo through the ages, their blood a dark refrain under the sun's red eye. The road stretched on, and the fire burned low, but something kindled in Lorin that night, small but fierce enough to hold.

• • •

While Lorin and Hikal plotted their craft in secret, the mountains concealed a challenge that would demand more than skill.

The days sped by as Lorin's party ascended the rocky road to Cragmoore, the air growing chillier with each step, a biting edge nipping at their cloaks and frosting their breath. Jagged peaks loomed closer, their granite faces streaked with iron veins that glinted like scars under the pale sun, while the wind howled through the passes, carrying the faint scent of pine and damp earth, a whisper of the dwarven realm ahead. The count of the days was lost, though it was well past a fortnight when they rounded a blind bend, the path narrowing between sheer cliffs, stumbling upon a dwarven encampment, a rough bivouac on the roadside.

Five stout shapes stood silhouetted against a campfire's glow, their camp a cluster of low tents of oiled leather, pegged taut against the wind, with iron ingots and bundled furs lashed to a nearby sled. The fire crackled, its flames licking a spit where a hare roasted, the air heavy with the scent of char and sweat-soaked wool.

All dwarves in the encampment leapt up at Lorin's party's approach, axes poised, their steel catching the firelight with a menacing glint. Clad in furs and leather, their beards braided with iron rings, they bristled, forming a wall of muscle and suspicion, eyes narrowing under heavy brows. The greatest among them, plainly the leader, stepped forth, a barrel of a dwarf, his beard streaked with gray, a scar splitting his cheek like a lightning strike. His axe, double-headed and etched with runes, rested easily in his grip, but his stance screamed readiness, a coiled spring of distrust. "What're you doing here?" he bellowed, voice a low growl echoing off the cliffs.

Lorin's pulse quickened—could words sway these dwarves, or was conflict inevitable?

CHAPTER EIGHTEEN

Tale of a Lost Prince — Lorin

As our troupe treads toward Cragmoore, Hikal's honeyed words sway wary dwarves, a campfire's glow heals old wounds, and a lost prince's shadow stirs Lorin's heart. Lorin, bearer of the elven writ, holds the key to Cragmoore's gate, where dawn's cold gaze tests trust's fragile chord.

*T*he guard barked, "We wish no visitors, return to your kind, or ye'll taste Cragmoore steel!"

Hikal stepped forward, his broad frame steady, hands raised in peace, and Lorin's breath caught, hoping the dwarf's kinship would calm the guards. "Greetings, friend," he said. "My brother, wife, and I were bound for Parcelridge for her healing. We met these wayfarers outside the city. They pose no threat. Hear them out and let us pass, I beg you."

The guard's gaze flicked to Hikal, softening a fraction, and Lorin's pulse eased slightly, though the axe's gleam kept him tense. The grip on the axe didn't slacken, and his companions muttered softly, their words sharp with suspicion. "Outlanders with a dwarf? What trick's this?"

Yarnell, his cloak flapping in the wind, faced the guards and bowed. Lorin watched, uncertain if diplomacy could sway such mistrust.

Yarnell announced, "We are on a diplomatic mission for the elven king to yours."

Lorin drew forth the royal writ, the parchment sealed with elven wax and the sigil of Arkiel's house unbroken. He held it high, his hand steady despite the chill, the firelight catching the seal. When the leader reached to snatch it, Lorin pulled it back, his jaw tightening.

"You'll see it, but you'll not touch it," Lorin said, his voice low and firm with a warning edge, "This bears the king's seal, meant for Tarul's eyes, not yours."

Lorin saw the leader's scarred cheek twitch, his hand hovering, then dropping with a grunt. "We care nothing for outsiders, elves least of all," he spat, the glob landing near a pile of freshly fletched arrows by the fire. "Yet a diplomatic envoy'll not be hindered, not by us, leastwise. It's late; you won't make the stronghold tonight. Rest here until dawn, and you'll reach Cragmoore's gates by midday tomorrow. You're light-armed, and your dwarf guide speaks for you, so I'll let you pass come morn. Show that writ at the gates; they'll settle your fate. It's beyond my grasp, I promise nothing but a night's shelter."

His tone held no warmth, but his axe lowered a fraction, and his men followed suit, though their stares lingered, sharp as the frost on the cliffs.

They waved off an offer to take watch. A younger dwarf with a braided beard said gruffly, "We guard our own," his hand never leaving his axe haft.

• • •

As the guards retreated to their posts, the troupe settled into the camp, the night's chill urging them toward the fire. Lorin and his companions fell to kitchen duty. The campfire's heat was a welcome balm against the mountain's bite.

Yarnell backed up with his hands in the air. "I confess I should never cook for others, a stray hound would turn its nose at my offering, more char than charm."

Fortunately, Hikal bore some craft, his hands as deft with a pot as with a hammer. Hikal turned Parcelridge's yield, gnarled roots, a clutch of wild onions, and a brace of dried hare into a fair stew, its steam rising, savory with a pinch of Cragmoore salt bartered from the guards, and vegetables gifted from the farmer.

The dwarves watched, their grumbles softening as the scent filled the camp, one muttering, "Least they ain't useless," though he kept his axe close.

"Best fare we've had since Ethrael departed," Lorin said, voice low but warm. "I'm sated, and the warmth drives back the cold." He glanced at the stream beyond the camp, its waters glinting silver and blue under the moon, a quiet mirror to the night's chill.

Hikal shrugged, stirring the pot with a wooden spoon, his broad hands steady. "Naw, friends, my wife's the true cook," he said, a wistful note creeping in. "She served the royals when Tarul and his elder brother were lads, and her stews make you weep for joy."

His gaze drifted, lost in memory, the fire's glow catching a flicker of longing in his eyes, and for a moment, the camp's tension eased, the dwarves' silence less hostile, their shared meal a small bridge against the mountain's cold.

• • •

As the fire's crackle softened the night, Lorin sensed Hikal's distant gaze, heavy with unspoken grief. Lorin's heart clenched, the name he bore in secret stirring unease he couldn't shake. "Friend, what ails you?"

"Pardon," Hikal said, voice soft. "It still grieves me. Tarul's brother, Barzul, was lost years ago. He reminded folk too much of his mother's death, set them ill at ease. Nor did his body do him any favors. He hadn't the look of a dwarf. She died in childbirth. Queen Lazula, 'precious jewel,' her name meant, was beloved. Though not his fault, too many could not forgive him for her loss. It broke the king's heart." My father's heart, Lorin thought, the title foreign yet heavy with loss he couldn't claim.

That name, his name, stung like a wound unhealed. I'm not that prince, Lorin told himself, though the truth gnawed at his resolve. Lorin leaned forward. "Why did he not resemble them? No ill meant, yet was she unfaithful?"

"Some thought so at first," Hikal replied, "yet she was steadfast to her king and mate. She fell deathly ill. The elves came, striving to save her. They labored months over her and the unborn prince. My wife deems their cures and magic warped him. He was defenseless in the womb. When her end loomed, they cut him free. The king and my people hated the elves for rending her, yet without it, both would have perished. Dwarves shrug off magic better than most, yet an unborn babe? It weakened him, stretched his frame, and shrank his brawn. In truth, he seemed more human than a dwarf."

Craving tidings of his early days, Lorin pressed for more. "So the queen's death in childbirth fueled the distrust for elves?"

"Aye," Hikal nodded. "We've got a pact with them. We're honor-bound to keep it. Yet it doesn't mean we're close. Goblins, cave elves, we fight the same foes, aid in strife, yet the days of shared feasts are gone."

Lorin hungered for more. "How was Barzul lost? Did battle claim him?"

"We deem him dead, though we cannot say certain," Hikal began. "In dwarf custom, every youth, lad or lass, faces a rite to claim full standing. Armed with but a weapon and the garb on their back, they're sent alone into the caverns beneath the hold for a week. Beasts often harass them. Endure, and they're full kin. Returning early is a failure. They can strive anew next year. It is rare to fail twice, unheard of to perish, yet Barzul came not back on his second try. The royal guard scoured the caves and found his sword bloodied, yet no body was found. They deemed him lost."

"So, how did Tarul rise to the throne?" Lorin asked.

"This was a terrible time for us," Hikal said. "During Barzul's second trial, King Qartul and Queen Kiran toasted with wine at a feast. Unbeknownst to them, cave elves had again poisoned the wine to destroy the monarchy. The king and queen died the day after Barzul went below. Tarul faced his rite beside Barzul's redo, but where Barzul failed, Tarul prevailed, the youngest dwarf ever to pass. He was crowned at once, losing mother, father, and brother in one stroke!"

Lorin drank in the tale. "Were Tarul and Barzul close?"

"Not especially," Hikal replied. "Tarul was ten years younger, born to Qartul and his second wife, Kiran. Barzul fit not the dwarvish mold, yet Tarul? Pure dwarf, like his sire. Barzul was the rightful heir, yet fate gave him no chance. I recall him fondly, gentle, like his mother."

Lorin's breath caught, the name Barzul striking him like a hammer on steel. That name, his name, echoed like a chain he couldn't cast off. Lorin's fingers tightened on his mug, its warmth a frail anchor against the past he shunned. "Barzul," he repeated softly, testing the word. "What was he like?"

Hikal leaned back, looking into the fire, his gaze distant as if seeing the past in the flickering flames. "A wild one, Barzul was. He was always underfoot in the forges, begging me to let him hammer scraps into shapes. He made a lopsided dagger once, called it a 'dragon slayer'. He couldn't have been more than five, but he'd swing it around like he was fighting off a whole army. He loved the mines, too. He used to sneak down there to chase glowbugs, those little lights flickering in the dark. I'd find him covered in soot, grinning like he'd found a treasure hoard. But he had a soft side, too. I remember him giving his royal cloak to a miner's lass who was shivering outside the forge. He didn't care that it was his best one. He said she needed it more. His father was proud of that, reminding him of his mother. It is said he had a heart as big as the mountain."

Lorin's chest tightened, Hikal's words stirring echoes of a past he could scarcely grasp. Was that boy truly me? Lorin thought the memories were a weight he couldn't fully bear. He swallowed hard. Looking to Hikal, he offered, "That boy sounds worth knowing. Yet gone from us,"

Lorin's hands trembled. He tried to picture his parents, Qartul's stern face, but nothing came, just the same hollow ache he'd felt since Keenroot. I am that lost prince, Lorin thought, yet the kings' warnings chain my truth. "Tarul is king now," muttering to himself, his voice thick with hidden longing for a brother he couldn't claim.

Lorin's throat tightened, the weight of Hikal's words pressing against the fragments of his past. He ached to claim his name, Barzul, but the kings' warnings to conceal his heritage kept him silent. Lorin's fingers tightened on his mug, its warmth failing to ease the truth he held. "Barzul's heart was worth fighting for," Lorin strained with buried truth, "may his family honor his worth, wherever he is."

Hikal raised his mug, a fierce glint in his eye. "To Barzul, and ending the cave elves' blight forever." Lorin raised his mug in return, the clink of clay a quiet promise in the forge's glow. But as he drank, a single tear slipped down his cheek, the faint echo of a child's laughter ringing in his mind, a spark of the boy he struggled to embrace.

The fire dimmed, its embers mirroring the fading weight of Barzul's tale in Lorin's mind. "So, how fares the realm under Tarul?" Lorin pressed, "Is it strong? Thriving?"

"Strong, yes," Hikal nodded. "Tarul's a fierce, cherished leader. Yet shunning outside trade hinders us. Mountains lack what woods and fields yield. We've goods that others seek, and we need theirs. I pray we'll mend ties someday."

"Tell me of Tarul's mother, the second queen."

"When Lazula died, Qartul and the realm crumbled. We rose again when he bound anew with King Rylak of the Tains clan. That bond was sealed with Qartul's wedding to Rylak's daughter Kiran, Lazula's youngest sister. Lazula was the eldest Tains princess, Kiran the least. Her name, 'Maiden of Iron,' suited. She was plain yet steadied Qartul's broken heart. Still, I doubt he ever loved her as Lazula."

Lorin spoke softly, "I searched the elven archives before we departed, yet the full tale eluded me. It is grievous. No wonder your folk mistrust outsiders. Thank you for sharing. We honor your fallen leaders' memory."

Lorin watched as Yarnell joined in, "Your tale's a treasure. I want to record it for King Arkiel when we return. He may not know it all, and grasping your sorrows could heal trust between elves and dwarves."

"Young bard, sharing our past with the elven king could aid us, yet don't paint us as weak, and keep it for his ears alone. It is not my right to bear our grief to the world. Can you agree to that?"

Lorin watched as Yarnell pledged, "I'll honor it. I'll pen it here and let you review it before we return. It will only be shown to Arkiel. Fair enough?"

"Thank you," Hikal said, easing. "I know it's much to ask a minstrel to hush a tale. It's late, let us rest. Tomorrow's weighty, and who knows what it holds?"

CHAPTER NINETEEN

Clang of New Ways — Lorin

Sit, friends, and let my lute hum a tale of Cragmoore's iron heart, where Lorin walks with a king's writ heavy as fate.

Hush now, for the dwarven gates loom ahead, their forges pulsing with secrets old as stone.

Will sparks of trust kindle 'twixt elf and dwarf, or will rocks fallen from the heavens forge a path none foresee?

Journey with me, as shadows dance and metals gleam!

The scent of roasted grain and herbs, sharper than yesterday's stew, stirred Lorin awake as the troupe ate in quiet camaraderie, warmed by the guards' softened glances, a stark contrast to last night's frost. The royal writ, heavy in his cloak, tugged at his thoughts, its burden a reminder of the task ahead. With dawn's light spilling over the horizon, the troupe stirred, ready to face Cragmoore's gates.

Bearing the writ's weight, Lorin led the troupe as they packed and pressed on, the distant rumble of Cragmoore's gates steadily tightening his resolve by midday. The sentries, eyeing them as outsiders, were all business with stern mistrust. Lorin's pulse quickened, but he kept his stance relaxed under their scrutiny. The guards held their arms poised, ready to act. Lorin and the troupe strove to seem harmless, keeping their movements calm.

The blacksmith stepped forward, saying, "I am Hikal, a realm blacksmith. I met these two on the road while bound for Parcelridge for my wife's healing. She and my brother went on.

These wayfarers aided us. They bear a diplomatic charge from the elven realm with a missive for our king." Lorin held the sealed writ aloft. The guard examined it, sizing them up.

The guard said, "Let us see those barrels. Powder, I'd wager."

"No, sir," Yarnell said smoothly. "Two contain wine, a gift for King Tarul. The third is scrap metal, as you can see. Beyond our dwarf friend here, we're no threat. Not a blade among us, only my bolas and a pair of dwarven hammers belonging to Hikal."

The guard, wary of incurring two kings' wrath, deemed them safe. "Follow my sergeant to the stables and stay there. I'll send word to the court. Give me the writ. I'll see it reaches the king."

Lorin's grip tightened on the parchment, his resolve firm as he spoke. "You must understand, I cannot risk losing this, for King Arkiel's wrath would be severe. I propose my friends wait at the stables while I bear it to the court myself. If King Tarul's displeased, I'll face his wrath. Search me if you must, I'm no threat."

The guard nodded, "I see why Arkiel chose you. So be it. Yet be warned: a man in the king's presence, unbidden? Rare as mithril! You roll the dice with your life."

• • •

Four guards escorted Lorin, leaving the bard and blacksmith at the stables. The echo of boots faded down stone corridors while Lorin braced for a long wait—royalty seldom rushed for commoners. Yet within an hour, royal-clad guards ushered Yarnell and Hikal into the throne room, where the king sat beside Queen Pykal, a stout female dwarf aptly named 'Fire Hearth'. Guards lined the walls as Lorin stood before the king.

"Come in, friends," Tarul boomed. His gaze flicked to Hikal. "Is this Nana's mate? I have fond memories of your wife's great food. Of course, Lorin would find you. Thank you for guiding these wayfarers. You have served the throne more than you know. They pose no peril to this court. I vouch for them. Guards dismissed." Hikal and the guards filed out, leaving only the king, queen, Lorin, and Yarnell.

Queen Pykal sat rigid, her grip firm on her throne's arms, eyes fierce with a protector's fire.

"Pykal," Tarul said, "these are two I met when I slipped off to see King Arkiel. We must mend our relationship with the elves. I took the first step by visiting him. He's sent these as envoys, a fit choice. Though I expected the healer Ethrael among them, it seems she was detained."

Lorin bowed, his cloak rustling softly. "Your Majesty, Ethrael tends a healing need in Parcelridge, yet I hope she'll join us soon."

"I am disappointed. She is a delight. So what brings you to my kingdom?"

"As you may recall, I am training to be a master blacksmith. My final work alone remains. I wish to learn from your smiths to complete my final task—and share elven techniques in return."

He gestured to Yarnell. "The bard performs for courts, thirsting for your tales, eager to offer his gifts." Yarnell strummed his lute, punctuating the words.

"Ethrael seeks healing wisdom of every kind. When she arrives, I humbly request that she be granted entry to your clinics. She'll bless your healers as she learns from them. I assume that King Arkiel's communique requests an exchange of skills between your two kingdoms. We are his answer to his offer."

King Tarul smiled, "I can think of no one better. I welcome you to my kingdom."

The queen's shadow loomed across the stone floor, a silent challenge. Queen Pykal rose, her voice a hammer's strike, resolute and fierce. "Strangers, what do you mean by this? You dare to bring your foreign ways to weaken my husband's throne or harm his people? Speak plain, your purpose touches my king and his realm, and I'll entertain no threat!" The throne room's silence grew heavy, all eyes on Lorin. He stood firm, his heart steady under her fierce scrutiny.

"Your Highness," he said, keeping his voice calm and firm, "we intend no harm nor burden. We come to share and learn, to strengthen ties between your folk and the elves. We'll lodge in the village, pay our way, and take only what leave you grant. King Arkiel sent two barrels of wine for Your Majesties, as a gesture of peace."

Pykal's eyes blazed, her stance unyielding as stone. "Wine from the elf king, again? Do you think I'd let my husband or his subjects taste his poison? I guard Tarul and this realm with my life. Your gift provokes doubt."

"No, my lady," Lorin said gently. "It is yours to savor, yet I'll drink from it at your bidding to prove it safe. Our aim is friendship, not peril."

Tarul broke in, patting his queen's arm, his voice warm yet steady. "Pykal, my shield, I drank at Arkiel's table, and I trust him. Yet to set thy heart at ease, Lorin shall taste each barrel tomorrow. When he stands strong, we'll feast to welcome them and see their worth. Sharing crafts is wise. I'll set quarters in the village and bid the guilds to welcome them."

The royals rose, Pykal's gaze lingering on them with a protector's vigilance as they swept out. As the throne room emptied, a quiet settled over the hall.

A servant entered and said, "I'll lead you to your lodgings. Follow me." He wrestled with himself as they walked, muttering, "It's not my place, but visitors? Strange! The king and queen shun guests. The queen guards her lord and folk with an iron will. We dwarves do not take kindly to change."

• • •

After Lorin and Yarnell dressed the next morning, Hikal knocked on the door. "I reckoned you hadn't reached the market yet, so I brought breakfast. After you eat, I'll show you around." The room's simple warmth, a stark contrast to the palace's grandeur, eased Lorin's tension momentarily. Hikal's familiar presence, forged on the road, steadied his resolve for the day ahead.

Another knock. It was the servant from the previous day. "I will lead you to the forge, clinic, and tavern."

Hikal leapt in. "No need, I'll do it. They're friends, and I would love more time with them."

"Pardon," the servant said, "the queen has called Lorin to taste the wine, as promised. After that, you can take over."

The servant led them to court, where two goblets gleamed under torchlight, presumably one from each barrel. Pykal watched keenly, her stance firm, guarding against deceit. The air grew taut, Pykal's gaze sharpening like a blade.

Striding forward, Lorin seized a goblet and drained it, the wine sharp on his tongue. It was the first alcohol he had had since he was injured. Yarnell snatched and downed the other, grinning, his eyes glinting with mischief under the flickering light.

Pykal waved them off with a dismissive flick of her hand. Leaving the court, they wove through Cragmoore's bustling streets.

Hikal reminded the servant of his offer to escort. Lorin caught Hikal's steady nod, a silent promise of support amid the dwarf's grumbling.

The man shuffled off, muttering, "Drinking in court before the queen? Friends with a dwarf? We dwarves favor not change!"

• • •

The first stop was the healing center, Hollow of Ylva. The hall's sterile air carried a faint hum of distrust, chilling the room. They had already received word that Ethrael would arrive later.

Lorin felt a pang of worry for Ethrael, hoping she'd navigate their mistrust. His mind raced, weighing how her elven grace might sway their hardened hearts.

The head healer said, "Just the thought of an elf in our midst gives us pause. Yet I'll not defy the king's 'request'." Their guarded glances suggested they hoped she'd never arrive.

A healer's glance lingered on Lorin, her eyes narrowing as if measuring the intruder's intent, heightening his unease. Lorin turned away, the weight of their stares lingering as they left the hall.

• • •

From the hall's chill, they stepped into the tavern's lively glow. The Hammerdeep Tavern was their next stop. Taverns are a bard's natural habitat. Yarnell was right at home. No introduction was needed; no hand-holding was required. A bard is a master at making friends. The clink of mugs and dwarven laughter filled the air, a warmth Lorin noted with cautious hope. A dwarf's fleeting smile met his gaze, a rare crack in their guarded reserve. With Yarnell settled, Hikal and Lorin lingered briefly, savoring the tavern's camaraderie, their thoughts turning to the challenges ahead.

• • •

The tavern's glow lingered in Lorin's mind as he and Hikal wove through Cragmoore's streets, the forge's rhythmic clang summoning their purpose.

At the forge, Hikal introduced him to the forge master, Torvok. Lorin laid forth his plan.

"I am unsure of my final work yet, but for now, I'd shape a staff as a gift for a friend who saved my life. I've brought scrap metal and odd rocks, and I deem they might serve. We need your aid with said rocks, as we do not know their nature. Mishandling them could sicken you. They're in a wagon at the stables."

Torvok eyed him. "If you're working on your final task, I expect you know your way around a forge. Yet I'll judge myself. This is my responsibility. I'll have the contents of the wagon fetched this afternoon. Until then, let me show you the workings of the forge and introduce you to the smiths."

Though unlike the elven forge, the layout felt familiar to Lorin, its rhythm echoing his past. He ran his hand over the anvil and waved it over the hearth, feeling its warmth. Sitting with the smiths, he proved his craft and bonded with them.

When the wagon rolled up that afternoon, Lorin unveiled the strange rocks. Torvok studied them, gloved hands lifting a small one with a grin. "I know these. But I've not seen their like in decades, nor in such numbers. My forerunner had one, head-sized, and named such stones 'god rocks'. They fell from the heavens, not of this world. Forge it right, and the deadly dust burns off. Yet it needs more than this hearth can provide; it craves the roar of the Dragon Forge. It is in the caverns, hottest we wield, fueled by unearthly flame!"

Lorin's heart raced—equal parts awe and unease.

"The former forge master, Master Garrim Firebraid, shaped one into a dagger once," he said, "Brittle, though, snapped when tested. He said it needed another metal. We tested all we had, yet none sufficed. At last, he deemed mithril the key, keeping it light and halting the break. The problem is that mithril is rare. It hasn't been seen here in over a century. Sorry, lad. You know Hikal already, so I'll leave you with him. Call if you have a need."

Lorin nodded.

"Thanks for the insight. I've already learned something today. Hikal and I designed this staff for my friend Ethrael, who will study at Hollow of Ylva. It is my side task until inspiration strikes for my final piece. I'll use scrap from my barrel to spare you trouble. I've not even peered within, Master Falere, my elven forge master in Keenroot, gathered it. It is heavy, brimful, so I've plenty for both."

Lorin and Hikal pried open the barrel, and their jaws fell, expecting standard metal, but instead finding gleaming mithril shimmering like starlight. Master Falere, friend to King Arkiel, had not given scraps but riches.

The 'god rocks' were now within reach. Lorin would craft Ethrael's staff with that blend first. The mithril's gleam sparked hope, a bridge for elven craft and dwarven trust. Both grinned, alight with zeal.

Leaving the forge's heat, Lorin carried the mithril's promise to their lodgings. He and Yarnell shared tales of their day. The dwarves had begun stiff yet warmed to them. Hikal's morning bounty still fed them, and they ate, bade goodnight, and drifted off, Lorin dreaming of new ways.

The day's triumphs, small yet sure, kindled faith in shared futures.

• • •

In the morning, Torvok returned to the forge with an aged she-dwarf on his arm. "I've unraveled the 'god rock' craft. Hot, stern toil, yet I'm eager to try. This is my forerunner's widow, Maela. She's here to meet you and show you his broken dagger and mold." Lorin noticed her hands tremble, as if reluctant to part with them, before they steadied.

She spoke softly, "See that black, glossy sheen? Pity it broke, the edge still sharp as the day it was forged."

Lorin gazed at the dagger, a fractured wonder. He took her hand and kissed it. "Your husband was a true master. I am honored to behold his craft. Through his craft, I can offer my friend a rare gift. I'm humbled by you both." She smiled, her expression softening at his words.

"Can I ask a favor?" Lorin added. "Could you leave the dagger and mold with Master Torvok? I'd love to study them as we labor, even glean insight. Though you know me not, trust your forge master to guard your husband's legacy."

At first, she hesitated, but then, with a proud nod, she relented.

"Thank you. I promise to honor his legacy. Anything I end up accomplishing will be because of him."

She handed the blade to the forge master and headed home, escorted by Torvok.

Hikal looked to Lorin, "Lorin, let us begin small, test the rock-metal blend with a simple object. A rod, maybe as a prototype for Ethrael's staff?"

"What of an eight-inch dagger with a long shaft?" Lorin countered. He envisioned the rod-dagger—a blade with an elongated shaft to mimic the staff's durability and compare against the widow's dagger.

"We'd try strength, durability, and edge, like her husband's, without wasting too much rock or mithril. We'll take his mold as a guide. The long shaft is used to test the durability of the staff project."

Hikal nodded.

Lorin and Hikal shaped the roughly shaped rod-dagger mold by midday. Together, they pored over the edge, and Lorin was uncertain how to sharpen it after forging. They wrought it as sharp as they could before the pour. Later that afternoon, Lorin watched as they cast a plain metal one to compare to the proper mix.

By morning, Lorin inspected the cooled test piece, which had been removed from the mold. Its heft felt right in his hand, though the imperfect edge was merely fair, fit for testing, not a proper blade. He considered honing it but agreed with Hikal's suggestion to leave it for comparison with the final blend. After cleaning the mold, Lorin spent the rest of the day studying the widow's dagger mold, hoping to uncover its secrets of edge and balance.

CHAPTER TWENTY

Echoes in Flame — Yarnell

Deep in Cragmoore's stony heart, where no sun dares pierce, the Dragon Forge breathes, a beast of flame and iron, its roar a hymn of fire that shakes the mountain's bones. I, Yarnell, bard of road and rhyme, linger in the tavern's smoky haze, where tales of its fury hum through the din, spun by smiths whose hearts bear heavier burdens than their hammers. Picture it, as I do, a cavern vast as sorrow, walls scarred black, streaked with blood-red molten veins, the air a sulfurous claw that grips the throat. There, they say, the 'god rocks' yield only to the 'Breath of Karrak', a fire fierce as a star's heart, tamed by none but the boldest. I strum my lute, its strings humming low, and weave their tale. For though I dwell among their grief and grit, my voice heralds their forge-born toil, a song of sweat, steel, and legacies wrought in fire, to echo beyond these halls.

*H*ammerdeep Tavern hulked deep in Cragmoore's stony gut, a cavern gouged from raw rock, its walls streaked with iron veins and quartz glinting under the sullen glow of forge-lit braziers, chains dangling, embers spitting in the smoky murk. The air was thick with molten steel's tang, peat smoke, and the dark kick of dwarven ale, black as coal, sloshed from casks hewn from the mountain's hide. Low tables of slate and iron ringed a roaring hearth, flames snarling in stone, and the growl of dwarf voices, gruff oaths, rumbles of barter, tankards clashing like hammers, thundered through, solid as the rock overhead. Yarnell had sung for many, but this was his first crack at dwarven songs for true dwarves, and they didn't care for outsiders; their beards bristled, eyes cut sharp as chisels, weighing him like he would filch their ore. He had paid dear for this perch, slipping a fat pouch of silver to Grimlok, the tavern's squat lord, his beard like wire, his scowl carved deep, his grunt of "You'll earn it or rue it, outlander" still ringing as the dwarf pocketed the coin and jerked a thumb toward the stage.

He stepped to its red glow, Yarnell, bard of road and rhyme, cloak patched, boots gritty with Cragmoore's dust, and cradled his lute, strings taut and eager. She was his new lass, now sweet as a mountain spring, more profound than the mines' hum, familiar yet bold as a grown voice. The patrons scarcely spared a glance. Grimlok leaned on the bar, arms crossed, eyes cold as slate. Yarnell struck the first chord, a low drone rolling out, rumbling through the rock like a delver's tread, snagging their ears. Beards twitched, gazes hardened, a mutter of "outlander's gall" rippling low, but he grinned, letting her spin an intro slow as cooling ore, each pluck a spark.

"Gather near, you of the deep," he called, his voice rough as gravel yet laced with a lilt to ease their guard, "for I have a song of hammer and vein, struck true for Cragmoore's blood, bought with coin and craft."

His lass sang fiercely, notes diving low, then soaring sharp. The tune was a saga of dwarves tearing iron from the earth's black heart, forges bellowing, steel unbent. Her tone bore it, sweeter than his old lute's cry, mature as a cavern's growl, each strum a pulse that stirred the hall. At first, they sat rigid, arms folded, tankards gripped like wards, a grumble of "What's he know?" passing beard to beard, Grimlok's scowl fixed, lips tight as if he'd demand the silver back. But as he wove tales of ancestors whose hammers woke the peaks, veins bleeding gold under their fists, their ice-cracked eyes softened to ember glints, fists eased. Grimlok's brow twitched, a flicker of surprise, and he uncrossed an arm, mug tilting slightly as he sipped, watching now, not glaring.

A burly dwarf, beard knotted with iron rings, slammed his tankard and barked, "Sing *Forge of Thrain*, bard, prove you've stones!" Yarnell flashed a quick smile and nod, his fingers leaping as strings snapped a march, bright and fierce, her clarity slashing the haze like a pick through shale, notes ringing bold as anvils struck. The hall surged, boots pounded stone, tankards crashed in time, a lass with hammer-scarred knuckles roared the refrain until it bounced off the walls, fierce and proud, an elder's growl weaving in like a hammer's echo.

Grimlok straightened, his scowl softening to a squint, then a half-nod. He thumped the bar once, a grudging beat, and a faint smirk tugged his lip as the crowd's frost thawed. Beards bobbed, laughs cracked, and a few clapped shoulders like he had earned a pint. Sweat stung his eyes as he pushed her harder, chords swelling, a storm shaking the cavern, their cheers a roar he rode until his throat scraped raw. The last note hung, low and sweet, and silence gripped the tavern.

Suddenly, a bellow of approval erupted, coins and iron bits clattering at his feet like fresh-struck ore. Grimlok met Yarnell's eye, raising his mug a hair, a dwarf's salute, thawed slow but sure, and Yarnell bowed, clutching his lute companion close, his chest hammering. She'd sung her first dwarf night, thawing some cold hearts, Grimlok's included, truer than he had dared hope. He deemed the coin well spent. His new mate showed herself a maestro, ready to ring through these halls and beyond.

• • • *(Lorin)*

By day, Lorin toiled at the forge, yet nights drew him to the tavern with Yarnell. He and his companions gained footing since arriving. Though locals, wary and bred to mistrust outsiders, still blame their queen's death on the elven kind. Yet nearness wore at their fear, for it was harder to hate those with whom they'd shared a brew. This mingling could heal some breaches.

Two months had passed since leaving Parcelridge, and Ethrael's absence gnawed at him. One night, after much ale with Hikal,

Nana entered limping. Hikal spied her first, hastening over, lifting her off her feet, and whirling her in gladness. After their greeting, they sat with Lorin and Yarnell. Hikal poured her a brew. She gazed into it, her visage heavy, seeking words in the foam.

He clutched the staff mold as if it might shield him. His darting eyes and faint trembling betrayed the fear in his heart.

Nana took a deep breath, her voice wavering, "I know what you'll ask—Lorin, she's not with me. We met, and she mended my leg. She's a ceaseless healer, skilled beyond measure, who worked harder than any I've seen. She ministered with care, giving all to the ailing. She gave me exercises, saying my limp would lessen with time. I owe her much. She took no coin and said Hikal's aid sufficed. We agreed to travel here together."

"But a week before we'd depart," she continued, drawing another deep breath, "I went by the healing hall to confirm. They said she'd vanished—no word given. It wasn't like her, for she oft spoke of her longing to rejoin you."

Lorin sat mute, broken. He rose in silence and shuffled home. For weeks to follow, he dragged himself to the forge, toiling until spent. He ate little, then fell into bed. He spoke only when pressed, his spark extinguished.

Yet one day, as he and Hikal shared a quiet midday meal in the tavern's shadow, a spark of hope stirred when Torvok burst in, breathless, "His notes say a blend of 20% mithril, 30% iron, and 50% rock will curb the dagger's frailty. Melt the rock in the Dragon Forge to cleanse it. Remove the rocks from the heat when they turn a black-red color. Once they cool to a glossy black, add the iron. The residual heat will melt and thicken the iron, changing the color to matte black. Immediately stir in the mithril, and achieve a glossy finish. Pour it swiftly into the mold. Brilliant man—I'd start small, though."

A gleam returned to Lorin's eyes. His hands twitched, and he clutched at the staff mold unawares. "We have a rod-dagger mold set from weeks past—poured with iron to compare against, too." Hikal ran and fetched it.

"Great minds!" Torvok beamed. "Let us wait till tomorrow—melting the rock may take hours, and I'd rather have time to spare than not enough. At dawn, I'll lead you to the Dragon Forge; your barrels will be there. Down a pint, for I hear your bard friend has a following. Hopefully, a brew and a hearty rhyme from him can lift your spirit."

Lorin's droop eased, though he was not wholly back. Hikal shared the rock lore with Nana and Yarnell, forge speech they could not understand, yet it fanned Lorin's ember.

Yarnell advised Lorin while strumming a gentle tune, "I know you are yet low, but heed me. Craft Ethrael's staff as a gift to greet her home, and your final work will swiftly follow. We'll fulfill the king's charge, then set forth to seek her. I suggest you train at the armory, for you were of no use in that mountain fray."

He took it fair, a spark of aim piercing his listless wait. Lorin mused that King Tarul could aid them. Perhaps he had a Parcelridge tie to probe. Yarnell, seeking to aid Lorin, penned a note on Ethrael's vanishing for the king, hoping to spark a path to her return.

• • •

Bolstered by this resolve, Lorin rose as dawn broke, its light swallowed by the mountain's black jaws. The three smiths—Lorin, Hikal, and Torvok—descended to the Dragon Forge. They trekked into the dwarven kingdom's belly, past halls of chiseled stone and veins of glinting ore, until the tunnels narrowed and the air turned to fire's breath, like creeping into a beast's maw. The forge's gates were massive blackened iron doors, banded with runes that glowed dull red, and locked tight with a snarl of gears and chains no thief could crack.

Hikal swore they'd hold a battering ram at bay, and Torvok, with a grim nod, worked the key, a slab of stone etched with dwarf-sign, heavy as a shield, its edges pulsing faintly with a ward's hum. He slid it into a slot carved deep, and only then did a second lock whir, a lattice of steel bars sliding across the seams, each tipped with barbs that would shred a careless hand. Hikal grinned, saying a rune trap lay beneath: touch it wrong, and a blast of fire greeted the fool. These doors were forged to keep any would-be robber at bay and punish them if they were picked.

Inside, the forge loomed at the mountain's heart—a cavern vast as a cathedral, its walls blackened and scarred, streaked with molten rivulets glowing red as blood, scars of heat no mortal fire could muster. The air hung thick with sulfur, a choking reek that clawed the throat and stung the eyes, sharp as a blade's edge. The heat seared unnaturally, a living beast, fierce enough to scorch lungs and blister hands, a roar of flame that could set a man's bones to trembling just hearing it told.

At its core blazed the Dragon Forge, a monstrous pit ringed with jagged rocky teeth, spitting fire of white and decorated with gold that reflected like a trapped sun. The forge was by the mountain's blood, what dwarves call the 'Breath of Karrak'. Only that fire, Torvok had bragged, could tame the 'god rocks', too stubborn for any lesser blaze.

The Dragon Forge flames roared high, a bellow rattling the heavy doors. Torvok had laid out the steps earlier. All chanted them back at each step. "Melt the rocks until they ran black-red, like lava kissed by night." The 'god rocks' were thrown in the smelting pot.

"Pull them out to cool until they thickened, still molten but dark." The smelting pot was removed from the heat and placed on the side to start cooling.

"Mix in iron with the pit's fading heat until it flowed matte black." The iron was thrown into the smelting pot and mixed well.

"Stir in mithril." The mithril was added and mixed well, giving it a glossy finish like wet glass.

"Pour it fast," Torvok warned, "or it'll set before the mold." They poured it swiftly into the mold, a slender and sharp dagger rod, its edges catching the firelight like a star snatched from the sky.

They stood in that inferno, lungs burning and sweat pouring, but they bore it out, a trio of shadows against the glare, and hauled it through those iron doors to the typical forge higher up to cool overnight. Lorin reckoned it craved a slow, natural set to harden true, and let the mountain's cool breath temper what its fiery heart had birthed. They trudged back up with their new booty, weary and singed. The forge's growl faded behind the sealed gates like a beast gone quiet. Doors locked tight with key, bars, and fire until the next dawn, or until some rogue dared test their strength.

Lorin dropped the rod-dagger in their hut before heading to the tavern.

Nana forbade ale, pressing water on them until they waddled, her trade well-known. No one questioned her resolve.

• • •

The next morning, the smiths, still bearing the forge's toll, hastened to the forge to see the yield, joined even by Maela, the former forge master's widow. They broke open the mold, and out fell a queer rod-dagger object, its hue striking, black as a starless midnight, yet glossy. Lorin touched it first, feeling it cool, then warming to his hand, light yet substantive. This object was far superior to the original iron casting, though its edge fell short, a puzzle none could fathom.

All day, they tried it, slicing and striking both ends. It would not bend or break, a god-sent wonder, a roaring triumph.

Maela trembled, clutching Lorin's sleeve. She wept, joy and grief entwined. "I am thankful to see my husband's work fulfilled, yet sad he did not."

Lorin turned to her with a tenderness granted a beloved grandmother. "Dear lady, this would not be without him, or you sharing his legacy. We owe you a debt. I cannot thank you enough. Yet here's a thought: with your permission, we could use his mold to forge a new dagger honed by what we've learned. I'd be honored to shape it for you, at no cost but your blessing. You'd keep his first attempt and have the culmination of his legacy, too. May I? We'd wield his mold with care and return it."

She sobbed. His companions swapped puzzled glances, yet Lorin knew, cradling her in his arms, letting her weep. When she steadied, she handed him the mold. Answer given.

In the days that followed, Lorin and Hikal ran the rod-dagger through every trial: strength, durability, resilience, and wholeness. Only the edge fell short. It was agreed that the widow's mold lessons would likely correct that.

• • •

As the rod-dagger's trials honed his craft, Lorin's thoughts turned to a greater work, one to forge a legacy beyond Cragmoore's flames. Hammers never fit his grasp. Short swords were more usable than long, but the latter were too weighty. The 'cursed sword' flickered into his mind, a longsword. The magic had tamed the heft. One wrought from 'god rocks' would be lighter even without the magic. Next step: a design.

Lorin collaborated with Hikal, reworking his old hammer sketch into a basic sword design. They agreed it would not provoke dwarven ire. None would perceive it as a slight against King Tarul. Many might call it a tribute, distinct from the royal arm yet resonant with its legacy.

Lorin sought out the king's servant to request an audience. The man chuckled, deeming it a fool's errand, but with a wry grin, he promised to deliver the plea.

As evening fell, the servant sought Lorin out and guided him through the shadowed streets to the palace, ushering him directly into the king's private chambers. No guards stood watch. The servant was dismissed with a casual wave of the hand.

Lorin stepped forward, the air thick with the scent of aged wood and flickering torchlight. "My lord," he began, his voice steady yet humble, "we've achieved a great triumph at the forge, and I'm resolved to craft my final work. Once it's complete, we'll find Ethrael. We believe she has been taken. But that's not why I stand before you. My final forge project is a longsword, similar to the 'cursed sword'. I know the hammer you wield was one I forged for our father. My memory's faded, yet I'd like to examine it, and, with your permission, draw inspiration from its form. Some here might bristle at this, but I intend no harm. In truth, I seek a quiet bond with my brother. To others, I'll say it honors dwarven ways and your crown. Will you grant this?"

"Brother," Tarul replied, warmth in his voice, "it's an honor to share our blood, even in secret. Here, study your youthful craft as you will; I cannot part with it, though, as I am sure you can understand. For my part, I'll ensure my folk know I see it as a tribute. One request, before you go, let me hold a farewell feast for you and your friends. Please show me your work openly. I'll bless them and speak of mending bonds with Arkiel's realm. I pray your healer friend is safe. I know it weighs heavily. You and Yarnell have done much to heal old hurts between us and the elves. I must go. A king's time is never his own. I'd love more time with you. Shall we say supper in a month? Nana and her mate are welcome, too. Farewell, brother!"

CHAPTER TWENTY-ONE

Fires of Fate — Lorin

Good folk, sit and lend your ears to a tale of fire and heart, where Cragmoore's Dragon Forge blazed with purpose. I, Yarnell, bard of fleeting truths and stubborn songs, sing of Lorin, whose hands shaped dagger, staff, and sword from 'god rocks' and dreams. With Hikal and Torvok, he braved the forge's maw, gifting the widow her blade, crafting a healer's staff, and forging a sword of dwarven might and elven grace, veiled for the final feast. Harken, for this refrain weaves a smith's resolve, a village's awe, and a legend's dawn! Thus, in those caverns of fire and stone, Lorin's legend took its first true breath.

With thoughts afire, Lorin could not sleep. All night, he remained awake, sketching rough plans for his sword. At dawn, he hid his sketches under his cot and headed down to the Dragon Forge, its heat awaiting.

Come morn, the forge thrummed with zeal. Hikal, Torvok, and Lorin descended to the Dragon Forge. The aim was to melt the matter and pour it into the molds for the dagger and staff. They held to the same crafting as before, yet with more material this time. It took nearly the whole day to process enough for both. As weariness was about to overwhelm them, they poured the molds, first the dagger, then the staff. They left them at the Dragon Forge to begin cooling, thereby avoiding harm to the castings. The forge was barred for safekeeping, and the three men practically crawled home.

"By the gods, the forge's heat has wrought a grievous toll on you, worse than before," Yarnell remarked.

Nana nodded, her gaze laden with concern. It had dragged three to four hours longer. The forge drained their vitality, as if sapping their life. She once more urged water and broth upon them before sending them off to bed. She drew a vow from each not to return for several days to restore their strength.

On the third day, the three smiths met at the forge and headed to the Dragon Forge to fetch the works. Their steps into the caverns were swift. They returned quickly. Due to the warm air, the molds were still warm, though no longer hot. Two more days of cooling in cooler air were deemed prudent. With the molds secured, Lorin turned to a vision born in solitude.

Lorin remembered the black sword from his dream in Keenroot. Concluding that it might have been a prophetic dream, he incorporated as much of the design and artwork as he could remember. Wishing this project a surprise, he kept it veiled from all. The design came together quickly, inspired by the king's hammer and the dream. By suppertime, he was pleased with the design. Come breakfast the next day, he began shaping the mold. He reckoned it would take at least a week.

The day came to free the works from their molds. All the smiths, Maela, and the villagers gathered to see the new works. The dagger, being the smallest, was chosen first. With great care to protect the mold, they drew it forth. The dagger was splendid. Its hue matched the rod-dagger cast before, yet it was of much better quality. Crafted by the former master, the mold had birthed a work as masterful as its first attempt. Unlike Lorin's test piece, this dagger's edge was keen as a razor and required no whetting.

Lorin gazed at the dagger, knelt before the widow, and laid it in her trembling hands. Tears streamed down her face. Speechless, she bade Lorin rise and clung to him as if her life hung in the balance. When she finally let go of Lorin, Hikal gave her the mold.

While the villagers escorted the widow home, a hush fell over the forge, anticipation rising for the unveiling of the staff. Save for Hikal, no one knew what to expect. Hikal and Lorin worked in tandem to free the staff from its mold, their movements precise yet tinged with excitement. Unlike the dagger's mold, which could be reused, the staff's was a fragile shell that had to be shattered. Should the casting prove flawed, a new mold would be needed, a daunting prospect. But the gods smiled upon them that day. The staff emerged flawless, its surface gleaming as if kissed by divine light. Lorin tossed the fragments of the staff mold into the forge's fire to be consumed.

The craftsmanship matched the design plans perfectly, with no blemish or rough edge to mar its elegance. Lorin, almost reverently, ran his shirt over its length to polish it, though the gesture was unnecessary. The staff already shone with a mirror-like sheen. The other smiths, each a master of their trade, gathered close, their keen eyes poring over every inch. They turned it in their calloused hands, searching for even the slightest imperfection; none could find fault. Murmurs of awe rippled through the group as they lauded its rare worth, their voices a blend of envy and admiration.

Lorin gripped the staff tightly as though it were a tether to Ethrael across the vast distance. Its weight felt alive in his hands, a silent promise forged in fire and metal. Despite its cumbersome length, he never let it stray beyond arm's reach, even when he wandered through the Dwarven Halls. Seeking their counsel, he carried the staff to the healers' sanctum.

Lorin presented the staff to the local healers, its glossy black form a testament to his craft for Ethrael. Forged from 'god rocks' and metal, it gleamed with a liquid sheen, ready to honor her healing art.

The healers marveled at it. Lorin marked the head healer's silence. "Madam," he said, "I highly prize your assessment. Do you think my friend will appreciate the staff? Is it fitting for one in her profession?"

"In truth," the healer replied, "I've never seen a more remarkable staff. The crafting is exquisite. The artwork is perfect for your friend."

Lorin smiled a bit but noticed a hesitation in the healer. "Is there something you're afraid to say?"

"Well, a slight suggestion: contrasting material could enhance its beauty. Though the black is unparalleled, marking the design work and the bulb atop with a light-colored metal, silver. Silver to lift the black. You might not know, but silver is known for its healing virtues. It is often used in our tools and even some salves. Yet you are the smith, and this is slight counsel for an already flawless work."

"I thank you," Lorin said. "I value your words and am grateful. Silver could easily be wrought into a highlight."

Lorin sought out a silversmith, and with his skilled aid, Lorin implemented the healer's suggestion. He was overjoyed with the result, but kept the final work veiled from all. Thus, the staff stood complete, a radiant gift for Ethrael's healing art.

• • •

Later, when the forge had quieted and the others had gone, Lorin finally allowed himself a moment alone with the finished staff.

He lifted it with both hands, breath catching as the forge-light ran along its glossy black length. Forged from the divine metal and rare 'god rocks', it seemed almost alive in the dim glow, its surface polished to a liquid sheen that reflected the embers like rippling dark water. The weight was perfect—solid, balanced, shaped not for war but for a healer's steady hand.

He turned it slowly, letting the details emerge one by one.

Silver vines spiraled up the shaft, their inlaid metal catching the light with a cool, radiant shimmer. Each leaf glowed softly, fine-edged and graceful, the silver lending the staff a purity he knew Ethrael would recognize instantly. The healer's suggestion echoed in him—*silver to lift the black*—and Lorin felt a quiet swell of gratitude. The contrast transformed the staff, making the dark metal look deeper, more deliberate, as though moonlight had decided to take root in its surface.

At the crown, the vines curled inward to cradle the bulb of the same glossy black material. The smooth orb rested beneath a silver cap that gleamed like frost, the divine stone beneath shimmering faintly, as though holding its own quiet pulse. The silver-framed bulb looked almost sacred, as if it protected a truth waiting for the right healer to awaken.

Near the grip, his thumb brushed over the gold rune he had etched by hand—the elven symbol of protection. It glowed with a faint warmth, soft against the black and silver. The rune's quiet light seemed to bless the staff in turn, bridging the contrast of metals, binding the craft with purpose.

Lorin exhaled slowly.

He imagined Ethrael's fingers resting where his were now, imagined the way her eyes might widen at the silver vines or soften at the protective rune. He had built the staff to honor her strength, her gentleness, her unyielding heart. Every line of metal, every shimmering vine, every gleam of silver was a piece of what he wished for her—healing, steadiness, and a future unmarred by pain.

Behind him, Hikal's voice broke the stillness with quiet awe.

"By the mountain's heart... Ethrael will treasure this."

Lorin swallowed, his grip tightening around the staff.

He hoped so.

He prayed so.

For in the fire-lit quiet of the forge, holding the staff he had crafted for her alone, he felt the truth settle in his chest:

This was no mere creation.

It was a promise.

• • •

With a design less intricate than the staff's, yet no less vital to his purpose, he deftly shaped the sword's mold in a mere week, his hands guided by a vision of Ethrael's strength. His tools carved the mold with precision, honing the blade's edge with meticulous care. He had studied the dagger's mold for how to craft the edge. He incorporated those lessons of the master's craftsmanship into his sword mold, a weapon destined for legends.

With the mold complete, he joined Hikal and Torvok to bring the blade to life. Together, they readied their tools, their resolve a symphony of craft.

Dawn broke cold over Cragmoore's peaks, its chill settling over Lorin as he, Hikal, and Torvok descended once more to the Dragon Forge, their third foray into its fiery heart. They braved that fiery heart again, molten 'god rocks' flowed under their skilled hands, shaping Lorin's sword. Their hammers struck in rhythm, forging a blade to weave elven grace with dwarven might, having forged the rod-dagger, then the widow's dagger and staff, and now his blade. As Lorin gently placed the filled mold down, he thought of the black sword and his future. Was he part of some great prophecy or an imposter?

As the cooling passed, he crafted a sheath. He kept this hidden, shielding the final yield from view. "All will be unveiled at the final feast," he said.

Thus, from the forge's heart, the blade of legend was born.

• • •

Lorin waited until the deep hours of night, when Cragmoore's torches burned low, and the halls fell quiet. Only then did he bar the door of his small chamber and kneel beside the cast blade. His breath fogged faintly in the cool air as he loosed the sword from the mold. Like the staff, the molding was destroyed, releasing its treasure, like a nutshell releasing its meat. His hands were trembling—not with fear but with the weight of what he was about to behold.

The mold had birthed the sword like a whispered secret. The sword gleamed up at him, black as starless midnight, its glossy surface catching the lone lantern's light in rippling currents. The sight of it struck him still. It was the shape of his journey, his destiny—the pain he had borne, the strength he had gathered, and the path yet unknown.

His fingers brushed the flat of the blade. It felt warm, almost living. A pulse of memory stirred.

Keenroot. The dream. The black sword held in a stranger's hands—the hands he now knew were his own.

The dream had felt like a prophecy then, a message he hadn't been ready to understand. Now, the blade before him matched it in every contour.

Lorin accented the sword with silver as he had the staff. He desired the sword and staff to be siblings.

He traced the carved runes hidden in the vine work accented in silver. Protection. Renewal. Connection. They glowed faintly beneath his fingertips, as if recognizing the one who had shaped them. He thought of Ethrael's steady hands, her compassion stronger than any weapon. But this blade was for battle, a weapon, a stark contrast to her healing staff.

The hilt balanced perfectly in his palm, ironwood warm against his skin. The dwarven knotwork bit into his grip with purposeful strength. Light from the lantern ran over the angular lines of the crossguard—stocky, unyielding, a guardian forged in stone and fire. Dwarven endurance and elven grace met there, fused into a harmony he felt in his bones.

He lifted the blade.

Not high—just enough for the lantern flame to shimmer across its length. In that wavering glow, the sword looked like it drank the shadows around it, as though it carried its own night within.

"This is who I am now," he whispered, the words barely reaching his own ears.

Broken man. Burgeoning smith. Companion. Protector.

The sword answered with silence, but it was a resonant silence—the way a held breath can speak before a vow.

He placed the blade carefully into its sheath. That, too, was beautifully wrought: midnight leather and blackened steel, silver vines threading through rugged dwarven runes. A union of worlds, just as he himself was becoming.

When he fastened the clasp, something settled inside him.

Not peace—no, not yet.
But direction. Purpose.
Destiny.

He wrapped the sword again and hid it beneath his cot, veiled until the Feast of Honor, when the king himself would see the truth of what had been forged.

Only then did Lorin lie down, exhaustion finally taking him.

Before sleep claimed him, he saw again that dream-sword gleaming in the shadows of his mind—only now, it was no vision.

It was real.

And it belonged to him.

This was a blade of destiny—born from prophecy, realized in the Dragon Forge.

CHAPTER TWENTY-TWO

Halls of Parted Kin — Lorin

Harken, ye of stout heart, to my song of Cragmoore's twilight feast, where stone and star entwine. In halls aglow with rune and flame, Lorin bestows a staff of solace, a sword of valor, binding kin across realms. My lute chants of alliance forged, while a throne's hidden heir stirs shadows of the past. Attend, for this tale weaves parting's grief with unity's eternal spark!

*I*n preparation, Lorin wrapped both the staff and the sword, with its sheath, in their own bed cloth. He wished the king to see his works first. Lorin and his companions donned fine garments for the occasion. Lorin, Nana, Hikal, and Yarnell arrived together at the festivity hall. Lorin felt a pang of sadness, knowing they'd part from their friends tomorrow, yet he yearned to find Ethrael.

As Lorin entered the festivity hall with his companions, he addressed Hikal, "You have been a great blessing to our mission, especially to me. I will always have fond memories of the time we spent together. I want to give a gift to show my appreciation." Lorin handed the rod-dagger to Hikal with heartfelt gratitude. Hikal smiled and placed it into his boot.

"My kin," the king stood and addressed the court. "It is time to bid farewell to our guests, Lorin and Yarnell, from the elven realm. They've shown us how much we may learn from one another. I deem it is time to repair our bond with our elven brothers. They took the first step, risking much by sending them to us. We welcomed them and held them as family. Now, we must trust them in turn. Two of us shall venture to the elven realm a year after their arrival. I hope they'll learn as much from the elves as we hope to share with them. I've penned a writ for King Arkiel to say as much."

"Now," the dwarven king said, a broad smile creasing his weathered face, "I'm eager to hear our guest bard share his craft. Many among my court have heard him at the village tavern, yet a king enjoys no such liberty."

The king turned to Yarnell, "Bard Yarnell, would you perform, please?"

Lorin watched Yarnell step forward, lute cradled in his arms, its polished wood gleaming like amber in the torchlight. The great hall, a cavern of stone and splendor, bore walls carved with runes glinting in silver and gold. Braziers roared at each corner, casting a warm glow over nobles in furs and gem-studded vests and common folk in sturdy wool, their faces ruddy from the mountain air. The scent of roasted boar and ale mingled with the hum of chatter filling the space.

"My lord," Yarnell said, bowing low, "what would you like to hear: a dwarven ballad, an elvish tune, or another melody?"

The king replied, his voice echoing off the stone, "You're the master of your craft." He sat upon his granite throne, its back carved with a great hammer, his iron-gray beard braided with onyx beads. "I leave it to thee, yet choose a tune to fit the hour, not those rowdy tavern songs." He chuckled, a sound like tumbling gravel, and the court's measured laughter rippled warmly through the hall.

• • • (Yarnell)

"Sire," Yarnell's voice steady despite the moment's weight, "I sing a song crafted in the quiet of a starlit night, inspired by Ethrael's tales of her lost home. It has yet to be performed publicly. You and your people will be the first."

He took his place between the throne and the commoners, standing on a woven rug dyed the deep crimson of mountain berries. The hall's murmur continued, heedless of the music to come, dwarves clinking tankards, a child tugging at her mother's sleeve, a noble adjusting his cloak. Drawing a breath, resting his fingers on the strings, he began.

Song: The Alliance of Stone and Star

Ho, the hammers ring, in the mountain's core,
Bold as war horns, through the caverns roar!
Dwarven boots march, with a steadfast beat,
Forging axes bright, in the molten heat.
Stone unbroken, hearts of iron stand,
Guardians of Aelthar, we defend the land!

Stone and star, together we rise,
Dwarves and elves, with fire in our eyes!
In the valley green, where the starblooms glow,
United we fight, where the brave winds blow!

Soft, the breeze sings, through the treetops high,
Elven arrows dance, beneath a starlit sky.
Silver voices weave, with the forest's lore,
Magic of the ancients, from the days of yore.
Moonlight in our hair, spells of starlight cast,
Swift as fleeting dreams, our foes shall not last!

Stone and star, together we rise,
Dwarves and elves, with fire in our eyes!
In the valley green, where the starblooms glow,
United we fight, where the brave winds blow!

In Aelthar's vale, where the starblooms shine,
Dwarven steel cleaves, through the goblin line!
Elven vines of light, bind the cave elves' blades,
Hissing in the dark, their greed now fades.

War cries shake the peaks, roots entwine the foe,
Victory dawns bright, where the brave winds blow!

But hark, the melody turns, sharp as crackling flame,
Dark fire spreads, with a curse's name.
Starbloom Grove burns, petals fall to ash,
Aelthar's rivers boil, in the inferno's clash.
Though we drive them back, to the shadows deep,
Our triumph's stained, with the scars we keep.

Stone and star, together we rise,
Dwarves and elves, with fire in our eyes!
In the valley green, where the starblooms glow,
United we fight, where the brave winds blow!

Oh, Aelthar weeps, for the grove's last light,
Yet stone and star, still burn through the night.
With axes and spells, we'll forge anew,
The alliance holds, ever brave, ever true.

· · ·

The hall stilled, the murmur fading as if the very stone held its breath. Eyes fixed on the bard, nobles and commoners alike, their faces caught in the glow of the braziers. A grizzled dwarf in a blacksmith's apron clutched his tankard, his knuckles white, a proud tear glistening in his beard as he recalled his kin's valor, though his jaw tightened at the memory of the fire. A young lass near the front, her hair a fiery red, pressed her hands to her chest, her eyes bright with awe at the alliance's stand yet misty with sorrow for Aelthar's fall.

The king leaned forward on his throne, his stern features a mix of pride and grief, his gaze distant as if he stood amidst the burning grove, hammer in hand. Yarnell was borne away, his fingers moving as if guided by the alliance's spirit. His voice rose and fell like the clash of steel, the whisper of starlight, and the roar of flames. It felt like the whole court lived the story, and none dared miss a note or word, each bound by the music's spell.

When the final note faded, a mournful chord lingered in the air like the last wisp of smoke. The hall sat in still, reflective silence, the only sound the crackle of the braziers and the faint drip of water echoing from some unseen cavern. He lowered his lute, breath shallow, and waited.

After a few breaths, the king spoke, his voice a reverent rumble. "Bard Yarnell, I'd heard of your gift, yet I've never heard such a stirring strain in all my days. That song wove our forges' fire, elven stars' light, our stand's triumph, and Aelthar's sorrow. I pray many of my people have seen your mastery and found new inspiration—to honor our alliance and rebuild what was lost."

He rose from his throne, his heavy cloak of bear fur sweeping the floor, and the hall erupted in applause, a thunderous roar that shook the stone. Dwarves stamped their boots, clapped their hands, and raised their tankards, their cheers a wave of warmth that washed over him. Many wiped tears from their eyes, their pride tempered by the song's tragic end.

"Were you mine to command, I'd conscript you to my court," the king continued, his eyes bright with admiration. "I know you must go, but please, visit again. You're always welcome here."

Bowing deeply and swelling with gratitude, Yarnell said, "I thank you, my lord. You honor me beyond words."

• • • (Lorin)

"Lorin, your turn," the king continued, "show the court what you've been working on. I know already of the kindness shown to Maela Firebraid."

Lorin rose, bearing the wrapped treasures, and approached the throne. A guard moved to take them, yet Lorin paused and looked to the king. The king waved the guard off. Lorin laid the first rolled cloth on the king's lap.

The king lifted the staff, gazed at it, and held it high for the court to see. "Truly a master smith's work, such fine craft. I trust this is for your lost friend. The craft is first-rate, light for its size, yet not too much so. She'll prize this gift." He passed the staff to the queen, who eyed it briefly before handing it to a guard. With Lorin still holding the sword to show, Yarnell took the staff and its cloth for safekeeping.

"Thank you, Your Majesty," Lorin said. He laid the second cloth, with the sword, on the king's lap. "Sire, a sword for myself, honoring the dwarven realm, its great might, and the time we dwelt here. I drew inspiration from your hammer. My lord, I await your true judgment."

The king turned the blade over in his hands, examining the artistry. He pulled the blade from the sheath. He ran his fingers along the flat of the blade and tested the edge before returning the blade to the sheath.

"Lorin, I have never seen such a blade. The craftsmanship is exquisite. Though I favor my hammer, I can see the appeal of such a blade. It is truly a brother to my hammer. The same smith could have made it. May it serve you as mine serves me. As you travel the world, all shall know you have kin in the dwarven realm. My brother made my hammer for our father, and it passed to me, a tie to my past. With this sword in your possession, I'll always feel your presence near. While you speak of dwarven traits, I see elvish threads, too. Forged for our shared future. Take this court's blessings with you."

Queen Pykal's visage hardened, yet she held her tongue. The king returned the cloth, sheath, and sword to Lorin, who sheathed it and bound it to his side. Guards stepped forth to disarm him; protocol dictated that no one was allowed to bear arms near the king.

The king rose. "Hold! None shall disarm this man. His sword and my hammer are kin. By honoring my blood, he's become part of it. Treat him as ye would Barzul, for I see Barzul's spirit in him. We may lack my parents and elder brother, yet the gods have brought Lorin to our court as a remembrance of days past."

Lorin knelt. "My lord, I thank you for your kind words. I am honored, and may the gods strike me dead if I were ever to bring shame to you or your people."

"Now, Lorin," the king went on, "I have gifts for you as you make ready to go. First, you may not have heard, but Maela Firebraid passed last night. Her dying wish was to gift the dagger you made for her. You blessed her final days, and this court will always be grateful. Remember her and her mate as fondly as she did you. The mold and the first broken dagger were given to Torvok, the forge master. Second, as I told Yarnell, you're always welcome here. I look forward to seeing you soon. Lastly, I'll send two guards to escort you to the elven realm. You should be safe once there. Now, let us toast with the elven wine you brought. Cheers!"

. . .

After a short span, the king whispered to Lorin and Yarnell. "Gentlemen, meet my queen and me in my chambers. There are weighty matters of state to speak." Lorin and Yarnell followed the king and queen at a reverent distance into their private sitting room.

"I've sent men to seek information about Ethrael," the king began. "We learned little, yet I'll share what I know. It seems Ethrael was pressed, not forced, to visit another realm for a healing need, though I do not know its nature or location. It is little, yet she's safe so far as we know. I hope this eases your burden a bit."

"Second," he said, turning to his wife, "this is for you, my queen. I know you have been uncomfortable with my welcome of these two and my opening bonds with the elven king. The rumors are that the elves poisoned my parents, yet we both know it was the cave elves. Moreover, when I visited the elven realm months ago, I found a kindred soul in Lorin. You may not believe it, yet he's my lost brother, Barzul, the rightful heir to the throne. Still, he veils his birth for our realm's sake. We cannot share this openly, yet as my queen, you must know. The elven king learned his lineage and cared for him as his own, with nothing to gain and much to lose. How can I shun ties with him if he can risk so much for my brother, who can never be named noble? I implore you to follow my lead."

The queen's eyes darted from her king to Lorin. "My lord, this overwhelms me. If this news were from anyone but you, I would reject it. I bear a mixed heart, certainly. He does not resemble a noble dwarf. Are you sure?"

Lorin spoke, "Majesty, you're right to doubt. The best we've reckoned is that my mother bore elven cures and magic while carrying me. It caused me to be less dwarven and more human in appearance. They say a dwarf babe lacks an elder's guard against magic. I lack a dwarf's frame and stamina. Magic sways me more than other dwarves, even now. A head wound cost me many memories, yet I hope one day to reclaim them. Even before my injury, I'd have been a poor monarch. I am sure you know, Father was always uncomfortable leaving the throne to me, and with my looks and lost memories, he was wise to do so. The realm thrives under my brother and you. I vow never to claim the throne."

The queen visibly relaxed, "Thank you. Losing a father, mother, and brother so swiftly was devastating. At least my mate has a brother again. I welcome you as family. I wondered at his strange words this night, warmer than his normal decrees. Now I see he shielded you as he might."

Lorin looked to both king and queen as a smile spread to his face, "I look forward to seeing an heir, my niece or nephew, rule one day."

Before setting off for Keenroot, Lorin met with Torvok. He entrusted the 'god rocks' and the barrel of spare metal to the master's keeping, vowing to return for them. He deemed it wiser to leave them with one who knew their perils than risk the dust poisoning other folk. Torvok decided it was best to leave the rocks and spare metal at the Dragon Forge, as he was the only one with the key.

CHAPTER TWENTY-THREE

Craft of Kindred Sorrow — Lorin

Harken, ye who tread the paths of valor, lend your ears to a tale of fire and shadow. My lute weeps for a brother forged anew in distant halls. From the dwarven deeps, Lorin returns, his hands bearing works of star-born craft, a staff and sword to mend and sunder. Yet a weight clings heavier than iron, for Ethrael, our healer, is lost, her fate a gnawing void in our hearts. Beneath the Keenroot's canopy, truths unfold, and secrets of lineage stir the winds. Gather close, for this song speaks of triumphs tempered by sorrow, of a smith whose flame may yet light the way.

*T*hat night on the road, as he fared back among them, strange sounds pierced the dark. Yet, with stalwart dwarven guards beside Lorin and his companions, no brigands nor goblins dared test their might. He paused briefly at Parcelridge, seeking additional information about Ethrael, but found none.

At the elven forest's edge, he pitched camp among the dwarven escort. During the morning meal, as he supped, two elven rangers stepped from the trees. Lorin bade warm thanks to the dwarves, who turned homeward while he and Yarnell pressed forth with their elven guardians.

As they entered Keenroot, Lorin and Yarnell were led straight to the throne room. Ever heedful of decorum, Lorin longed to wash the road's dust from his face before facing royalty, yet the rangers wouldn't allow it. Their escorts departed, leaving them alone until the king himself entered, unshadowed by guards.

"I trust your journey bore fruit?" he asked, his gaze settling on Lorin.

"Aye, sire," Lorin replied. "King Tarul warmed to your vision, welcoming each other's folk now and then to share crafts and kindle trust between realms. He's pledged to send some of his own next year. Here's his missive, and I wager it speaks the same. I finished my smith's final work, yet heavier tidings weigh on me, for we've lost Ethrael." He poured forth all he knew, every thread of her tale, and besought the elves' aid to track her.

"I'll see what may be wrought," the king said, "though I can promise nothing. May I behold the works you created?"

"Of course. This dagger hails from a mold cast by an old dwarven forge master, named Garrim Firebraid, now gone to his rest. His first blade was too brittle and broke, yet his studies birthed this one. The blade was crafted from rocks discovered during our journey. The dwarves called them 'god rocks'."

"The black hue enchants," the king mused, turning it in his hands. "So light, so flawless in balance. Such metal I've never seen, truly one of a kind."

"For your patronage of our path, and all done for me, I gift it to you."

"A token of the dwarves and you," the king said. "I'll cherish it. It shall not stray from me." He drew a dagger from his boot and slid the new one into its place.

"This, my lord," he continued, "is a staff I forged for Ethrael, wrought from the same rocks. Its markings speak of healing arts, a tribute to her care in mending me. I pray I may yet place it in her hands." A tear gleamed in his eye.

The king examined the staff and passed it to Yarnell.

"And here, my final labor, a sword. Its sheath and blade woven with elven and dwarven designs, their union reflecting my heritage. I saw it in a dream. I believe it was prophetic."

"It warms my soul, you have such a magnificent blade. Remember, I told you the gods have great things in store for you. You're a rare soul, Lorin. From life's harshest strokes, you shape triumph. You'll be sung as he who bridged elf and dwarf relations anew. Though your true blood may abide shadowed, both kingdoms are indebted to you."

Lorin bowed at the high praise. "Sire," Lorin said, "until Ethrael's fate be known, I'll hone my craft with this blade. There is also the matter of returning the 'cursed sword'. I mean to be ready when the hour strikes."

"Wisdom guides you," the king agreed. "Mine own guard shall train you, yet hear me one request more. As we said, the 'cursed sword' knows you for a wizard. Study with my court mages, too, you may find whispers of truth you have yet to grasp."

Lorin weighed the words. "No harm in exploring new things. If magic stirs in me, I'll wield a fresh tool. If not, I'll add it to the tally of my stumbles."

• • • *(Yarnell)*

Yarnell petitioned the king, "My lord, I have crafted a song titled 'The Sorrow of Barzul'. I promised it would only be for your ears. May I sing it for you?"

"I would be honored. Let's retire to my private chambers."

Later, in the king's private chambers, Arkiel's voice broke the silence, soft but commanding. "Bard Yarnell," he said, "you've returned from the dwarven lands with a tale of sorrow that touches on a lineage close to my heart. Will you sing it for me now?"

The bard bowed low, his lute companion cradled in his arms, its polished wood warm against his chest. "My lord," his voice steady despite the moment's weight, "I learned this tale from Hikal, a dwarven blacksmith, who shared a guarded dwarven tragedy, the royal lineage of Lorin, whose true name echoes in this song. With your leave, I'll sing its lament."

Arkiel nodded, his expression a mix of anticipation and sorrow. His gaze flickered briefly to Lorin, a silent acknowledgment of their shared secret. "Proceed," he said, leaning back in his chair, his hands resting on its arms. The chamber's stillness wrapped around us like a cloak.

He stood at the center of the room, the moonstone floor cool beneath his boots, the enchanted orbs casting a soft glow on my lute's strings. Lorin remained by the door, his presence a quiet weight, his eyes downcast as if bracing for the truth he could not yet grasp. Yarnell drew a breath, fingers finding the strings, and began.

The Sorrow of Barzul (A Dwarven Lament)

Beneath the mountain's ancient keep,
Where stone and shadow softly weep,
There shone a king, Qartul by name,
His throne a spark of golden flame.
Beside him stood his jewel so fair,
Lazula, with her radiant hair—
Her laughter warmed the halls of stone,
Her love the heart of dwarfdom's home.

Oh, Barzul, child of sorrow born,
Through grief and loss, thy name is worn.
The strings lament, the heart does rend,
For dwarven light that met its end.

But woe, the cave elves' venom struck,
While Barzul grew in Lazula's womb.
Her light grew dim, her life forsook,
Her unborn babe faced certain doom.
Wood elves, with blades and magic cold,
Cut Barzul free, his life to hold—
Yet stretched his frame, his dwarfhood torn,
And Lazula died when Barzul was born.

Oh, Barzul, child of sorrow born,
Through grief and loss, thy name is worn.
The strings lament, the heart does rend,
For dwarven light that met its end.

The king's great heart was rent in twain,
His realm a shroud of endless pain.
Yet Kiran came, of iron made,
Her strength to soothe where grief had flayed.
A second son, pure dwarf was he,
Tarul, their hope, their legacy—
But fate, a blade, would strike anew,
And poison's breath the night ran through.

Oh, Barzul, child of sorrow born,
Through grief and loss, thy name is worn.
The strings lament, the heart does rend,
For dwarven light that met its end.

At feast of joy, where wine was poured,
The cave elves struck with traitor's sword.
The goblets clinked, then fell to dust—
Qartul and Kiran, betrayed, unjust.
Their sons, now grown, to caverns deep,
Faced trials where the shadows creep—
Tarul returned, a king to claim,
But Barzul vanished, lost to shame.

Oh, Barzul, child of sorrow born,
Through grief and loss, thy name is worn.
The strings lament, the heart does rend,
For dwarven light that met its end.

His sword was found, with blood defiled,
The gentle prince, the mourned child.
No trace remained, no hope to cling,
And Tarul rose, a grieving king.
The dwarves, they mourn their fallen line,
Their hearts a wound no years define—
For mother, father, brother gone,
And Barzul's name in stone lives on.

Oh, Barzul, child of sorrow born,
Through grief and loss, thy name is worn.

The strings lament, the heart does rend,
For dwarven light that met its end.

A single note, a fading sigh,
The lute's last tear before it dies.
Oh, Barzul, lost beneath the stone,
Thy sorrow claims us, flesh and bone.

• • •

After a few breaths, Arkiel spoke, his voice a reverent whisper that seemed to echo in the small space. "Bard Yarnell, that was a song of profound sorrow and truth. 'The Sorrow of Barzul' carried the light of Queen Lazula, the shadow of betrayal, and the loss of a lineage the dwarves have mourned in secret. You've honored their memory with your craft."

Arkiel rose from his chair, his silver robes shimmering, and stepped forward, his applause a soft, solitary clap that felt more like a tribute than a celebration. "Such a tragedy explains much of the dwarves' mistrust and the shared foes we face," his eyes meeting Lorin's, a silent acknowledgment of their shared truth. "You've given me much to reflect on, bard. I thank you."

Yarnell bowed deeply, his heart swelling with gratitude and the moment's weight. "I thank you, my lord. It is an honor to sing for you."

Warmly, the king said, "Go now, I release you. Rest awaits, and training begins. My thanks, once more, for service to the crown, or more accurately, should I say, crowns."

"My thanks, my lord," Lorin replied.

• • • *(Lorin)*

After sleeping off his travels, Lorin ventured to the forge, eager to show Master Falere his craft. He swelled with pride for his craft, anxious to present it to his master, the first to fan his smithing flame. Falere greeted him with genuine joy, gladdened to see him return whole. When he unveiled the staff, Falere grasped it with time-worn reverence, his hands tracing its length in silent awe. He sought flaws he knew he'd not find, yet lingered longer to drink in its elegance.

"My first thought leaps to the material," Falere said. "This color, I've never seen it. Tell me, is it as stout as a staff must be?"

Lorin's face shone with pride. "Aye, Master. The silver adornment yields, yet the core beneath outstrips any strength I've known, made from what the dwarves call 'god rocks'."

The smith gently tapped the staff against the stone floor with waxing vigor. He peered at its base, finding no scuffs or marks. His gaze drifted to the carvings. "These signs bear meaning, I wager. Speak of them."

"When I dwelt among the dwarves," Lorin began, "I consulted with their healers. Their tokens I wove here, marks of healing and mending. At first, the staff gleamed solid black, yet their headmaster suggested silver accents for grace and to echo silver's healing lore."

"Wondrous!" Falere breathed. "Words fail me save to say: well wrought. This stands as thy final work, a triumph. Good job."

"Master," Lorin said softly, "this is but a gift for Ethrael, the woman who snatched me from death's embrace. It is not my final piece."

"Ah, where is she? I'd thought to see her at your side."

Lorin's voice wavered. "She's not here. We've not laid eyes on each other for many months. My heart is troubled, Master. This was my thanks for all she has done for me and for what she means to me. I pray I'll be able to present it to her."

"She'll prize it," Falere said gravely. "If the gods hold any grace, you'll set it in her hands. Yet tell me, did this toil steal all your time, leaving your true work undone? I'd not fault you, though I'd mourn the loss."

"No," Lorin replied, a spark returning to his tone. "I finished it! If you remember, before I left Keenroot, I'd meant to forge a hammer, as you did when I was last here. Yet after wielding one and shaming myself, I turned to a sword instead. Brother to the staff, in truth." With that, he drew forth the sheathed blade.

Falere's breath caught. "The sheath alone outshines the staff, such craft. Elven grace mixed with dwarven might and silver common to both." He eased the sword free with reverence, testing its balance, its heft, its edge.

"Light as a whisper, yet fierce. This black blade bewitches me, and the edge is matchless. My friend is a master indeed. Pray, teach me what you've learned."

Falere sheathed the weapon and pressed it back into his hands. "I thank you, Master. I'd not have shaped this without your guiding flame."

"Young man," Falere countered, "the fire was always within you. I but fanned what the heart already held."

He shared all he learned in the dwarven kingdom, stories of dwarven forges and sturdy smiths. He recounted tales of the 'god rocks', rod-dagger, widow's blade, Dragon Forge, and his craft's secrets. When the day's toil waned, he trudged home. Weariness clung to him, yet a smile crowned his face, a quiet victor's smirk.

CHAPTER TWENTY-FOUR

The Blade's Resolute Forge — Lorin

I, Yarnell, bard of distant roads, weave tales in Keenroot's fleeting dusk, a wanderer drawn to this saga, my heart pierced by Ethrael's vanished light. Lorin, for her sake, hones his blade in strife, his will forged for magic's craft, ready to tread any path to call her home. In halls of hope, fields of steel, and taverns aglow, our song resounds with grief, resolve, and quests yet to bloom.

As Lorin teetered on slumber's brink, a knock broke the stillness. A familiar servant from the court spoke, her voice soft yet pressing, its urgency piercing the fog of Lorin's weary slumber. "The king bids you bring something of your friend Ethrael's to his mages, for they claim it might aid their scrying to seek her. I know nothing beyond. Bear it when you come to the palace tomorrow. Good night." With that, she turned and retreated into the dark.

Lorin rubbed his weary eyes and grumbled, his heart shadowed by the weight of another loss he could not reclaim, as if his hidden name, Barzul, bore yet another curse, the faint echo of his own uneven breaths mingling with the room's stifling gloom. "I'll visit the mages tomorrow, but what can I give them? All Ethrael had was with her in Parcelridge. I can search her hut, yet I hold scant hope."

That night, Lorin had another dream. He faced a goblin champion with his black blade. He easily countered the champion's advances. At one point, the sword even attacked the goblin without Lorin holding it.

At dawn, Lorin trudged to Ethrael's humble dwelling, Yarnell at his side, his steps heavy with the dread of finding naught to aid her scrying, as if each empty corner mocked his shadowed vows. As he recalled, it stood bare of her traces. "I failed her," he slumped into the chair. His heart was heavy with Ethrael's absence, as if his shadowed past had claimed another sworn to his care. The hut's barren chill felt like a silent curse.

"I've no idea what to do, for there's not even a rag on the bed," he said, kicking at the floor in despair.

A few moments passed. A memory fought to be heard. A smile spread on his face as he stood, talking to no one, "Hold, what of the bedcloth! She wrapped the 'cursed sword' in the bedcloth. The last time I saw it, it was still about the sword at the palace. Thank the gods!"

Lorin and Yarnell ran to the palace, Lorin clutching a frail hope. His heart quickened at the thought of the bedcloth binding him to Ethrael, as if its threads might restore the honor he owed her steadfast heart.

Finding the mages, he said with excitement, "Ethrael had little, naught save the garb on her back. Yet she wrapped the 'cursed sword' in her bedcloth to keep it safe. Will that serve? Last I saw, King Arkiel had the sword."

"If she used it before, it could," said the mage, robed in shadow and wisdom, as he stroked his chin. "We'll request the king to lend it to us. It'll take time, yet I daresay we can still track her."

Lorin grinned at the mages, scratching his head, a flicker of hope kindling in his chest at the thought of finding Ethrael. "I thank you," Lorin said. "The king has pressed me to train with you, for he claims I've some gift for magic. Yet I begin my sword craft today, so I'll come tomorrow. I mean to strive with the guards in the morning, then study with you afternoons."

The mage arched a brow. "We'd normally require more hours to hone the craft, yet we'll yield, as 'tis the king's will. Tomorrow after midday, then."

• • •

Lorin approached the training grounds, Yarnell trailing behind, where the guards sharpened their art, his heart braced with a defiant resolve to prove his sword's worth, his chest tight with the weight of impending judgment. Lorin felt a wary respect for the elves, their frames gleaming with sinew, chiseled and sure. Though they lacked the dwarves' brawny heft, their prowess, precision, and form were perfect. Some clashed in duels, others strained at drills, while a few smote straw-stuffed foes.

Lorin met the trainer's gaze, sensing the scrutiny sizing him up, his resolve hardening against the challenge. "So, you fancy yourself a warrior? A touch long in years to begin this career," the trainer added, stern posture fueling Lorin's resolve. "I wouldn't even take you as squire if his majesty hadn't commanded it."

"I understand," Lorin said, a quiet amusement stirring in his chest at the trainer's doubt, his heart alight with the anticipation of proving his blade's craft.

The trainer squinted. "You need your gear and swear five years study, dawn to dusk, no shirking. Even in dreams, I demand training."

Lorin felt a spark of defiance in his chest at the trainer's misjudgment. "Hold, you've got it wrong. I'm not here to join as a guard; I wish to grow fair with a sword," his defiance flaring brighter, "And five years of training all day? No, the king has me set for afternoon study elsewhere," his resolve unyielding, "But I brought a blade I forged myself," his resolve sharpened by the chance to defy such scorn.

The trainer barked a laugh. "Let's see this sword you've patched together. You'd fare better fishing a broken one from the scrap heap, higher worth, I'd wager."

Lorin drew back his cloak to unveil the sheath, his posture steady with a fierce pride in his craft, his heart braced for the trainer's reckoning, undaunted by the guard's doubt. The smug grin on the elf's face wavered. Yarnell smiled at the sight. The guards' smug grin completely fell when Lorin revealed the black blade.

Lorin had a surge of defiance in his chest, his heart ablaze with the challenge of proving its worth. "This fair enough? Is it as good as your scrap swords?" Lorin asked, a pulse of satisfaction in his chest at the trainer's faltering composure.

Lorin watched with bated breath, his heart confident in the quality of his craft, while the trainer tested the blade. His jaw slackened. Its edge was unyielding, its balance true. He clanged it against his steel, eyes wide.

"I've never seen such a marvel," he muttered, yielding it back. "Normally, a work of art is no war tool, yet this... I'd trade my firstborn, had I one, to possess it. I'll train you if only to see what it can do."

Lorin felt a swell of quiet triumph in his chest, his craft's worth affirmed, as if this blade might yet carve a path to redeem his shadowed past.

• • • (Yarnell)

With Lorin holding his ground, his triumph a beacon, Yarnell slipped off for a tale, his heart tuning to the songs that bore their shared grief. To the tavern, his heart eager yet steeped in grief for Ethrael's loss, to regale the patrons with the saga of his wanderings.

The elven tavern in Keenroot, known as the Silver Leaf, was a haven of warmth and song, its walls crafted from smooth ash wood, their surfaces carved with delicate vines that shimmered in the glow of enchanted lanterns, rekindling Yarnell's heart's deep fondness for its familiar beauty. The ceiling was a lattice of woven branches through which glimpses of the starry sky peeked, and the air was rich with the scent of honeyed wine and freshly baked bread. Elves filled the space, their laughter a melody of its own, some clad in silken tunics of emerald and gold, others in simpler garb, their silver hair catching the light as they raised their goblets in cheer. It was here, amidst the revelry, that he took the stage, lute in hand, to share the tales of the journey to Gooseberry,

Parcelridge, and Cragmoore, though the weight of Ethrael's absence hung heavy in his heart.

The tavern's keeper, an elf named Lirien with eyes like polished jade, had called him to perform after hearing whispers of their travels. Her summons warmed his heart with purpose. "Sing for us, bard," her voice a lilting song, "of the roads you've walked with your companions. Our folk crave tales of the world beyond Keenroot's borders."

With a bittersweet smile, he knew the songs would carry triumph and loss. Standing on a small platform of polished oak, the crowd's chatter faded as the first notes were strummed on the lute. As a bard, he took some liberty with some of the lyrics to make the ballad more exciting.

"Good folk of the Silver Leaf," he said, his voice ringing clear as his heart thrummed with anticipation over the hum of the tavern. "I'm Yarnell, a bard who's walked far with two brave souls, a healer and a man of hidden strength. Tonight, I'll sing of our journey to Gooseberry, Parcelridge, and Cragmoore, where we faced trials, found triumphs, and bore a loss that haunts us still. Sit back, raise your goblets, and let the songs begin!"

His heart soared with the crowd's fervor, their goblets glinting in the lantern light, when he launched into the first song, 'The Curse of Gooseberry.' The lute's strings danced with a lively yet haunting melody, and the notes were quick and sharp like the rustle of leaves in a storm. His voice joined, bright and bold, each word painting the tale: a village gripped by fear, folk sickened by a curse born of sky-fallen rocks, their dust a poison that seeped into the earth. The wise and gentle healer stepped forth, her hands a balm for the afflicted, while her companions, a man of quiet strength and a bard with a song, stood by her side. The music swelled as she broke the curse, her courage a light in the darkness, the village saved, their gratitude a harvest of hope.

The elves clapped and cheered, their voices delighted, his spirit lifted by their joy. He moved into the second song, 'The Shadows of Parcelridge.' The melody shifted, the notes slower, more ominous, like the creak of ancient trees in a haunted wood. Yarnell's voice deepened each verse with a brushstroke of danger: a forest path to Parcelridge, where shadows moved with cruel intent, bandits clad in cloaks of midnight, their blades hungry for blood. The man of hidden strength fought with a ferocity born of heart, his fists a storm against the foe, while the healer's quick wit turned the tide, her herbs a smokescreen to blind their foes. The bard's song rallied their spirits, a tune of defiance that echoed through the trees until the bandits fled, the path cleared, and Parcelridge welcomed them with open arms.

The crowd's cheers grew louder, their goblets raised high, but a shadow crept into his heart, preparing for the final song, 'The Storm of Cragmoore.' The lute's strings thrummed with wild, tempestuous energy, the notes a whirlwind of sound, like thunder rolling over jagged peaks. The bard's voice rose, bold yet tinged with sorrow, each word a gust of wind: a mountain pass to Cragmoore, where a storm raged with fury, its winds a howl of icy wrath, its rain a deluge that threatened to sweep us away. But the healer was no longer there. She'd stayed in Parcelridge, her heart bound to the sick she tended, her hands a balm for their suffering. The man of hidden strength and the bard pressed on, the man shielding them from the gale, the bard's lute a beacon of warmth through the storm until they reached Cragmoore's gates, their journey a testament to their endurance, though their hearts ached for the healer left behind.

The melody slowed, the notes turning soft and mournful, a lament for the unknown. The song of Parcelridge's sorrow: the healer vanished, her fate a mystery, leaving her companions to grieve and wonder. Had she been taken by foes, lost to the town's shadows, or called by some greater purpose? The song ended on a single, trembling note, a question that hung in the air like a fading echo, the tavern's cheer dimming to a reflective silence.

The elves sat quietly for a moment, their goblets lowered, their faces a mix of awe and sorrow, the weight of the healer's disappearance settling over them. Then, slowly, they began to clap, their applause a gentle wave, a tribute to the journey's triumphs and losses.

"To Yarnell, the bard of the Silver Leaf!" one elf called, his voice bright but tinged with empathy. Soon, others joined in, their cheers a wave of warmth that washed over him, though their eyes held a shared understanding of loss.

Lirien approached with a goblet of honeyed wine in her hand, her smile soft with compassion. "A fine performance, Yarnell," she said, pressing the goblet into his hand. "You've brought the roads of Gooseberry, Parcelridge, and Cragmoore to life and honored the healer's memory with your song. Our folk will speak of this night for many moons. You are welcome here anytime."

Yarnell took a sip of the wine, its sweetness a balm after the songs, and nodded. "I'd be honored," he said, his voice warm with appreciation, though his heart still ached for Ethrael.

He shared, "There are more tales to tell, and I have a mind to craft a new song for Keenroot's beauty, and perhaps one to seek answers for our lost friend."

His heart stirred with gratitude at the elves' cheers, their voices a chorus of hope. He stepped down from the platform. The weight of the journey was lightened and deepened by sharing its tales. His spirit lifted, yet burdened by Ethrael's absence. The Silver Leaf hummed with life, and he knew the adventures and Ethrael's mystery would live on in the hearts of those who'd heard them that night.

As time wore on, Yarnell scarcely glimpsed Lorin save at supper, where he'd gulp a meal and fall into a deep slumber. The lad was wrung dry, body and mind taxed to its brink. Yarnell's heart ached for Lorin's unyielding toil. Lorin seldom spoke of his lessons, and the magic arts eluded Yarnell's grasp. Yet Lorin's weary form stirred a deep concern for his steadfast endurance.

The forge had wrought him strong, yet the guards' rigor carved his sinew sharper still. Knowing Lorin, he cast his whole soul into it, his heart ever pushing him to ensure on Ethrael's return.

CHAPTER TWENTY-FIVE

Guilt's Shadow, Duty's Call — Lorin

In Keenroot's ancient annals, Lorin's saga wove a thread of valor, resolute, through gathering shadows. Goblins, their malice a blight upon the forest's heart, stirred war's grim tide, and the king's call, steadfast, summoned a warrior yet unproven. Lorin, blade-bearer, stood poised, his spirit unsteady, where duty clashed with doubt. The village, abuzz with dread, murmured of bloodshed's cost, yet none foresaw the path unfolding, a quest to sunder the cursed sword's legacy. Thus began a verse, somber, of fealty and sacrifice, etched in fate's unyielding forge.

*L*orin was summoned abruptly to the palace. As he entered the throne room, his heart felt unsteady beneath an unspoken summons' weight. King Arkiel sat enthroned, guards arrayed about him, their steel-clad forms a chorus taut with sudden strain, as if called unawares. The air, heavy with purpose, pressed upon Lorin's chest.

"Countryman," the king began, his voice resolute, steadfast, "the number of squads of goblins is ever increasing in our forest, destroying it and killing our people. Seek their camp, bind them for questioning, halt their trespass. We need information."

Lorin scratched his head, brow furrowed, his thoughts awhirl. "Sire, I grasp their call, yet why me?"

"You've trained," the king replied, his gaze piercing Lorin's doubt. "This is a chance to test those skills in the field. I must know when you're ready for the greater quest ahead. Forget not; you must return the 'cursed sword', and when we find your friend, your blade may be needed to free her."

Lorin faltered, his sureness wavered. He'd swung steel for months, yet in his last encounter, he was more a danger to himself than to the adversary. Still, he dipped a swift bow and stepped out, veiling the unease singing beneath his skin.

As Lorin stepped from Keenroot's palace, his unease a silent shadow, the village pulsed with dread, whispers rippling through cobblestone streets. Elders murmured of war's shadow, while young blades sharpened steel, eyes alight with defiance.

The elven band searched for about a week before they found the goblins. There were a dozen of them. With the five guards, they were outnumbered 2-to-1. They watched and waited primarily to see if there were others. But as the sun set and most of the goblins were sleeping, the elves and Lorin surrounded the camp. Slowly, they crept up until they were just outside the light of the fire.

Only one goblin was awake, guarding the camp. An arrow flew and killed that goblin without a sound. To their credit, they gagged and bound four other sleeping goblins before any stirred. A fight ensued, and two more goblins were killed before it was all over. Nine of the original twelve enemies would be brought back to the palace as prisoners. In the scuffle, Lorin had killed one of the goblins.

Lorin had found himself face to face with a goblin bearing braided bone-charms woven into his hair—Skarn, though Lorin didn't know the name. This goblin barked orders with a tremor of reluctance, as if command had been thrust upon him unwillingly. He lunged at Lorin with a crude spear, his attacks forceful but scattered. Lorin parried, steel ringing in the night. One mistimed thrust left the goblin open, and Lorin's blade cut in a swift arc, ending the clash as Skarn collapsed among the roots and leaf-litter.

Once all of the goblins were disabled, the backpacks and provisions were inspected. Not much was found of interest, but there were a few notes in one of the bags. No one could read them, so they brought them back to the palace as well. The hope was that someone would be able to interpret the strange language. The heads of those killed were brought bagged, the fire extinguished, and the bodies left for the forest animals to pick clean.

Returning home, shaken, his first kill weighed heavily. Now two deaths weighed upon him—the earlier fight and this one, this reluctant goblin leader who had met his blade by necessity rather than malice. But the village's fervor swelled as the prisoners were marched in. The bags containing the heads were in the guard's hands. Lorin passed unnoticed, the clamor a distant echo. His thoughts dwelt on the death blow he dealt.

• • •

Days later, Lorin, still haunted by his kill, sought solace in Keenroot's quiet, resuming his magic studies as the village's unrest faded to a murmur. The rest of the guards, hearing of the excursion, pressed him for details, but he was dismissive, withdrawn. Finally, one of the elves on the hunt, a veteran, took him aside.

"Lorin, I can see you are struggling with what happened in the field. I understand, for I, too, have felt that burden. You have to remind yourself; it was him or you. You have been trained to protect yourself. But more importantly, you were serving the crown. If you had failed, they would have killed our entire squad and likely would have come to kill women and children here in the village. They knew they were in our territory and understood the consequences that would follow. Always remember this feeling. The taking of a life, even an enemy, is a somber thing. It may be necessary, but still a life nonetheless."

"But you don't understand, I didn't just kill him, I enjoyed it. I didn't even think of him as a person, just a thing to vanquish. I didn't know that could happen." The thought chilled him—did he even have a soul left?

"I am glad to hear it. Too many don't have the heart you do. You are not a killer. Your training and instincts took over. Such thoughts can arise even when we slay for sustenance. One life is taken, but their sacrifice helps the village to survive. This was very similar. I will leave you to your thoughts, but I suggest that you get back into your normal practice routine tomorrow morning. It will help you clear your head."

Lorin lingered in Keenroot's stillness, the veteran's words a faint ember in his heart. The weight of a life taken, even justly, pressed heavily, yet duty called, resolute, unyielding. He gazed at the village's torchlit paths, their glow a fragile guard against war's encroaching shadow. The black sword at his hip seemed heavy, its legacy a chain binding him to Ethrael's fate. With a breath, he steeled himself, vowing to wield it not for vengeance but for her salvation.

A couple of days later, Lorin, bearing the veteran's counsel, joined a larger contingent of Keenroot's army in the courtyard. While the troops stood nearest the platform occupied by the king, most of the village scattered about the perimeter to listen in.

In Keenroot's courtyard, whispers swirled like autumn leaves, the village's heart taut with dread. Women clutched children, their eyes scanning the horizon for goblin shadows, while elders muttered of ancient feuds reborn. Lorin stood among them, his gaze fixed on the king's platform, the weight of their fear a mirror to his own, yet kindled by a spark of defiance.

King Arkiel looked over the courtyard and drew in a deep breath. "My countrymen, the goblins have invaded our homeland. Although it is currently in relatively small numbers, we need to send a message. This is our land, and we will defend it. Any goblins found will be eliminated on sight. I hope the warning will be heeded, but we need to be prepared. I will send dispatches to our nearest allies informing them of the situation."

Things did not sound good. It seemed like the elves were gearing up for war. Yarnell said, "I do not want to get conscripted. I'll leave in the morning."

Yet fate had other designs. At the pronouncement's end, a servant cornered both Lorin and Yarnell, ushering them into the throne room.

"My friends, turbulent times are ahead. What I withheld from the other guards was that we translated the goblins' notes. It appears that their king is seeking revenge for the loss of his family, the beheading, when Lorin was originally injured. Additionally, they are aware of the sword's heritage as a goblin killer. The plan is to kill Lorin and steal the sword. So, the time has come for Lorin to return the sword."

"On the morrow's dawn, Lorin will take the sword and deliver it to the parents' home of the sword owner. They will want to have it returned and have the skills to protect it. As the goblins are actively looking for you, I will provide a mode of quick transportation. Come by the palace in the morning, and I will have the sword, a letter for the magicians, and a steed for your journey."

The king sighed before he continued, "I am afraid my mages have not been able to ascertain the location of your friend. When you return the sword, you might ask if they can help you."

Lorin's shoulders sank. "King Tarul and you have tried already. Likely, she is beyond reach."

The king steadied him. "They wield other arts and may prevail where we could not."

Lorin forced himself to hope for the best. "Very well, I shall ask them."

"I hope you thrive on this path and find her safe," the king added. "I'll cast in a few coins for the way. I wish you success on this mission and pray you will find your friend unharmed. I hope you will return. You are ever welcome."

That night, as Lorin trudged to his cabin, the king's words of hope a fragile shield against his doubts, he drifted to a restless sleep. A goblin snuck into Keenroot's stillness and seriously injured Yarnell. An arm was sliced, as was his stomach. Yarnell cried out in pain, Lorin awoke, grabbed his sword, and dispatched the intruder. Lorin bound Yarnell's wounds, searched the attacker's remains, and cast the lifeless body out of the hut.

Lorin faded into Keenroot's palace shadows, Ethrael's staff heavy in his pack, its runes a silent cry for her return. The 'cursed sword' pressed against his hip, a grim weight of battles past. He dreaded that the mages' hold might offer no hope.

"She lives," he whispered to himself, forcing defiance.

The king's charge burned, resolute, yet doubt clung like mist. He recalled the goblin's lifeless eyes, their malice now his burden, and vowed to wield the blade for redemption, not wrath. Keenroot's lights flickered, a beacon for his return, should fate allow. Lorin tightened his cloak, the night's chill a harbinger of trials ahead.

At dawn's light, Lorin gathered provisions for his journey. He said his goodbyes to the Master Falere, guards, and mages. Yarnell headed to have his wounds looked at by the healers. The guards disposed of the corpse, searching the area for further threats.

• • • *(Dravok)*

Torchlight jittered along the obsidian walls of Goblinhall as Dravok entered the great chamber with the battered survivors of the second squad. Their armor hung crooked, faces drawn tight with fear. None dared lift their eyes.

King Gorath sat upon his obsidian throne like a mountain waiting to fall, breath rumbling from deep in his chest. Krogar, the king's champion, towered beside him, tusks bared, grief and fury flickering across his yellowed eyes.

Dravok dropped to one knee, head bowed low. "My king... we return," he rasped.

Gorath's claws dragged across stone. "Where Skarn?" he growled. "He led the squad after my kin slaughtered."

Dravok swallowed hard. "Skarn... dead, my king."

Silence fell like a hammer.

Krogar stepped forward, breath hot and sharp. "Dead? By who?"

Dravok's voice shrank. "The... same human, Champion. Same one who kill your son."

Gorath leaned forward, eyes narrowing into burning slits. "Same human?" he hissed. "You sure?"

"Yes, my king," Dravok said, voice trembling. "Skarn faced him in night raid. Human strike fast. Too fast. Skarn fall. Others fall. Elves take the rest."

Krogar's fists clenched until blood beaded along his claws. "That human... he took my son. Now take Skarn? I'll tear him apart with my bare hands."

Gorath's breathing deepened, heavy as rolling thunder. "What he use? Magic? Trickery?"

"No, my king," Dravok replied quickly. "Just steel. But he... different now. Stronger. Fought like... like he not same human we faced before." He hesitated, shame burning in his throat. "He frighten us."

A low rumble built in Gorath's chest. "One human should not grow so strong. Something else behind him... something hidden."

Krogar spat on the floor. "Then we crush him before he grow more."

Dravok bowed lower. "My king... there more." He forced the words out. "One goblin from second squad... he break from us. He go to elf-village. Attack human's friend."

Gorath stiffened.

Dravok continued, voice cracking. "Human kill him too."

Krogar snarled, tusks flashing. "He kill in dark, kill in huts, kill in forest—this no normal human!"

Gorath rose slightly, shadow stretching across the hall. "Recall squads. All but few."

Krogar blinked, surprised. "We leave forest?"

Gorath shook his head slowly. "No. Leave small fang-pack in trees. Hidden."

The king's claws flexed. "They bite elves. Annoy. Make fear live in branches."

Krogar grinned, savage and satisfied. "Good. Let elves jump at shadows."

"And if human show," Gorath growled, voice dropping to a cold whisper, "they kill him."

Dravok pressed his forehead to the stone. "As you command, mighty king."

Gorath waved him away, but before Dravok turned, he caught a flicker in the king's gaze.

Not just rage.

Fear.

And fear, when it reached the throne of Goblinhall, was a seed that never stopped growing.

CHAPTER TWENTY-SIX

The Blade's Burden Returned — Lorin

Greetings, friends, draw near, for I, a wandering bard, free of any realm's tether, offer a tale of Keenroot's halls and the wilds beyond. I watched Lorin, brave yet unseasoned, mount Windrider, a pegasus fleet, gripping a cursed sword, departing Keenroot's ancient court. Across vast skies, goblin arrows faltered below, and I admired his resolve. Far from elven lands, in a tower bleak, he met mages Kael and Lysara, presenting their daughter's blade, stolen by brigands' hands. Their grief awoke, secrets stirred, while goblins lurked close, wards trembling. Lend your ears, for Lorin's path twists sharp, the sword's weight heavy, his fate entwined with perils unseen. Hear now, as I sing.

*L*orin reached the palace with a light pack, prepared for a steed's journey, his sword, Ethrael's staff, and a spare shirt stowed in a sack. Having never sat on a steed, he deemed it would be a wild ride.

The king met him in the courtyard, yielding the 'cursed sword,' a writ for the mages, and a map to their hold. Lorin searched the map, tracing the path to the mage's hold.

"My lord, I've never ridden a horse, and this seems a long journey. If I read this rightly, it would take weeks even if I were a seasoned horseman."

The king grinned. "I understand. Dwarves favor not steeds, I know. Yet I never said you'd be riding a horse."

Out strode a fair stallion, muscles strong and steady. No handler led it, and it trod straight to Lorin of its own will, proud, with purpose.

The king gave Lorin a ring and motioned him to wear it. Once on his finger, Lorin's eyes widened, and he heard the stallion speak in his head.

"*My lord, I am Windrider, herald for my kin,*" the beast said. "*The king told me of your quest and its haste, and my family and I would be honored to aid you.*"

Then, with a faint stir, the stallion shook and spread two vast wings. It was no horse but a pegasus. The king grinned as Lorin stood, jaw fallen, stunned by the marvel. A speaking steed was unusual, but a pegasus beyond expectations. Pegasi were objects of legend.

Lorin roused swiftly, his heart stirred. "Windrider, I know not what to say. This is a great honor. I've heard of your kind only in old tales, yet they do you scant justice. I fretted over this trek, yet now I feel heartened. From my soul's depth, I thank you for joining me."

The pegasus dipped his head in a slight bow. "*My lord, the foe draws near, so we had best depart. Climb my back and grasp my mane to hold fast. Unlike clumsy steeds, we may speak—no need to tug me. I'll begin slowly until you gain your balance in flight. It is a different experience from walking.*"

Lorin turned to the king, "Sire, I'll bear the sword back where it came and return soon, hopefully with Ethrael. I know not what lies next, yet I can see no home but here."

The king smiled. "Lorin, it warms my heart to hear you call this your home. I deem you'll wander some, yet you have a place here while I reign."

• • •

Lorin steadied his breath, Windrider's wings poised, the vast unknown beyond Keenroot calling, his quest now truly begun.

Lorin slung the 'cursed sword' around Windrider's neck, then mounted the pegasus's back, hands twined in the thick, silken mane. His fingers trembled, not from fear alone but from the weight of the unknown. How might one ride a creature born of the sky, when earth has been your only friend? When Windrider was sure he held fast, he leaped skyward, wings beating steadily, and took flight. He rose slowly to ease Lorin in; the flight was striking.

The first rush stole Lorin's breath. The ground fell away, the courtyard shrinking to a pattern of stone and shadow. Windrider's wings thrummed, a deep, rhythmic pulse that vibrated through Lorin's bones, steady yet fierce... muscles straining to find balance in this unfamiliar motion. His stomach lurched, part thrill, part terror, as the earth tilted and swayed far below, no longer a solid thing but a distant dream. Could he, a dwarf bound to stone, master the sky, or would the cursed sword's weight drag him to ruin, and as always, would Ethrael's fate be his burden?

Lorin could scarcely fathom the view. The nearest he'd come was peering from a mountaintop, yet its bulk hid half the world. Atop Windrider, all stretched open and fair, no trees, no stones, nor rivers marred the perspective. The land spread wide: green forests, golden fields, bright rivers, and sharp distant peaks... clouds drifting in the vast sky. Lorin's heart raced, awed by the height and vastness, as if he'd entered a realm beyond mortal reach.

Windrider's voice broke through, warm and steady in Lorin's mind, a guide to steady him in the sky. *"Ease your grip, my lord. Let your body sway with my wings. The sky is no foe to fight but a partner to trust."*

Lorin nodded, though his knuckles stayed pale. Slowly, he loosened his hold, letting his hips rock with the pegasus's cadence. Each beat of those wings lifted them higher, steady and strong.

As they set forth, they spied a small band of goblins below, their twisted forms scuttling like ants across a clearing. A couple of arrows, crude shafts, wobbled upward. But Windrider soared too high, and those barbs fell in vain. Lorin glanced down, his pulse quickening, yet the danger seemed distant as if the sky shielded him. The goblins shrank to specks, their malice no match for the pegasus's grace.

Windrider snorted, a sound like a gust of pride. "*Let them waste their quivers. The ground is their cage, not ours.*"

Lorin and Windrider spoke the whole way, their words carrying over the wind. Lorin asked of him and his kind, each answer painting visions stranger than the last. He learned they dwelt amid the clouds, nesting right upon them, their hooves treading mists as solid as stone. Thus, folk scarcely see them, for their nests lie hidden within the heavens' veil. Windrider spoke of storms they raced for sport, of stars they grazed beneath at night, their light brighter than any forge Lorin had known. The rider's voice grew bold, his questions growing eager, and Windrider answered with patience as if glad to share the sky's old tales.

The flight stretched long, yet time seemed to bend. What would have dragged weeks afoot dwindled to one endless day with wings. Lorin's fear ebbed, replaced by a quiet awe. His hands no longer clutched but rested, fingers laced in the mane like a friend's clasp. The wind rushed past, now steady, and he found himself leaning into it, eyes wide, taking in the world's expanse. When dusk crept near, the sky glowed gold and crimson, clouds bright with light. He wondered if this was what gods saw, the world clear and vast.

• • •

Windrider's hooves met earth, the tower's stark shadow looming, its wards humming, a new trial awaiting Lorin's courage.

Windrider alighted smoothly at a gate, a path stretching to a tower. His hooves touched the earth with barely a jolt, wings folding quietly. Lorin slid down, legs wobbling as the ground felt too still, too heavy after the sky's vastness. This tower, vast and grim, held Ethrael's hope, yet its wards whispered danger, daring Lorin to prove his mettle or falter.

Lorin touched Windrider's warm, solid flank and whispered, "Thank you." The pegasus dipped his head, eyes bright with purpose, and Lorin knew this flight had changed him. He would forever see the world in a broader perspective.

Lorin had barely grazed the gate when a jolt flung him back, knocking him flat in the dust. When he blinked awake, a robed man stood over him, staff glowing like it held a thunderstorm in check.

"Who are you?" the man asked, voice low and steady, like a river carving stone.

Lorin hauled himself up, brushing off his tunic. "I am called Lorin. I swear I come not to stir strife," Lorin said quickly. "I'm on a quest from King Arkiel." The mage's grip on his staff loosened a hair.

"A claim hard to trust, yet coming astride a pegasus sways me to belief. Such beasts are famed judges of worth and shun ill. My name is Kael."

The pegasus, white as a winter moon, had kept Lorin's hide intact. Windrider bowed to Lorin. "*Keep the ring. I hope we will meet again. Call me when you need a swift return to the elf king.*" Then he sprang skyward, rising swiftly into the dusk.

Lorin turned back to Kael, "I have a gift for you. Yet may we take this within? Goblins hunt me."

Kael nodded curtly, and the gate swung open, the wolf's head knocker snarling as Lorin passed.

• • •

Stepping past the snarling gate, Lorin entered the tower's heart, blue torchlight guiding him toward the library steeped in secrets he surmised. He pulled his focus back to the purpose of the visit, returning the sword, and more appropriately securing Ethrael's return.

The tower itself was a proper marvel, and not the cozy kind. Could this bleak hold, steeped in secrets, yield Ethrael's redemption, or deepen the sword's curse? It rose tall, with jagged black and grey stone. The top twisted, hooking sideways, angled toward the sky, and the base sprawled wide, dotted with arched windows leaking a dull orange glow, like a dim forge. Vines snaked up the lower walls, thick and dark, looking more like they'd choke you than allow climbing.

The iron fence encircled it tightly, with tall bars spiked and humming with blue light, and runes scratched into the metal. Down the hill, a good stretch from the tower's shadow, sat an orchard, rows of twisted trees, branches heavy with fruit. It was set apart like the tower didn't want it too close, and Lorin saw a haze over it, maybe wards or something older keeping watch.

Inside, the lady of the tower met him, silver robes catching the blue torchlight, all grace and iron in one. The walls were carved with shifting swirls, and a big staircase spiraled up, steps worn smooth.

"Fetch fare fit for a guest," she told some servants, then fixed Lorin with a look. "Sir, we seldom suffer visitors; your purpose must be of great weight. Follow me to the library, where we may weigh your errand's heart."

Lorin followed her to a round room, shelves packed with books clear to a domed ceiling painted with stars that twinkled like the night sky. Some tomes glowed, others were chained shut, probably cursed, knowing mages. A long table sat in the center, dark wood carved with wolves and dragons, and the mistress took a seat. Lorin squared up, ready to spill his tale about King Arkiel's quest.

The lady gave Lorin a cup of tea. "My husband shall join you soon. I entreat you to partake and renew yourself. I must tend the readying of our evening meal."

Lorin sank into a seat and began to sip as the lady left him alone.

The man entered, robes shed, yet clutching his staff as a lifeline. "As I said, I am Kael, and you met my wife, Lysara," he said with courteous form. "What seeks the elven king of us?"

"I come to—" Lorin began.

Kael rose, voice sharp with practiced anger. "I am no vassal of his throne to be called at his will!"

"Hold, my lord," Lorin said, hands raised. "You misunderstand. He sent me to restore a lost article. And I bear a personal request to ask after."

Kael eyed Lorin with a piercing gaze, studying him closely. Then his demeanor showed hope.

"Can it truly be? Suffer me a moment to fetch my wife—should this be what I hope beyond hope, her presence is required."

He hastened out, calling fervently, "Lysara, come straightway!" He returned, leading her in with zeal, both trembling, gladness mixed with fear of disappointment.

"I ask you, show this gift from the elven lord," Kael said, voice trembling with anticipation.

Lorin drew forth the 'cursed sword'. "King Arkiel said you crafted this for your daughter."

"Verily, we did so with the utmost care," they cried as one, their voices ringing with truth. "I know not the full tale," Lorin pressed on, "yet brigands slew her. I found it, and the king bade me bring it back to you."

They took the sword eagerly, as if it were precious. "We offer our deep thanks," Lysara said, voice firm despite her emotions. "You can't grasp the weight of its return. Years have passed since we last heard from her. We harbored fears of her demise yet lacked certainty. This brings scant comfort, yet affirms what we dreaded."

Their grief mirrored his own doubts—could this blade, heavy with loss, foreshadowing redeeming Ethrael, or lead him to ruin? Lorin gave them room to grieve. The sword's curse clung heavy, not mere steel but a vow, how would he wield its power, and return unbroken?

When he thought they were ready, he continued, "The sword's worn some, yet it holds magic still. It aided me, a mere novice, to weather a goblin attack."

He sank back into the seat and sipped his tea, sharp fare, yet he drank it down, too courteous to complain.

After a span, Kael said, "Young man, your tale holds. Much remains unsaid. Some you know, some beyond you. This blade bears rare virtues. Pray, eat with us this eve, and abide beneath our roof. You are safe here. Come morning, we shall speak of a fit reward for your deed. This blade's virtues, tied to our daughter's spirit, hold secrets yet veiled. Come dawn, its true might may stir, a power to guide your path, unveiled in light."

As Kael's words lingered, a faint hum stirred the library, the sword's hidden power whispering, secrets poised to unravel in the dawn's light. Lorin's gaze fell upon the 'cursed sword', its blade glinting, alive with secrets. Kael's words echoed—rare virtues, truths veiled. Could this weapon hold Ethrael's salvation, its magic a key to greater power? Lorin's resolve hardened, dawn promising the blade's true might, a force to reshape his path, its weight a vow. Its edge seemed to pulse, a silent call, urging him toward a destiny yet unwritten, its secrets bound to the unveiling of dawn.

CHAPTER TWENTY-SEVEN

Veiled Truths Revealed — Lorin

I am Yarnell, a bard whose lute thrums with tales gathered from road and hearth, now lingering in Keenroot's shadowed halls, awaiting Lorin's return. From this mage-lit town, I hear whispers of him at a distant tower, a young wanderer I once knew, his stride weighed by a strange sword. Rumors speak of his nights with mages, trading tales of battles and 'god rocks', dark as a raven's wing, his voice steady despite a burdened heart. They sought his secrets, so the stories go, while that blade, said to hold hidden power, stayed ever at his side. Word carries of Ethrael, his friend, caught in the Fayes' veiled realm, beyond our grasp. And Luna, a maiden with fire in her eyes, spoke for her father's honor, her plea thick with hope. Here in Keenroot, I weave these threads of steel and choices yet unmade, my song poised for Lorin's next step.

At supper with the mages, Lorin recounted his adventures since finding the sword, wisely concealing his princely blood. He kept his past buried, wary of these mages' keen eyes. Kael and Lysara listened with gentle grace, posing few questions, focused on the 'god rocks'. He hadn't traveled on foot, yet the pegasus flight exhausted him more than he'd expected.

When his head met the pillow, Lorin slept through the night, dead to the world. He dreamed again of the black sword glowing as he fought back hordes of goblins.

Dawn's light spilled through the mage tower's windows, stirring Lorin awake. As the sun broke through his window, he washed, then wandered down for breakfast. A young maid smiled at him as she entered the chamber, perhaps to tidy. Having forgotten something to drink, he received a cup of tea from an older dame. He mumbled thanks and sipped the tea slowly.

• • •

Kael and Lysara entered carrying the sword, placed it on the table, and sat. The servants gathered, the entire household anxiously awaiting Kael's words.

"You cannot fully grasp the service you've rendered this house," Kael said. "You should be told the sword's tale."

Kael leaned closer. "You have gleaned shards of our daughter's path with this blade, and yes, it spoke to her, lending its might in conflict. What has eluded you, however, is that it is not merely forged with spells but harbors a human spirit."

"Allow me to explain. As we wove common enchantments into the sword, Firmin sought our aid. Firmin was deathly ill, fated to perish at winter's close, and begged us to protect his family. This was no mere farmer, but a renowned swordsman, a servant to kings, seasoned in quests, famed for goblin-slaying, and our occasional ally. The night before, goblins struck him with a poisoned shaft to the back, meant to kill him outright. But the venom instead stilled his limbs. Assuming him dead, they ransacked his home, seizing gold and spoils from his adventures. By fortune's grace, his wife and child were away, gathering winter stores in Parcelridge, thus spared from the goblins' wrath."

Kael stilled, tone steady. "When he had gathered enough strength, Firmin came to us, knowing the poison would eventually claim him. We struck a pact: we'd protect his family if he allowed us to bind his spirit to the sword. Until you came last night, his kin thought him lost to the poison's grip. We deemed it unwise to burden them with news of his soul dwelling in the blade. Yet when we held it yesterday, it spoke to us, confirming your tale."

Lorin absorbed the words, rubbing his chin. "My lord, this explains much. I wielded the sword far beyond my skill." A spirit in the sword? His mind reeled, torn between awe and unease.

Lorin continued, "I bear many questions, yet here's the first: why was it named cursed if a spirit provides aid from within?"

Kael extended his hand, brushing the sword with reverence. "A keen question. The spirit within affirms that a sword cannot serve two masters. Many swordsmen, ever prideful of their craft, lacked the means to commune with it, nor would they cooperate with the sword's will, thus resisting its guidance. You and our daughter bore no such vainglory. You let Firmin's mastery hone the wielding. Though the blade bears wear marks, the spirit abides in strength. We mean to yield it to his family as rightful due. We owe you our deepest thanks. You mentioned a favor; what might we do to repay your service?"

Lorin addressed the mages earnestly, expressing how it gladdened him to restore their household, even if his own family was astray. He told them of Ethrael, how she drew him from death's edge, how she was lost now, and how dwarves and elves failed to find her.

"King Arkiel thought you might wield rare arts to find her," he said, handing Lysara an old bedcloth. "Use it if it helps. Either way, I'm glad I restored your daughter's sword to you."

Kael and Lysara took the cloth and stepped out, speaking softly, leaving the sword on the table. The elder dame and the teen drew near, their hands on the blade, tears falling, their expressions mostly glad yet tinged with sadness. Lorin, sensing the moment's intimacy, moved to the library.

In the mage tower's library, amidst shelves of weathered tomes, Lorin reflected on the sword's history and magic. Kael and Lysara met him there.

"Lorin," Kael said formally, "it may take a week, yet we shall strive our utmost to find your friend. For now, pray tell more of the 'god rocks'."

Lorin explained how the 'god rocks' were poisonous until blasted in the Dragon Forge and how he shaped them with dwarven aid. Kael and Lysara hung on Lorin's every word as if it were gold. After Lorin finished, Kael and Lysara asked if he had any fragments of the 'god rocks' left.

"Sorry, none with me," Lorin said. "They're dangerous to touch raw, but I possess the sword and staff I crafted from them. Forged with other metals, the sword and staff retain the distinct, glossy black color of the 'god rocks'." Lorin handed his sword to Kael, then the staff to Lysara.

Lysara gave a swift smile, which faded quickly. "Lorin," she said, "we know this is a great request, yet might we examine the sword and staff while we seek your friend? Your service to us has been rare, yet as seekers, this unusual rock grips our minds. Be assured, no harm shall come to them."

Lorin paused for a moment. "If King Arkiel trusts you, I suppose I can, too. Tend them as I did your daughter's sword." He hesitated, his trust in the mages a fragile thread, yet Arkiel's faith swayed him.

Still at the mage tower, Lorin reflected on his training. During the months of training with the guards and mages back in Keenroot, Lorin took the opportunity to rest that week, roaming the woods near the mage tower. The teen maiden, Luna, often went with him, showing him her favorite spots and sharing tales of her father from days past. Memories of Keenroot's drills lingered, but Luna's tales eased Lorin's restless heart. Lorin and Luna grew to be great friends.

· · ·

As autumn's chill deepened, Lorin gathered with the mages again. One night at supper, he, Kael, Lysara, Luna, and Vetra, her mother, sat around the table as Lysara spoke.

"We bear tidings. Our scrying has revealed that your friend is dwelling in a realm, but we cannot pinpoint her location further. She has entered the Realm of the Fayes, known to common folk as the fairies. Their land bends to strange and magical laws, shielding it from our sight beyond its bounds. They are reclusive, scarcely mingling with outsiders. Armed with this information, the elves might fare better in your quest."

Ethrael, alive but trapped? His chest tightened with hope and dread. Lorin stirred. "Well, that's more than I knew before. I'll seek her out. How may I find this realm?"

Kael cautioned, measured as ever. "It lies but a few days' journey, and we can yield a map. Yet we advise you to wait. Entry is granted only to their kin or those summoned by their queen. An attempt now would prove futile at best, but more likely deadly."

Kael said, "I will dispatch a missive to King Arkiel, advising him that you will remain with us for a time and that Ethrael is trapped in the Realm of the Fayes. I will urge him to use this knowledge to entreat the Faye queen on your behalf. I have heard they have some limited relations."

Lysara waited patiently for Kael to finish and quickly spoke up, "We have tested your sword and staff; some findings merit discussion before you leave. First, the material within these works readily lends itself to magic. Though we vowed to study, we've dared to etch an enchantment on each. Henceforth, they may hold magical power, which you could draw upon to wield spells, provided you master them. We can teach you a few simple ones before you leave, suited for a traveler like you. Moreover, they shield you. Should magic strike, they absorb a portion of its force. See this as our thanks for restoring our daughter's blade."

Lorin's eyes flared, "My lord and lady, that's a great gift. I thank you. Ethrael shall rejoice too."

Kael pressed on, addressing Lorin further. "Second," he said, all learned and wary, "this is a personal plea, and you are free to say no. Should you hold more of these 'god rocks', I'd be grateful if you could shape a staff for me. I'd pay you well for your effort, of course. I trust the design to your judgment. You have proved yourself a smith of rare worth."

Lorin rubbed his chin. "My lord and lady, I know not when I'll next return to the dwarven realm, yet I'll consider it. Could you teach me some magic arts? The elf king says I bear some hidden gifts to wield that sword, a wizard's bent he says, yet I've stumbled thus far."

Kael nodded, measured as ever. "Maybe you do hold such skill."

"When may we begin the training?" Lorin asked, voice alight with hope.

"First, there abides a third matter," Kael said. "We could shift the spirit from our daughter's sword to yours, a crafting of scant effort. The choice, however, rests with you."

Lorin shook his head defiantly. "I cannot allow it. It's back with its family now. I'll not tear them asunder for my gain." Lorin's heart wavered—honor bound him, yet the sword's call tugged.

Lysara leaned nearer, "You mistake our aim. We've weighed this as one—by 'we', we mean our entire household and the sword spirit as well. This blade will outlast our mortal days. The spirit within craves purpose. He trusts you completely. Our sword's quality is inferior to yours. It would be a great boon for him."

Luna stepped in from the hall, her voice soft yet steadfast. "I beseech you, sir, grant this favor for my father. To sit on a shelf, gathering dust, would be torment and unbearable. He was—is—a soul of valor and adventure. He yearns to combat the world's evils, especially the goblins, for their treachery. He deems it in your hands that he might still achieve righteous deeds."

Lorin rubbed his chin. "You offer a convincing plea. Can I speak with the spirit myself? I'd hear it from him. I'll not enslave any to service, not even a magic sword." To bind a soul against its will—he couldn't stomach it, no matter the sword's power. He recalled Ethrael's slavery and the burden on her soul.

Excitement shone on Kael's face. "Such a humble inquiry. We did the same for our daughter and Firmin's family. Lay your hand on the sword."

Lorin placed his hand on the hilt. He felt the sword warm, like a faint pulse beneath his fingers.

Kael touched the blade, murmuring arcane words.

'By the gods, lad!' a voice boomed in Lorin's mind, rough and loud as a war horn. *"It is a pleasure to speak with you. I've been stuck with just my thoughts for years. How fare you, Lorin?"*

Lorin blurted aloud, "Are you the sword?"

Kael broke in, calm and sure, "Your grasp forges a direct path to the spirit. You need not speak. Merely think your words to him."

Lorin thought, *"Are you the sword?"*

"Yes, Greenling," the voice roared back. *"Lorin—or Barzul, whatever you name yourself—I'm Firmin, and I'm delighted to speak with you. To your query, yes, I'd leap from this rusted heap to your magnificent blade if you'll have me. We'd be a mighty pair, felling any ill you set your gaze upon. I owe you a blood debt for bearing me back to my wife and lass, having thought I'd never see them. Luna's grown fierce and fair, and my woman's yet the fire in my bones, so to speak. You gave me that, and I'm forever grateful. Abiding in this rusty shell benefits them nothing. Let me go forth and fight. Maybe we can carve some coins for my family along the way."*

Firmin's voice echoed Luna's plea, and Lorin felt the weight of their trust settle—he couldn't deny them. Lorin spoke aloud, "Guess I'm the lone naysayer here. Go ahead and transfer Firmin from your sword to mine."

The entire household smiled broadly, and Kael nodded. "If you yield both swords to me, we can work the shift at midnight. The full moon lifts our craft's might, and it will be complete by breakfast."

CHAPTER TWENTY-EIGHT

Haldir's Harmony of Spirits — Lorin

Gather 'round, ye lovers of lore, for I, a bard, sing of Lorin's saga, where steel and spirit forge a mighty bond! His sword, imbued with Haldir's cunning soul, gleams with runes that flare like stars in a smith's fire. A hammer's strike wove their fates, their harmony a dance of trust. Lysara, deft mage, reshaped Ethrael's staff in secret, its Starbloom petal a guiding light for Lorin's quest. In drills, he honored Luna's tears, his mind honed sharp as forged steel, though memories flicker like fading embers. Haldir, the hidden hero, steadies his hand, their unity a flame against the dark. Lift your tankards, for this tale of warrior and blade burns fierce, a beacon for battles yet to blaze!

Come morn, after they'd supped on a modest meal of bread and smoked fish, Kael approached Lorin with a quiet reverence. The candlelight from the night before had long extinguished, replaced by the morning sun. In the mage's hands rested Lorin's sword; it looked similar, but something had changed. He extended it toward Lorin, his eyes steady with unspoken trust.

"He's ready for you," Kael said, his voice low, as if speaking of a living thing.

Lorin reached out to his sword, his fingers brushing the hilt, and the moment he grasped it, a jolt coursed through him, sharp and clear, like a hammer striking true on glowing steel. The sword seemed to hum in his grip, an eager resonance that pulsed up his arm and settled in his chest. The runes etched along the blade flared to life, their glow keener than ever on the old steel, a vivid blue that danced like liquid flame. It wasn't just a weapon returned, it was a companion reawakened.

He stepped back, giving it a few swings through the crisp morning air. The balance held, perfect as ever, but there was something more, an intimacy in the way it moved with him. His strokes were tighter, smoother, as if the sword anticipated his intent before his muscles fully committed. The spirit within it pulsed with a fierce vitality, it seemed to meld with his own, guiding his hand with a subtle nudge here, a steady pull there. It wasn't control, it was harmony, a bond forged in battles past and now renewed.

He paused, holding the blade aloft, its tip catching the first rays of dawn. He could feel it watching him, not with eyes but with a presence that pressed against his soul. "*You've missed this, haven't you?*" Lorin murmured, a faint smile tugging at his lips. The sword's runes pulsed once as if in answer, and he chuckled softly.

Kael, leaning against a nearby tree, crossed his arms and grinned. "Looks like he's glad to be back where he belongs."

Lorin lowered the blade, resting it across his palms as he studied it. The spirit within wasn't just power but loyalty, a comrade that had stood with him through blood and shadow before Lorin knew him. Feeling their warmth, he traced a finger along the runes and whispered, "*We've more work ahead, old friend.*" The glow flared brighter for a heartbeat, a silent vow shared between man and steel. At that moment, they were not merely warrior and weapon but two halves of a single will, ready to face whatever the universe would bring.

• • •

As Kael's silhouette faded when heading to the tower, Lysara drew Lorin aside with a gentle but deliberate tug on his arm. Her voice came soft yet crisp, like the rustle of leaves caught in a sudden breeze. "My dear," she began, her eyes flickering with mischief and caution, "I took some liberty with Ethrael's staff, a secret I've kept from my husband. He deems himself the sole warden of magic in this house, a gatekeeper of its mysteries, yet my arts sway to the divine and natural beyond his rigid grasp."

Lorin tilted his head, intrigued, as she continued. "I shifted his chant and reworked the staff's essence. Now, it holds only magics of clerics, druids, and rangers, threads of the earth, and the gods' will. Your sword, though, keeps the arcane kind fit for mages, wizards, and sorcerers, wild and unbound as it should be. Given Ethrael's healing proclivities and gentle hands that mend more than they rent, I thought this was more faithful to her ways. A staff of life suits her better than a tool of raw power."

She paused, glancing toward the tower where Kael's voice was faintly instructing the household staff. "I beseech you to keep this from him," Lysara added, her tone dipping lower. "He'd think it beneath our house's worth, a dilution of his grand designs. But we both have a share of magic; your sword and her staff are the same, balanced like two sides of the same coin."

Lorin's gaze drifted to the sword in his hand, its runes still faintly aglow, then back to Lysara. He felt the weight of her trust, the quiet rebellion she'd woven into her craft. A slow nod came as his answer, his voice steady but warm.

"Lysara, I thank you. Ethrael will value it. I hope she will tell you someday when we find her. She's not one for grand speeches, but her passion runs deep."

The path to Ethrael lies ahead, he thought, like steel awaiting the hammer's shape, and I'll forge it true.

Lysara's lips curved into a knowing smile, her eyes glinting with satisfaction. "Then it's settled," she said, stepping back with a grace that hinted at the power she wielded. "Let the sword sing its arcane song with you, and let Ethrael's staff bloom in her hands. Kael needn't know the finer threads we've spun."

Her eyes glinted with knowing. "Take this, too, a Starbloom petal, plucked from Keenroot's archives, its spark tied to Ethrael's lineage. Keep it close, the Grove's light may guide your path to her."

She pressed a shimmering petal into his hand, its warmth pulsing like a distant star. Lysara returned to the tower.

Lorin tucked the petal into his pouch, its faint glow lingering in his mind, a beacon for Ethrael's path.

. . .

With the petal secured, he tightened his grip on the hilt, feeling that familiar hum ripple through him again. The sword seemed to approve, its spirit pulsing in rhythm with his own, a comrade, now paired with a counterpart in Ethrael's newly blessed staff. The road ahead would test both Ethrael and Lorin, but with Lysara's subtle art, they were armed not just with steel but with a bond that ran deeper than magic alone could forge.

Holding the sword aloft, its runes catching the morning sun, Lorin let his thoughts drift inward, speaking silently to the spirit within. "*Should I call you Firmin from now on?*" he mused, testing the name against the blade's vibrant hum.

The response came swiftly and coarsely, a rumble like a whetstone grinding steel. "*No,*" the voice growled in his mind. "*I'd not have enemies sniffing out my past, like hounds on my family's trail. I'm not Firmin anymore, that life's ash. Call me Haldir, stout and sly. Means 'hidden hero', fits me to the bone.*"

Lorin's lips twitched into a faint smile. "*Haldir it is,*" sealing the pact. As the name settled, he realized something he'd overlooked. The spirit had already named him Barzul, a name whispered in secret. It struck him then: the sword had heard it all, those hushed councils when elf and dwarf kings laid bare his hidden heritage. No secrets lingered between them now, fair's fair, and the blade's glow pulsed as if in agreement.

. . .

Lorin practiced with his new weapon and companion. He tried exercises he had learned at the elven kingdom.

Haldir encouraged Lorin. *"Truly, not bad for our first run, though."*

As he sheathed the blade, catching his breath, Luna stepped closer, tears gleaming in her eyes. "I thank you so much, Lorin," she said, her voice trembling with joy. "I can see my father in your movements." Her father's shadow fights through me, he thought, and I'll wield this blade to keep his honor sharp.

Lorin grinned, wiping sweat from his brow. "Now that we may speak back and forth, people will deem me some grand swordsman. Any fray I win is your father's doing, be proud of that." Her face lit up, a beam that rivaled the sun filtering through the leaves.

The sword hummed softly at his side, Haldir's presence steady and approving, a hidden hero, as if shining through another's hands for his daughter's memory. Together, they turned home. The bond between man, spirit, and steel forged anew in the quiet of the woods.

As they trod back to the hold, Luna said, "I wish you could stay longer. I want to know my father's new comrade better."

Lorin said, "Strange, I was thinking the same thing. It would serve me well to learn some of Kael's magic arts and train here for a while." He was thinking: my past lies buried, but I'll hammer its embers until the truth sparks free.

• • •

Stepping into the tower's shadowed hall, he saw Lysara and had a question for her. "Have you the means to unearth my buried memories? In dreams, I glimpse fleeting shadows, hammer strikes, the glow of embers. When others recount my youth, those tales resonate within me, yet no firm recollection takes root." The mystery of Lorin's lost memories hung in the air, a puzzle waiting to be solved.

She regarded him, her silver robes catching the candlelight, her voice resonant with erudition yet tempered by empathy.

"Your dreams offer a propitious indication. They suggest the injury to your mind is neither profound nor irreparable. Permit me a hypothesis: the conduits to those memories have attenuated rather than the memories themselves being effaced. Dreams and those visceral intuitions traverse pathways distinct from your conscious faculties; much like an evocative fragrance that summons a dormant memory. It presents a most fascinating conundrum I shall endeavor to elucidate further."

• • •

Lorin settled into a cadence, mornings sparring with his sword, afternoons studying with Kael's arcane direction. He'd toil until his sinews sang with strain, then wrestle magic until his vision swam, collapsing each eve spent mentally and physically. He'd lay Haldir on the dining table when not in hand, where Haldir's gravelly timbre traded tales of ancient frays with any soul bold enough to lend an ear.

Months unfurled, Lorin waxed formidable, muscle taut beneath his skin, intellect honed like a blade's keen edge. No lost memories returned, but his thoughts rang clear, steady as a hammer's rhythm on heated steel. My mind's forge shapes sharper each day, he thought, yet the past remains a foe unslain.

His swordplay surged with precision, drills honed sharp as a blade from the forge, each thrust a strike, each parry a guard. He and the sword melded tight, their bond shedding words for instinct; the spirit's curt counsel, "Shift your stance, lad," or "Tighten that grip," whispered now, a murmur in his marrow. Their bond, forged in combat, was a connection that transcended words.

CHAPTER TWENTY-NINE

Echoes of Dwarven Honor — Lorin

Gather 'round, ye dreamers of glory, for I, a bard, weave Lorin's final verse, where steel and heart clash in the Faye's twilight! Ethrael's fate beckons, her staff's glow a star in his soul, guiding him through glades where shadows whisper treachery. Haldir's blade, rune-forged and fierce, hums with dwarven fire, its spirit steadying Lorin's hand against a queen's veiled traps. His raw magic surges, tempered by Kael's tomes and Jarek's brutal spars, yet doubts linger like forge smoke—can he save her? A dwarf's vow, "Protect your own," thunders in his chest, each step a hammer's strike toward truth. Peril coils tight, the Faye's secrets unraveling as Lorin faces his crucible. Hoist your tankards high, for this saga's crescendo burns bright, where courage and blade carve a hero's path through the dark!

*H*is brow creased as Lorin scratched his head. "Kael, my magic's not progressing. I've got the gestures down, but no spark comes. Were the sword and Arkiel wrong about my ability?"

Kael's frown deepened, thoughtful. "I've wondered the same. Your aptitude shines, yet you lack the mana mages channel. Wait here." He returned with Lysara, her steps graceful, robes catching the light. "We'll scry your body for magical proclivities, a standard test for novices we neglected in your case."

His breath caught as Lysara's magic probed, a tingling surge stirring memories of Ethrael's patient lessons, her voice guiding his clumsy gestures in a firelit hut. He needed this power to bridge the void of her absence. Fists clenched, hope battled doubt—could magic save her? The mages sat, eyes closed, as if hearing a silent hum. The dwarf held still, tense as a drawn bow.

After murmurs, Kael spoke firmly. "It's clear: you have innate potential, but your mana pool is near absent—an anomaly. Your essence repels arcane currents."

Lorin ventured, "I've dwarven blood in my veins. I've heard dwarves often resist magic."

They scanned again, nodding. Lysara's voice was precise. "Your dwarven heritage explains much. Magecraft mastery is beyond you, but you could wield mana through your sword."

Kael's gaze sharpened. "Your dwarven blood resists a mana pool, yet it channels raw magic—a primal force, wild as a dragon's temper. It's rare, rarer than elven sorcery, and demands discipline. The college may hone it, but your blade's the key."

Gripping Haldir's hilt, its hum steadied him like Ethrael's hands once had. If magic were his path to her, he'd master it, peril or not.

"Thanks," he said, voice low. "Keep my dwarven lineage secret. It could endanger my family."

Kael nodded. "We'll honor your trust. Bring the sword to your lessons. We'll train you to draw mana from foes and shape it into spells. Your blade will be your conduit, like a mage's staff. I expect swifter progress now."

"We've practiced spells, but what about ones to boost my blade? Shields, dodges, strikes, tied to the sword, not separate?"

Kael's brow arched. "A sharp idea. My lack of martial skill blinded me to it. Our lessons hold value, but elven bladesingers weave spell and steel. I have a tome on their art somewhere, more descriptive than instructional. I'll fetch it."

"Can you teach me some?" he pressed.

"I know a few," Kael said. "One coats your blade in flame, another in frost. My wards can shield you in close fights. We'll start tomorrow. Also, your magic differs from mages like me. It's a rare gift called 'raw magic'. I'm sending a letter to the magic college to inquire about your admission."

With magic's secrets unfolding, his thoughts turned to steel, eager to hone another skill for Ethrael's sake.

•   •   •

Sweat dripped from his brow, each drop glinting like sparks as he braced his sword after a grueling bout. Haldir's blade hummed faintly, runes pulsing blue. Chest heaving, he muttered, "*This training's fine, but I fear it'll crumble when blood's on the line. Foes don't fight clean. How do I brace for the unpredictable?*"

Haldir's voice rumbled in his mind, coarse as a war-worn shield. "*Drills forge your form, lad, but battle tempers it. Trust me when it twists wild. Keep your grip firm, wits sharp, and we'll cleave any fool who stands against us. I, too, felt that unease when green. You've grown stouter since our first fight. Still, a true foe's untamed. Find a sparring mate. Even a green and reckless one will test your mettle. Parcelridge crawls with sellswords. Pick a pup needing the grind. Iron sharpens iron.*"

His eyes flared with resolve. "*Jarek's in Parcelridge. He dreamed of swordplay last we met. Green but tough, good stock. He'll do.*"

A memory from Parcelridge burst into his thoughts. "*I've got a question gnawing at me. A bard in Parcelridge said that when the girl held you in a fight, he said you sang? I've never heard you sing. Was that just bardic flair?*"

Haldir vibrated in Lorin's hand. "*Ah, actually no. You remember she was from a magical family. She often cast a spell on me to sing when she was in battle.*"

"*I might have to learn that spell someday. That would shake up the opponents.*"

"*It sure did. We should go talk with Kael.*"

Lorin sought out Kael, striding purposefully. "A sparring partner would boost my confidence. Can Jarek join us here?"

The mage stroked his chin, gaze measured. "We rarely admit outsiders, but your presence enriches this house, and I'd see you stay. Your arcane studies need work, and Firmin's return lifts Veyra and Luna's spirits. I'll send for Jarek in Parcelridge, your name omitted to avoid prying eyes. My occasional calls for aid there won't raise unwarranted suspicion."

As Kael's words settled, the warrior awaited Jarek's arrival, restless for an actual test.

• • •

The next morning, the lad arrived at the tower gate, broad and twitchy, hands calloused more from plow than sword. "You sent for me?" he asked, voice thick with a country drawl.

Kael met him, staff in hand. "Your name?"

"Jarek. Heard you wanted me."

Kael waved his staff, opening the gate. "Close it and follow." He led the newcomer to the library, where the dwarf waited in the shadows, Haldir at his side, sizing up the lad. Jarek stood hulking, a blade-dreamer with more grit than polish.

Kael's staff tapped the floor, voice sharp. "You seek the mercenary's craft, yes?"

The lad shifted, boots scraping. "Yessir. Been swingin' a blade when I can. Folks say I've got grit, but I ain't had no proper training. Fended off varmints after our stock, but can't afford tutors. I'm green as grass, strong but untested."

"A mutual gain awaits. I need a sparring partner for a friend. It will hone both your blades. Train with him. Consider it a favor to me."

"Kind of you, sir, but as I've said, I've no coin. Back home, we'd barter, plow a field, fix a fence, but I've naught for a gent like you."

"I'll provide lodging and meals. Train with my friend, sharpen each other. Payment can wait. I hear you're honorable. In time, I'll call a task. Agreed?"

"Yessir."

"One more thing," Kael added. "Your selection wasn't random. My friend, your sparring partner, chose you. He's changed since you knew him."

Lorin stepped forward, hand on Haldir's hilt, broader and grittier than before. The newcomer grinned, lumbering over for a bear hug, then pulled back, eyes searching. "Where's Ethrael?"

"She's not here. We'll talk later, but this training might help find her."

Jarek blinked, stunned. "Ethrael got taken in Parcelridge, didn't she? Heard an elf lass vanished. I tried trackin' her, hit nothing. Hoped she'd found you."

"No," Lorin said, shaking his head. "Not sure if she was grabbed or ran. I've got a lead, but we can't move yet. I'm sharpening up for what's needed. Good to see you, though. I need a moment while you settle in."

Heart heavy with Ethrael's name, he slipped away to face his guilt alone. He wandered into the orchard.

• • •

The tower stood as a beacon from the orchard.

Under a gnarled apple tree, Lorin clutched Ethrael's staff, its weight a heavy reminder.

"Ethrael," he whispered, voice cracking.

The trees gave no answer. His chest tightened, guilt clawing.

Her voice had been his lifeline in that moonlit hut, reading tales to mend his shattered mind. Her silver eyes, fierce with quiet strength, had held him together. Her trembling hands, hidden from others, steadied his soul.

Now she was gone—somewhere in the Faye lands—and doubt gnawed: had she been taken, or fled?

The not knowing seared him.

"I should've stayed with her," he muttered, slamming a fist against the tree, pain flaring.

"If only the Faye queen would answer Arkiel's plea, I'd have a path to find her!"

He struck the ground with his fist as tears rolled down his face.

"I can't lose you," he said, voice raw.

A buried memory surged: his father's voice—A dwarf protects his own.

He'd failed her. He pressed the staff to his chest, its warmth a reminder of her touch. A cold breeze swept the orchard, rustling the leaves overhead. It felt wrong to Lorin that the world continued moving while Ethrael was missing.

Each sound, each shifting shadow seemed to mock his helplessness. He lowered his head, gripping the staff until his knuckles whitened.

You trusted me, he thought. And I wasn't there.

The weight of that truth nearly buckled him.

He vowed, "I'll face any peril."

Straightening, he wiped his face.

"Hold on, Ethrael. I'm coming."

Resolve hardened, he returned to the tower, steps heavy but sure.

As night fell, he steeled himself for the dawn's drills.

• • •

Post-breakfast, they hit the courtyard, swords drawn. Jarek gawked at the black sword. "That's a strange blade. Where'd you get it?"

Grinning, he said. "Forged it myself. Remember our dwarf kingdom trip? Used those poisoned rocks from the wagon. Dwarf tricks smelted it clean. Balance is perfect. Been training with a swordmaster. Let's start with his drills, then go free-form. Good?"

The lad nodded, slow and sure. "Reckon so."

His swings were wild, raw as a plow horse, but grit shone, absorbing basics fast. The lad's blade arced, grazing an arm. The sword's hum surged, guiding Lorin's parry. Their blades rang, sparks flew. Dust whipped up as Lorin shifted, each strike burned by Ethrael's absence.

Between bouts, Jarek panted, grinning through sweat. "You're sharper now, friend. Ethrael'd be proud."

His chest tightened, her name a spur. "Gotta be," he said, adjusting his stance.

By week's end, the newcomer's swings tightened, plowman's strength finding rhythm. Lorin nodded, seeing a warrior born, a brother in their shared fight. Exhausted, they ate and split. Lorin to magic lessons; Jarek to rest.

Over meals, Lorin was frustrated with his slower magical progress, unlike the forge's instinctual ease. But he figured, each spell strengthened his arsenal. Autumn leaves fell as their blades met daily, Lorin's strikes growing surer. Weeks of sweat sharpened his edge, but Ethrael's memory lingered, a constant ache, awaiting word from King Arkiel.

After months of hoping for the Faye queen's word, her note arrived. The queen had approved his visit to her realm to see Ethrael. Her approval was reluctant, her message a warning: Seek her at your peril.

Lorin's heart pounded. The note's words, a threat, but why? His fingers tightened on the note, knuckles whitening. He pictured her in that realm of twisting glades. Gripping the note harder, breath catching, he imagined her fate uncertain with her silver eyes calling through the void. The warning stirred a chill. Would he find her, or face a queen's trap? He pushed fear aside, his resolve firm. Once in Faye's domain, he'd be under the queen's rule. He steadied himself.

After endless months, he'd finally reach her. "Progress at last! I'll leave at dawn. Where's this Faye place? How do I get there?"

Luna piped up, but shy as a fawn: "Um, a map, perhaps? I could sketch one by morning if you wish. I used to trace Papa's old ones, and I reckon they're decent, to aid you."

He felt the sword's blade hum. "*That's my girl!*"

Clapping, he grinned. "It's settled, I'm off at first light!" Lorin's heart raced at the thought of Ethrael. He steadied his breath, her memory grounding him. His fingers brushed the Starbloom petal in his pouch, its faint glow a promise of her light. Ethrael's fate lay ahead, but his own past, shadows of hammer strikes and embers, felt like a locked forge. He might never reclaim it, yet her silver eyes called him forward. A dwarf protects his own, he thought, and that was enough for now.

His sparring partner cut in. "Reckon I'll ride with you."

Kael interjected firmly. His tone brooked no argument. "That cannot be, regrettably. The Faye shun outsiders. I marvel that an entry for Lorin was gained. The Faye's glades twist minds, snare souls, only the chosen walk free."

Kael stroked his beard in thought. "Moreover, I have a small task to offset your debt, a simple fetch from Parcelridge, no great ordeal. You'll escort Luna for supplies, goblin mischief's spiked, and I'd rest easier with you guarding her."

Lorin nodded, relieved Luna would be safe. His shoulders tensed, torn by duty, yet a pang hit him. His comrade's strength would've bolstered his quest.

Lorin's eyes fixed on the distance, steeling for a solitary trek. The blade's runes flickered, hinting at danger, as if sensing a shadow in the Faye realm's call. He squared his shoulders, ready for the unknown. Ethrael's light would guide him through the Faye's deceit.

• • •

Sleep dragged Lorin into darkness, but it was not the darkness of rest.

It was cold.

Expectant.

Alive.

A pale glow seeped through the black, and the world changed around him.

The Fey lands.

Silver trees rose in impossible spirals, their branches stretched like arms toward a swirling violet sky. The air hummed with an ancient pulse that made his bones ache with familiarity he could not explain.

A figure stood among the trees.

"Ethrael?" Lorin whispered.

She turned. Her face was strained, frightened. Bands of faint silver light circled her wrists, pulsing with each heartbeat. Her hair drifted weightlessly, as though suspended in deep water.

"Lorin…" Her voice trembled. "I can't find the path back."

Lorin stepped toward her, but the earth slid away beneath him, stretching the distance no matter how he fought it. "What's holding you?"

Her form flickered, dimming around the edges. "I agreed to help. I didn't know—"

Her voice broke.

Something moved in the mists behind her.

A shadow tall as the trees, crowned in thorns of moonlight. But before Lorin could see its face, the air shivered… and another presence flowed into the dream like silk.

A woman's voice. Soft. Ageless.

Beautiful in the way winter is beautiful—cold enough to kill.

"Child of iron," the voice whispered, curling around his ear. "She walks where your mortal feet cannot follow."

Lorin spun, but there was no one behind him. The voice came from everywhere. From the roots. From the sky. From inside his mind.

Ethrael gasped, reaching toward him. "Lorin—please—don't let me—"

Her form faded like breath on glass.

"ETHRAEL!"

But the Queen's voice drowned his cry.

"Fear not. The healer serves a purpose in my realm."

A pause.

A breath of frost.

"Pray she is strong enough to survive it."

The forest cracked. Light shattered.

Lorin jolted awake, heart slamming against his ribs.

Ethrael slept peacefully across the dying fire—unaware of the cold whisper curling through the night.

Unaware of the thin line of frost now etched across Lorin's palm...

...in the shape of a delicate crown.

EPILOGUE

Song: Haldir's Starlit Oath

In Keenroot's glade, where starlight weaves its spell,
A stranger lay, by death's cold hand compelled.
Ethrael's hands, with healer's grace divine,
Restored his spark, her Starbloom dreams to shine.
Through Aelthar's ash, her vow to mend took root,
A grove's lost light, her heart's unyielding pursuit.

At forge's heart, Lorin's hammer found its song,
A dwarven prince, where Barzul's blood belongs.
The cursed sword, with goblin-slaying might,
Unveiled his kin, throne lost to night.
Through Cragmoore's halls, his heritage awoke,
A brother's bond, in iron oaths bespoke.

From heaven's fall, god rocks in fire were shaped,
A staff for her, a sword where stars escaped.
In Dragon's Forge, *with dwarven craft refined,*
Elf and dwarf as one, their legacies entwined.
His blade gleamed black, a beacon fierce and bright,
To carve a path through sorrow's endless night.

Goblins struck, their wrath for blood repaid,
Lorin's blade, in guilt, their lives unmade.
To mages' tower, the cursed sword he bore,
Its makers wept, their grief an open sore.
Yet Ethrael's fate, in Faye's veiled realm confined,
Drives his heart, her loss a chain that binds.

Haldir's spirit, swordsman's soul of old,
Now hums in Lorin's blade, with runes of gold.
Forged anew, its glossy edge a star,
To cleave the dark, its might shall carry far.
With magic bound, this sword shall shape his tale,
A hero's path, where future quests prevail.

Sing the blade's unyielding vow, oh kin,
Honor's fire burns where shadows dim.
Starbloom's glow shall guide his way,
For Ethrael's light, he'll face the fray.

Beyond the veil, where Faye's dark secrets dwell,
Ethrael waits, her fate no tongue can tell.
With staff and sword, her spark in hand, he'll strive,
To break her chains, and bring her home alive.

Raise your voice, let Keenroot's anthem soar,
Lorin rides at dawn, to Faye's enchanted shore.
Haldir's fire, Starbloom's grace, his guide,
His dwarven oath shall free her from the tide.

ABOUT THE AUTHOR

James Selvy, a newcomer to writing fantasy fiction, is a native of Arizona and long-time resident of Tucson where he spent 36 years supporting the troops in the defense industry. Now he writes the kind of stories he loves to read—where adversity isn't a dead end but a steppingstone, and where each journey is a chance to stretch yourself to become a better you.

With the steady hand of a technical mind—tempered by a touchy-feely vibe—his debut novel, Cursed Sword, is a testament to the power of friendship, resilience, and the magic of hope. When he's not writing or tending to his two wiener dogs and a Bernedoodle, you'll find him enjoying desert life and dreaming up the next great adventure.